Silver's REBEL

SILVER BROTHERS SECURITIES

LACEY SILKS

MYLIT PUBLISHING

To the introverts on the outside
who feel like extroverts on the inside.
be the REBEL within you !

"Okay, Sam. You've got this. He's just a mysterious
bartender who eats women for breakfast, lunch and dinner,
and you can be his dessert."
~ Samantha Connor, Silver's Rebel

FROM THE AUTHOR

I originally wrote Dazzled by Silver in 2013. When I reread the story in 2021, I found a great need for improvement. Once the ball was rolling, the novel developed into something I didn't expect. The fresh plot, a new point of view, deeper connections and storylines, finally completed the story.

If you've never read this emotionally charged and page turning romantic suspense, I hope the new tension, conflicts and character motivations satisfy your every craving. The Silver family has wrapped its talons around my heart and has helped me through the most difficult times of my life. I expect them to take you on that same adventure filled with love, laughter, and plenty of smut.

He makes the rules, and she breaks them.

In a shadowy world where danger lurks around every corner, Samantha Connors finds herself targeted by an enemy she never saw coming. Her only hope is Gabriel Silver - a magnetic billionaire bodyguard with a mysterious past and rules of steel. Their connection is electric and utterly forbidden.

Gabriel's life is a fortress of secrets and broken trust, built on the ashes of a lost love torn away by the mafia's brutal games. Samantha, a wild-hearted rebel with a taste for trouble, becomes the unsuspecting pawn in a deadly game neither of them could anticipate.

When their worlds collide, the sparks erupt into an inferno. Gabriel's mission: protect Samantha at all costs, even if he has to break every rule. But the free-spirited Samantha refuses to be caged or controlled. At every turn, she tests his limits and challenges his darkest demons.

With every rule broken, the stakes climb higher, leaving Gabriel and Samantha to face the ultimate question: Can they trust each other enough to survive?

Silver's Rebel is the second novel in the *Silver Brothers Securities Family Saga,* and can be read as a standalone romance. Intended for a mature audience.

When I woke up this morning, I didn't expect to run into my past.

I parked across the street from the club and turned off the ignition. The dark alley seemed like a good place to keep an eye on the crowd. Less than fifty feet from me, New York's nightlife awakened. Tonight's surveillance would be easier than most.

Sit. Watch. And wait.

I lifted my hands behind my head and lowered the driver's seat a quarter down. I'd take babysitting a twenty-one-year-old client over digging for coffins with lifeless bodies, any day. Kendra had brought more trouble to the company than any of us expected, but if it weren't for her family more would have suffered. Besides, after ten years, she was more than a client. She was family.

Papers shuffled behind the bin, drawing my attention. A pinch of fresh adrenaline squeezed through my veins, reminding me of my investigating days. I rolled down my window. The sound of speeding taxis, revving engines, brakes, honks, and sirens blended into the night's tune. Much closer, laughter echoed from the street where a line of guests wound around the corner for the opening of my friend's new night-club, Kissed.

I groaned inwardly. Crowds meant trouble, and trouble for someone like me was akin to pissing on an electric fence wire. There was nothing pleasant about an electric current zapping through your balls. I knew that from experience on the ranch.

I cranked my neck to the side. As if on cue, a woman stepped out of the vacant building and into the alley. She glanced behind her and tiptoed on the balls of her feet to avoid the clinking heels from connecting with the pavement. Wrapped in a pair of leather pants, her ass swung back and forth as she hurried behind a garbage container.

"What are you doing?" I whispered.

She reached behind her, unfastened her pants, and squatted. The garbage container kept her hidden enough that unless someone walked out the side door from Club Forever, no one would see her. The sound of a powerful stream fizzed in the distance. I held in the chuckle when she sighed with relief. She finished fast, shook her booty, and zipped back up. The rebel double-checked her bearings beyond the container, brushed her hands over her thighs, straightened her shoulders, and stepped over the pool of pee to hurry out of the alley.

Her confident stroll faltered when she finally spotted my car. The young woman glanced behind her and then back to the only way out of the alley, past my vehicle. She reached inside her purse and picked up her pace.

This night could only end in trouble. I could sense these things.

"You're every kidnapper's wet dream," I called out as she hurried by. It probably wasn't my best opening line, but it had been a while since I'd been around... people.

She turned towards me, braced on her high fuck-me-now heels, and removed her hand from her clutch, pointing a nozzle to my face.

"You sick bastard!"

I gotta hand it to her—I didn't expect the pepper spray. I should have.

I reached my hand out to block the stream before she pressed the button. "Wait! Don't! I mean no harm."

She held her finger steady on the button. Her arm stretched forward, and my attention lifted from the nozzle to her bewitching eyes. Our gazes locked like in some fucking happily-ever-after movie, and all I could do was suck in a sharp breath, because I thought I was seeing a ghost. Her upturned nose, rounded cheeks, a blonde side-braid, and lips that begged for kisses were a heartless reminder of everything I'd lost. The uncanny resemblance stopped my heart. I blinked repeatedly until my body shook, pushing the flooding memories away.

"What's wrong with you?" She lowered her hand, stepped away from the club's side entrance, and moved closer to my car.

I'd practiced controlling these attacks before. This one was nothing new, but it had been a while since I'd had one. I recalled the guided therapy words in my mind, and my pulse finally slowed.

Fucking embarrassment.

"Nothing. I'm fine," I barked back.

The second-long pause felt like an hour. The fresh memories haunted me and were the exact reason I stayed away from people. I simply wasn't good company. But I wasn't about to let her walk inside Club Forever, either.

"You don't want to go in there." I pointed to the side door.

"I wasn't going to, but now you have me intrigued. Why do I not want to go in there?"

The fresh grunt vibrated deep in my lungs. Her voice, her demeanor, and piss-off attitude were a grave reminder of how I'd failed to keep a rebellious girl like her safe.

Because Club Forever likes to keep its women there—forever. Or so I'd heard. I didn't tell her that because we were in an alley, and it was dark. I didn't want to scare her more than I already had and get bear spray in my face.

"Club Forever is not for girls like you."

"How do you know what kind of girl I am?"

"For one thing, the kind who can't hold her bladder."

"That's not my fault. I had to hydrate for tonight. I'm celebrating. And what are you doing in a dark alley?" she asked, as if I were the beautiful woman — which I wasn't — strolling down dangerous streets.

"I'm not the one who can't find a bathroom."

Her cheeks flushed red through the darkness.

"You're a rebel. And trouble. That's what you are." I pressed the button on my steering wheel. The car door lifted open in a lazy semi-circle. I stepped out and leaned against the hood like Magnum P.I. Well, I sort of was one. Just a little younger and with better gadgets. She shifted from one foot to another uneasily. I approved of this extra caution around strangers, but she shouldn't have been in a dark alley in the first place.

"You get off on watching people relieve themselves?" she asked.

"No. I get off on making sure vulnerable women stay safe. This alley isn't safe. You shouldn't pee here."

That part was totally true.

She chuckled. "Was that a pun?"

"Maybe."

She placed the can of bear spray, or whatever poison I'd avoided, inside her sparkling clutch and secured the square accessory underneath her armpit. The gesture guided my eyes straight to the beautifully wrapped corset top around her body. It complimented the curvy ass in her tight leather pants.

"As you can see, I'm safe. And I don't need a man telling me what to do. Besides, isn't it past your bedtime?"

I laughed, shaking my head. "Yeah, sure. But if you had a man like me, he'd never let you pee in an alley."

She shivered.

"Then it's a good thing I don't have a man like you because I'd pee in my pants. The line's too long." She pointed across the street.

"That's a contradictory statement. You're going to Kissed?"

Was she even old enough to be there? Her timid nod, just a subtle gesture, reminded me of someone. Someone who was innocent and good-hearted, yet stubborn and definitely born to make trouble. It was always the quiet ones who got me in trouble. I let out a shallow sigh.

"It's my friend's opening night," she said, tucking a stray strand of hair behind her ear, and I realized I must be staring at Samantha Connor, Kendra's friend. I was supposed to have met her a while back, but my wounds had been too fresh and my mind too absent to care about work – and anyone hanging around Kendra was work. After failing as a private investigator, I'd stepped down the ladder and joined my brothers, James and Hunter, at the surveillance department of Silver Securities.

"Wouldn't your friend have you on a guest list?" I pointed my thumb over my shoulder and back to the street. "You know... to avoid the line and peeing in the alley."

"Possibly."

"I'd check that out before I peed with rats."

She tilted her hip and placed more pressure on her right foot. Her ass stuck out provocatively to the side. She blinked three times with her mascara-heavy lashes, smiled through those innocent lips, and blushed. This girl would cause trouble tonight, and she didn't even know it.

"But if I avoided this alley, I wouldn't have met you," she chirped. That voice sang through my ears with familiar tones. It flowed right through my veins, awakening the dormant memories in my heart.

Suddenly, an alley was the last place I wanted to be.

Fuck.

Seeing her now, I couldn't help but wonder whether we'd met before. In a different life, perhaps. She tilted her head to the side and her braid spilled onto her cleavage. I imagined that same hair scattered over my chest. Her gaze slowly lowered to my groin, and I realized I was hard.

She cleared her throat, making me feel like a total pervert.

"Ahem, I better go." Her voice broke with nerves. She turned around once more before stepping onto the sidewalk and called out, "I'll check the guest list, and thanks for the tip!"

Samantha ran off towards the nightclub, leaving me alone in the alley. I'm not sure how long I stood there thinking about her and my new assignment, but it would have been much longer if my cousin and partner at Silver Securities hadn't pulled up in his Bentley.

Julian Silver rolled down the window. "Hey, Gabe! You're going to be late!"

I checked my watch with a grunt. "I'm never late."

He turned off the ignition, and the headlights faded.

"Was that Kendra's friend?"

"Sure was."

"She hook you? Kendra's been teaching her self-defense."

She'd definitely hooked me, but not in the way that Julian thought.

"Thanks for doing this." He reached out the window and handed me a file.

"I want to say you owe me, but you already owe me." The words scraped my throat like rough gravel. Life's bitter taste had remained in my mouth ever since the funeral.

My watch beeped with a three-minute warning. "I have another minute. Give me the brief."

"Kendra made a deal two nights ago and fell through on another one tonight. This time she stiffed the wrong people.

Hartley's one of them. There's a buzz of retribution. They're coming. I don't know how long we can keep her under the radar, especially now that she's opened Kissed. People are going to ask questions. Her profile is in jeopardy, which puts Silver Securities in jeopardy as well."

"Figures you'd fall for a troubled girl," I puffed out.

"It's not her. It's the drugs." Julian always defended Kendra, but the man also loved her like a fool. And Silver Securities owed her.

I reached out and lowered my hand to my cousin's shoulder. "I know. We'll get her out of this and past it. I won't let her out of my sight. She's family."

Julian could have done this job just fine. So could Tristan, his younger brother. But when you fooled around with a client, life got complicated. Kendra tested my aunt and uncle's patience daily but they loved her like a daughter. My older brother had a sick daughter to care for, and Hunter was barely out of diapers, focused on adventures underneath a different skirt every weekend. His twenty-three-year-old energy bounced off the walls.

"Kendra has ways," Julian reminded me.

"I'll read the full file first thing in the morning. Tonight, I'm on duty." I nodded to the nightclub across the street, where trouble lingered.

"All right. Call me if you need me. I'm not far away."

I looked him directly in the eye and followed up with an overenthusiastic thumbs-up.

He rolled his eyes. "Get your life in order, Gabe. Decent work will do you some good."

Whatever.

He turned his ignition, and the car purred. Julian glanced across the street once more, shook his head, waved, and left. I locked my car and walked across the street to the club's back entrance. The busted lock reminded me to change it.

I crossed through the back to the private area where Ace and Axel Wagner were waiting in a corner. The brothers were each holding a glass of iced bourbon. The orange liquor glistened in the dimmed lights. We shook hands, and I sat across the table.

"What's going on?"

The waitress must have had seen me when I entered because she came with my favorite drink.

"Thank you." She left us in the private corner.

"Guess who bought the place across the street?" Ace asked.

"Your father bought it. Everyone knows that."

"Not Club Forever. The property beside it."

"Hartley? He already has the hotel on one side."

I lifted my glass to my lips, but stopped.

"Why does Scar need a strip club again?"

"It's a back-up plan… we found out something new. The organization is growing." The brothers eyed one another in a way that made the hairs stand up on my arms.

"Scar believes Infinity will operate in the building next door. Rebels will be sandwiched between the Hartleys. It could be our in."

"Rebels?"

"The new strip club."

Axel moved in closer. "This is an opportunity Silver Securities cannot miss. Hartley knows no limits. The longer the DA waits, the more brazen he becomes."

I set the drink down and leaned in. "Get Julian involved. I'm not in that business anymore. The case belongs to the Flintstones."

"Until someone you love gets involved."

That's why I don't have anyone to love.

"You're connected. We're all connected. And if Infinity operates across the street, your girl's business is in trouble."

"Kendra's not my girl. She's a client. I'll talk to the team, and we should set up a meeting. Obviously all Silver resources are yours.."

Resources were not the issue, and my empty offer felt a little nasty, but I wasn't in a fucking good mood. I hadn't been in a long time.

My focus shifted to the small crowd around the bar. "Enjoy yourselves tonight. The drinks are on the house."

The brothers clinked their glasses and relaxed in the cushioned seats.

I jumped over the bar and removed my leather jacket.

Morgan, the other bartender on duty, frowned. "You're late, and the crowd's thirsty."

I stuffed the jacket underneath the counter and washed my hands. "I'm not late."

"Well, it'd be better if you were here a few minutes early to prep."

"It'd be better if I got paid for this job."

That was a lie. I didn't need any payment to help family. Besides, a couple of extra hundred bucks wouldn't exactly change my wealth portfolio.

"That kind of attitude will get you in trouble with the boss."

"She's your boss, not mine. Where is Kendra, anyway?" I asked.

Morgan shrugged as a glimpse of a blonde braid caught my attention from the other side of the bar. "And that one? What's she drinking?" I pointed to Kendra's friend from the alley.

"A virgin Mary."

"Maybe not such a rebel after all." The devilish smirk that lifted in the corner of my mouth was new. I didn't expect it, but it had been a while since a woman had lifted my spirit.

"What, Silver?" Morgan asked.

"Nothing. Let's do this."

"Apron." She handed me the black fabric with an extra large pink lip print glowing in the dark.

"No, thanks."

Her laugh echoed above the hum of the crowd. "Come on. This place is gonna get crazy. Someone's bound to spill one on you."

"I. Don't. Spill. Things." I lifted my hand to stop her reply and pointed to the side of the bar where the blonde 'rebel' was sitting on a stool. "I'll take that side. Let me know if you see Kendra."

I stuffed the horrid apron underneath the counter and strolled around the corner of decoratively stacked beer mugs.

She was sitting at the bar cross-legged, sipping on her tomato juice.

Gross.

As much as I hated tomatoes, I wouldn't hold that against her because I knew someone else who loved the fruit. And I loved her dearly.

Get a hold of yourself.

She lowered her gaze to her breasts, and I blabbered the first thing that popped in my head.

"Find anything in there you like?"

Chapter 2

Sam

Music drummed deep inside my chest while a conversational hum carried through the club. The dance floor filled as women dressed in short skirts and tight crop-tops competed for attention. I wasn't sure whose attention, but it was working, because men did what they knew how to do best: drooled.

Kissed had to be the perfect spot to find a one-night stand. I sat at the bar in the middle of my best friend's nightclub and watched a voluptuous bartender work her magic behind the marble counter. Her plump boobs jiggled inside her clingy tank top. The black cotton fabric hugged her perked yet ample breasts, giving the salivating men at the bar plenty to fantasize about. She was working it, and it showed by her overflowing tip jar.

Implants?

I watched as she reached for the top shelf. Her breasts bounced in slow motion as she stepped off the bar ladder. She left to the other side of the bar, and I side-eyed the seats beside me before peeking down my corset top to compare.

"Find anything in there you like?" I jumped up at the manly voice behind the counter, and my mouth dropped open.

"I... I... I dropped a peanut," I babbled.

The barman's heated stare lifted from my boobs, meeting my confused eyes. Recognition slowly set in, along with a wave of heat that started at my cheeks. "It's... it's you."

His mouth lifted at one corner.

"It is. Gabriel Silver. My friends call me Gabe." He reached his hand over the counter for mine.

I returned his businesslike shake. His sky-blue eyes sparked with maturity and promise. I wasn't Kendra or the heavy-topped bartender, but I hoped to make a better impression than someone who lost a peanut down her chest.

Or a girl who peed in an alley.

Gabe's attention remained on my face, like he couldn't get enough of it, which made me blush that much more. He rested his arms on the counter, his weight forward. I swallowed hard through my dry throat, miraculously remembering his introduction.

"Samantha Connor. You work here?"

A shade of shame heated my cheeks as I suddenly wished we'd met under different circumstances. Anything would have been better than him catching me peeing in an alley, and I hoped forgiveness was one of his better qualities.

"You could call it that. Are you Kendra's friend?"

I was Kendra's only friend, but admitting that would mean she was my only friend as well. At least, my closest friend. The past few years searching for my birth-mom hadn't been easy. After I lost my mom to cancer and Dad in a freak shark accident, I found myself alone in the world, searching for my biological family had become a priority. Point was, all I had now was Kendra and a few work acquaintances.

"Yes, and you? I mean, you work here, so you must know her." I'd never have put him for a barman, but the brawn strength and confidence would make him a perfect bodyguard.

"Yeah, I know her. I'm surprised we haven't run into each other before."

Me too.

His stare consumed me, heating my body from head to toe.

I bit my lip. What Kendra told me when she invited me to join her on the opening night of Kissed was right: tonight would be a good night.

"Mr. Silver?" Someone called for the buff barman from the other side.

Silver, Silver, Silver... I ran the last name in my mind, but it didn't click.

He leaned in, his shirt that was a size too tight yet oh-so-perfect, scrunched up in all the right places. "Excuse me a moment. Don't leave."

His gorgeous blue eyes dazzled like gems. Their brilliant contrast against his tanned skin and chocolate-brown hair that was a little too long—yet perfect again—made me hold my breath as he turned around. The bangs shifted, revealing a silver streak of maturity and experience. He left, and my stomach completed its two-point-five somersault. I exhaled hard, took a moment to myself and swiveled around on my stool to regroup. The music picked up its beat.

I bounced to the danceable rhythm, my legs swinging back and forth.

Okay, Sam. You've got this. He's just a mysterious bartender who eats women for breakfast, lunch and dinner, and you can be his dessert.

I reached back for the frosted glass and took another sip of my virgin Mary. Condensed water dripped onto my lap, staining my pleather pants. As the second verse began, with Gabe busy on the other side of the bar, a sweet, pungent scent of roses swirled around my nostrils. I perked up at the familiar scent.

"Kendra! You're here!"

My bestie scanned me and gave a nod of approval, then wrapped her arms around me in a hug. Her straightened hair tickled my cheek as she whispered, "You're early."

I took another whiff of her classic scent of roses and fresh auburn dye.

"I couldn't miss your opening night," I grinned, then squirmed as all girlfriends do when their best friends reach their lifelong goals. If someone had told me after meeting at an ancestry group, where we both broke down, that we'd be hugging it out six months later, I wouldn't have believed them. "I can't believe it's your opening night."

Great boobs, glorious hair, great everything. I was certain that tonight would be Kendra's best night. I just knew it. As I added all the attributes my best friend embodied, the bundle of nerves in my chest grew. What if I flew under radar tonight? But then again, I was spending the evening with Kendra, who had delivered on promised nights of fun since the day we met.

She looked me over once more, and I couldn't help but ask, "You approve?"

"Much better than your pencil skirt suit."

"I wouldn't wear office clothes to a club!"

Her laugh carried across the bar, turning heads. I no longer minded the attention and focused on the blinding light that twinkled overhead and the spinning room. I grabbed the counter to steady myself. It was either the virgin Mary or the sudden overcrowding room that was getting to me. Sweat dripped from underneath my arms.

"Did I not tell you I have an awesome sense of style?" Kendra tapped my nose with her finger. I blinked twice, and the room came back to normal.

Earlier in the week, she'd sent me a link to buy the corset top and the skin-tight pleather pants. I wasn't sure how I'd remove them later, but I tried not to worry about that part. Hopefully, the problem of pant removal would fall into the hands of a handsome stranger. The pants clung to my body like another layer of skin.

The heat in the club was unbelievable. Or was it just me? I fanned my hand in front of my face.

"So? Anyone yet?" Kendra scanned the bar like she was on a hunt. Poor girl. She was in love with a man who couldn't return that love, and my heart ached for her. Our search for our families had brought us together, and although we'd met only recently, Kendra had felt like family from day one.

"Anyone what?" I asked.

"Anyone you fancy? I'm making sure you get laid before the sun's up."

I shook my head. "Shh. Lower your voice. Everyone can hear you."

She laughed again. "So? That's the point. If you advertise what you want, you get what you want."

I was all for 'getting some,' but not at the expense of my reputation and embarrassment in the middle of a nightclub. "Don't you have more important things to worry about tonight? It's your opening night."

She'd been working her ass off for months to get this venture going. I thought she'd be taking it more seriously by now.

"This club was a success from its inception. Besides, I have people for that."

I set the virgin bloody Mary on the countertop. The half-empty club had filled up like an overflowing dam. The security let in a handful of people at a time, and only those on Kendra's exclusive VIP list made it inside. Thank goodness Gabe had suggested I checked the VIP list.

"You look great!" I raised my voice over the loud music, but the volume lowered just as I finished my compliment, turning a few heads my way.

"Thanks!"

Kendra paid no attention to anyone else. Her silk halter blouse draped over her breasts in folds and waves, leaving little to the imagination. She must have taped the collar because when she leaned over the bar and lifted her hand for attention, the fabric held firm against her skin.

I peeked at my boobs again to make sure they stayed put.

No fear there!

Those suckers would be lucky to fall out. I did not need tape. My twins had peaked at sixteen, so there was no danger of indecent exposure from me.

"What are we drinking?" Kendra flung her body my way. Her hazel eyes held a shade of red, and I wondered whether tonight's preparations had finally tired her. Kendra had dreamed of opening a nightclub on Fifth Avenue for years. And now, the three-level Kissed club, with a posh lounge and a rooftop garden overlooking Manhattan, was the talk of the city.

"A Virgin Mary."

"Virgins are fine, but not in a drink."

I squeezed my knees at the comment. Unfortunately, it had been a while. A long while. Casey wasn't exactly the giving kind, and masturbation could only get a girl so far. Kendra had been on a mission to fix me with someone since the day I vowed to stay single and cried crocodile tears in her lap. She'd failed. Miserably. Not her fault, but my own. Work had taken the lead in my life, leaving me no time to play as I climbed the corporate ladder for a promotion. My sex life was dead.

"This place is amazing. I still don't get how you managed the investment." I grabbed her attention with the one thing I knew Kendra loved talking about, and that was herself. She had been searching for a partner to help with the establishment for months.

"I found a silent partner." She winked my way and just as

quickly turned her attention to the muscled bartender, waving him down. "Gabe, two orgasms!"

I sat upright.

She leaned into me and whispered, "You need to relax, Sam. Here, take this. I'm prescribing fun for tonight. Nothing else." Her lips quickly took mine in a delicate kiss that left a little pill on my tongue. She pulled away and winked. "Now swallow."

A wave of nerves sprinkled over my arms, but Kendra was my bestie, and I was very ready for a bit of fun.

I deserve this, I reminded myself. A one-night stand was exactly what I needed to get back up on the horse.

One night. Nothing more and nothing less.

I sipped on the Virgin Mary and waited for the pill to hit my stomach. The sound of a plummeting mistake echoed back. I wanted to ask Kendra how long it would take for the pill to kick in, but I forgot my words as soon as I saw Gabe stroll over from the other side of the bar. His sexy grin stretched across his face. He beamed with confidence as he set two shot glasses on the counter in front of Kendra. A whiff of his strong cologne displaced my balance. The tantalizing scent circled my lungs like an aphrodisiac.

Gabe reached for a bottle on a higher shelf. His shirt lifted above his belt, exposing his toned backside. Delectable shivers tingled in all the right and wrong places on my body, overstimulating my senses. He grasped the bottle's neck, and from that point, I couldn't look away. As he prepped the shots, flipping the bottles in the air, the muscles in his arms bulged and twisted. A tattoo of a thorn peeked from underneath the edge of his short sleeve. It encircled his bicep, appearing to pierce his skin in random spots with inked drops of blood.

I had no tattoos because I preferred to live pain-free. Also, the fear of needles was real.

Gabe tossed the bottle in the air like a pro. His strong

fingers caught the flask on the way back down, where he gripped it and tilted the bottle, ready to pour the liquor.

Fucking sexy as hell.

I shifted in my seat. The onslaught of his manly moves made me think of Casey's lack of any moves and how much I needed something firm and stable… someone, someone with experience like Gabriel Silver. Where did Kendra find him? The music faded in and out, and I wondered why the sound system was wonky. Sweat dripped down my back. The room spun. I glanced back at the thick crowd of bodies moving over the dance floor like a swarm of ants. Claustrophobia had never been a good friend to me.

"He's good with his hands, isn't he?" Kendra played with the end of my braid, bringing my attention back to her. She seemed rather calm and playful for an opening night.

"Yeah, he is," I replied in a dreamy voice. If Gabe heard me, he didn't let on. Should I have said it louder?

Argh!

Gabe excused himself towards another customer. "One sec."

"Where did you find him?" I asked as soon as he left.

"He's a friend of a friend. They're cousins. We're one big happy family."

I wasn't sure whether that was sarcasm, because the room was spinning.

"But you could almost say I found him in heaven." She giggled, swaying back and forth on her stool. "I'm fixing you up with him tonight."

"What? Wait, you're not serious, are you?" My heart pounded in my chest as I lifted my gaze in slow motion to an irresistibly sexy grin. Gabe pushed the shot glasses forward, drawing my attention to his talented fingers and hands.

"To great orgasms! I hope they please you as much as I like to please." He winked, turning on the charm and I heated all over again. The silver streak near the bangs matched the mysterious sparkle in his eyes. The scar across his brow lifted each time he looked at me. It must have taken an effort to lay that on someone his size.

More sweat dripped all over, and I made a mental note to use the ladies' room as soon as possible. Yet I didn't want to leave.

Did he even know we were being set up?

I snuck another peek at my hopefully-soon-to-be adventure. In the shadow of his longer hair, his piercing blue eyes dazzled like gems. A spark of mystery glistened in their center. They stood out against his tanned caramel skin, and just like that, my hormones threw a party in my pants. Evidence of experience and charismatic personality vibrated against the counter as he served the guests. He was older, but I wasn't about to age discriminate against that body and experience.

His stare encouraged a new rush of heat below my navel. My muscles lost their tension, and my attention shifted to the half Virgin Mary I was finishing. Maybe it wasn't a virgin after all? An icy shiver sprinkled over my body, and I concluded my hormones were working overtime this evening.

My corset tightened, and I breathed into the top of my lungs, which lifted my lemon-sized breasts into Kendra's face. She, of course, appreciated the closer view, crossing my comfort line.

"Nah-ah," I shook my head, and she let out a laugh. Her warm breath tickled my cleavage. I closed my eyes for a moment and pretended that it was Gabe.

"Kendra?" I swayed in my seat. "I don't think your Virgin Marys are virgins."

Gabe chuckled from behind the bar as he pushed another set of shots forward. The gesture forced my gaze up to meet his, and we had our moment again. The one where he stared at me and I stared at him and neither one of us blinked. And then I blinked.

Shit!

His eyes held mine with piercing intensity until I looked away. Immediate regret consumed me, but sweat was dripping into my eyes, and it stung so hard I couldn't concentrate. I must have blinked a lot because Gabe asked, "You okay?"

I forced a grin and a nod his way. Kendra reached for the fresh shots and slid one glass my way. "Cheers! To Kissed!"

I clinked my shot with hers. "To Kissed."

She brought the glass to her lips, tilting it up. I followed the stretch of her bare neck down to her ample cleavage, giving me a pause. I shook off the novel sensation and followed her motion. The sweet cream hit my tongue with its coffee flavoring and slid to the back of my throat. The liquor spread through my veins, and my growling stomach reminded me to keep a count of how many I had. Or was it too late for that? I'd heard it wasn't good to drink on an empty stomach, hence why I'd forced down the tomato juice.

I breathed in the blend of over-perfumed air. The more people gathered on the dance floor, the hotter it got. A cloud of scents and sweat circled around me. It was nothing short of arousing, but it was also becoming harder to breathe. We each took a Sambuca shot next. The sweet anise taste would definitely be harder on the head. I hopped off the bar stool and tried to dance off the spinning by shuffling my feet in place, but it didn't help so I sat down again.

"That was one hell of a shot," I said to Gabe, then poked my elbow into Kendra's side. "Kendra, give him a tip."

"I'll give him a tip if he can make my orgasm last longer than a swallow."

I burst into uncontrollable laughter and lifted my hand to cover my mouth.

"All you have to do is ask, K." Gabe grinned.

Was that all it would take? To ask him? Kendra must have known him well, since he was working at her nightclub, but then how come she'd never introduced us before? I hadn't exactly made meeting new people a priority the past year, but at least my nine-to-nine work routine gained me a promotion.

"Hey, are you sure you're okay?" Gabe asked, bringing me back to the present. Touched by his concern, I smiled back and just as quick, all the nasty things I imagined him doing to me came flooding back, flushing my cheeks. But he didn't have to worry. I was a big girl, and I could handle two shots. Or three. And a small white pill. As I took in his mature body, I decided I could handle him and his experience as well.

I sat a little higher on the stool to lean over the counter. Gabe came forward at the request of my beckoning finger. When he was close enough for me to whisper in his ear, I took my chance. "I prefer a screaming orgasm. It has more kick and leaves a lasting impression."

Gabe pulled back with a smirk. "Definitely a rebel."

The sweet pinch of his approval registered deep in my belly. His mouth curved half way, encouraging the butterflies in my stomach to go wild. This time, he was the one who leaned in first. I bit my lip and moved forward until we were pressed cheek to cheek and skin to skin. The smell of his musk, mixed with alcohol, intoxicated me as he whispered, "I'll remember that when I'm off the clock."

Fuck me!

Oh, he was perfect, all right. Gabriel Silver ticked off all my one-night stand boxes, and so many more. He reached out and brought his index to my chin, pushing it upward. "Your mouth troubles me, Sam. What can I do to take those troubles away?"

I collected the last nerve remaining and offered, "A one-night stand and no strings attached deal kinda thing."

He chuckled. "Kinda thing?" His brows lifted. "One night with me, Samantha Connor, and you'll be begging for another."

Tipsy, I held his stare with confidence, ignoring his cocky tone. "And I'll take two of those screaming orgasms as collateral. Once I know you can deliver, you can kiss me. Once I know you can kiss, we'll discuss further."

WTF, like seriously?

Why would I make a stupid rule to keep these damn pants on until he kissed me? Twice!

"I thought you said a one-night stand?" he asked, half-laughing.

I watched his chest vibrate, but I wasn't sure whether it was from his growl or because the music had gotten louder. The club had filled the last few minutes. Kendra swiveled on her stool, took me by the elbow, and I hopped off the bar. She pulled me away, cutting off my time with Gabe. He grabbed her wrist before we left and warned, "Keep it clean, Kendra."

She slipped out of his grip and swung her torso over the bar. She whispered something in his ear that I couldn't hear, slipped off, and took my hand again.

"Come on, Sam. It's time for some fun."

I liked this Kendra. For months she'd been closed off, working on the nightclub. And I liked that she'd been my rock through the good times and the bad.

The room spun some more, and we joined the crowd on the dance floor. I lifted on my toes to search for Gabe, but I couldn't see him over the sea of heads and bodies. At some point, I was sure I could hear him calling my name, but when I turned towards the sound, the room spun too fast. I lowered my head and tightened my grip on Kendra's hand.

The crowd pressed more tightly around us. The smell of sweat, perfume, and alcohol floated above us. Bodies ground one against another, and my claustrophobia spiked. I spun in a circle, hot and flustered. The music dimmed to a single-toned hum. I concentrated on my breathing, but there wasn't enough air to pull into my lungs. Disoriented, I searched for the front entrance.

I can't breathe.

I wanted to find Gabe, but Kendra pulled me elsewhere. Or was it somewhere?

"Look up." She pointed to the glass ceiling. In its reflection, a bundle of moving bodies, fog and lights, overwhelmed my senses. Someone was swinging on a swing. An aerialist dropped her silks, and the crowd gasped.

"Whoa!" I lifted my arms up in the air, swinging around like I was part of the show.

When I lowered my head, I noticed cages made of steel bars propped up throughout the club. Within, dancers wearing what I would have called floss rather than a bikini were writhing against the bars. I could have sworn they hadn't been there before, but by now I couldn't tell where I was either, nor what was real and what was not.

"Better than Club Forever?" Kendra's hopeful voice rang in my ear.

"Fuck Club Forever!" Thank heavens she never let go of my hand. I followed her through the dancing crowd. "This place is amazing!"

She squeezed my hand. "There's another thing we have they don't."

"What's that?"

"A private rooftop terrace."

"What? Whoa!"

"Are you ready for some fun?"

I sure was. My senses were working overtime. I wanted to dance, but the crowd had grown even larger. Another steady inhalation cleared my mind enough to concentrate on Kendra's guiding hand.

"Come on. It's time to get your life back. You'll never fall prey to Casey's flimsy dick again."

I giggled. But truth was truth. My ex's dick *was* flimsy, and my best friend knew me better than anyone. Casey was a boy, whereas Gabe was a man. Where was Gabe?

Lightheaded and overwhelmed, I followed her between the dancing bodies. The heat, the grinding, the smell of sweat, and the constant noise buzzed in my ears like a blender.

"Kendra, I'm not feeling so well."

"Come this way. You're claustrophobic, remember?"

I nodded. We finished crossing the dance floor and made it to around a wall at one end of the club. A couple wearing tomato costumes passed by, and I shook my head. It wasn't even Halloween. And I hated tomatoes.

"Did you see that?" I gasped. "I need air."

I couldn't breathe. Kendra guided me to the stairs behind the wall, where the crowd was thinner. We passed a couple of bodyguards and went up a staircase. The click of a lock registered in my ears at the top. She opened the door, and it felt like I was walking into a private pink boudoir.

I watched Sam fall backwards in slow motion and lunged forward to catch her limp body. She fell into my arms, and our combined weight brought us down to the the hardwood floor. Sam landed on top of me. I rolled her to the side and sheltered her from the gathering crowd around us.

"She's unconscious. Give her some room!"

"Sam? What's wrong with her?" Kendra pushed her way through the crowd. Her reddened eyes and smeared mascara made my friend look more like a hooker than a business owner. I sent out an alert to Julian who now pushed through the crowd towards us. He took Kendra underneath her arm and held her steady while I gathered myself back to my feet and lifted Sam into my arms. She mumbled something underneath her breath.

"What's wrong with her?" I asked. "What did you give her?"

"Nothing." Kendra's eyes doubled in size. Our client was proving to be trouble again.

"I saw you give her a pill, K. What was it?"

A small crowd gathered around us. Someone snapped a picture, and Kendra covered her face.

"Come on, Silver. We can't do this here." Julian grabbed

Kendra's hand. "Get her out of here. We'll re-group at the office." My cousin guided the security, dispersing the crowd.

Sam rested against my chest like a baby, drooling on my shirt.

"Wait! Where are you taking her?" Kendra panicked as I turned toward the exit door with Sam in my arms.

"Home."

"I'm coming with."

"No, you're not," Julian warned. "You're coming with me."

She slipped her wrist from his grip and pulled back. "Like hell I am."

I watched as Kendra sneaked back into the crowd. Julian shook his head and swore under his breath.

"She's your problem tonight, brother. I've got my hands full."

My cousin bolted after her, and that was the last time I saw Kendra or Julian. As I stood with Sam snuggled in my arms, a light flashed on the upper floor balcony as someone snapped another photo. The disco lights spun, blinding me, and when I looked at the area again, it was empty.

I turned away and carried Samantha through the club's front door. Outside, the sting of the fall midnight air woke her.

"Where am I?" She shifted in my hold as I searched for the car keys in my pocket.

"Whoa! Hold on!" The keys jiggled in my palm, and then I watched as in slow motion they dropped to the drain hole. But it was the keys or Sam.

"Don't move," I whispered in her ear. "I'm taking you home."

The clang of metal against metal echoed.

"Were those your keys?" she asked, blinking through her long lashes. I hurried around the corner to where I'd parked my car. I pressed my thumb to the door, and it slid open. This latest emergency feature came from my kindhearted older brother. He was a genius and pretty much too good for anyone.

At thirty-nine, my brother's unexpected baby had given him a head full of silver hair that complemented the salt and pepper beard.

I seated Samantha on the passenger's side and clicked her seatbelt.

"Orgasms…" she moaned, "screaming orgasms."

I chuckled, closed the passenger door, walked around to my side, and turned the ignition.

"Where's home, Sam?" I asked, but after no reply, I texted Julian who got the address from a semi-conscious Kendra.

Apart from Sam's sighs and a few horny moans I couldn't understand, the rest of the ride remained quiet. All right, maybe the moans weren't that quiet because my dick replied with hard intent. I parked in front of her home, removed her from the car, and carried her up the dozen steps to the front door.

"Sam, I need your keys," I whispered. She shifted in my grip, and her ass rubbed against my hard-on.

"Under the mat." She snuggled deeper into my chest.

"You hide your keys under the mat?" I let out a frustrated breath.

"I had no pockets."

"How about your sparkly clutch?" I remembered from the bar.

"I don't know where that is." She braced her forehead on my shoulder as she tried to look for the purse, as if that were going to help.

"Don't worry. It's probably at the club. I'll find it." Holding her steady, I widened my stance and carefully crouched to the ground. I lifted the doormat but found no key, and Sam was back asleep in my arms.

Fuck!

Just once, I wished that an evening could go somewhat smoothly. But then I remembered who I was, and the fact that my life had never been normal *was* normal. I laughed out loud until the echo reminded me it was well past the middle of the night. Someone turned on a light in the window across the street and peeked through the blinds.

I carried Sam down the steps. I placed her back in the passenger's seat and removed a small box from the glove compartment.

"Stay there." I whispered, but by then she was snoring so hard the barking dog across the street didn't even wake her. I hurried to the front door and picked the lock, went back to get Sam, and carried her inside. The snooping lady across the street turned off her light.

I removed my shoes and braced another dozen steps as I carried her upstairs to the bedroom. Her lilac and vanilla scent overpowered me. I swallowed hard and slowly set her on her bed.

I sneezed. A cat meowed and brushed against my leg. The second-long panic as I recalled I had cat allergies gave Sam enough time to spring back up to a standing position. She lifted her arms high in the air. "Help me with the corset."

She turned around. Her sweet aroma assaulted my senses and messed with my memories, sending all my blood flow to the only part of my body aching for relief. I fiddled with her corset ties, looping the long ribbons out of their crisscross pattern, loosening them one after another until the top was wide enough to slip down her body. I stepped back like I'd been burned. Her skin, curves, and unique scent drove me crazy. This was too much and not enough. It was too soon. She reminded me of everything I'd lost. The irresponsible path she offered could ruin us both.

She cupped her breasts and, wearing nothing but the sexiest pair of pleather pants I'd seen on a body, she turned back around to face me. Sam swayed on her feet.

"Help me get the pants off." She giggled, and I groaned.

How could I pretend that a half-naked, beautiful, appetizing woman wasn't standing in front of me? How could I pretend she didn't look like my younger wife?

I took a step closer and reached around to her ass. Her chest — with her hands between us — pressed against mine. Her warm breath left a trail of need on my arm. I lowered the smooth zipper, grabbed the leather at her hips, and helped her shimmy out of the tight pants. She let go of her breasts and, giggling, climbed underneath the covers. She sank in between the pillows. I pulled the comforter and blanket over her, breathing out with a little relief.

"Come to bed, Gabe," she whispered, patting the spot beside her.

Everything inside of me shut down. Her murmur hit me deep in the chest, and I didn't know whether to scorn her for taking a pill from Kendra or to give in and join her in that bed. I'd sink deep between her legs, forget about the past, and focus on pleasing her in the present. Once I forgot about everything before tonight, we'd be beautiful. Somewhere in my fucked up mind, I wanted her to be the woman I found, not the one I'd lost.

I located some makeup remover on the bathroom counter and dabbed a bit on a cotton pad. Sam stumbled into the bathroom, lowered her black lace panties to her knees, and sat on the toilet.

I turned around to give her the privacy she didn't appear to need.

Fucking Kendra. What the hell did she slip her?

Kendra's lifelong enemies spared no morals. I was working on a hunch, but I didn't like what it was telling me. Kendra didn't have many friends. She was lucky to have found Sam, but how? I had so many questions I wanted answered, I didn't know where to begin. How had Kendra kept this friendship, and whom had she crossed?

Sam wiped herself and turned on the shower. I sat on the covered toilet seat and waited while she washed. Beyond the bathroom door, a set of fairy lights flickered on a timer. They twinkled all over her bedroom, and the scene brought a smile to my face. At one point, Sam sung the lyrics, *I touch myself.* She had a great voice, but all the sweet offers she sang made me that much hornier. She wrapped a towel around herself and crossed steadily back to the bedroom, where she slipped underneath the covers again. The cat remained on the other pillow by her head.

A text came in from Julian: Kendra said Martinez is going after her friends.

Fuck.

Kendra could have jeopardized Sam's security.

"What's wrong?" Sam asked.

"Nothing. Close your eyes."

"How can I close my eyes when yours are so beautiful, Mr. Silver?" Her drunken voice held need. She writhed in her sheets with yearning. I reserved the last ounce of control I held for this moment, although a jerk-off session was inevitable before the end of the night.

Julian had to be wrong, but I suspected he wasn't. And if that were the case, Sam was in trouble.

I smiled. "Close your eyes, Ms. Connor."

She returned my smile, but listened. The fairy lights twinkling above sparkled over her face.

"You had an exciting evening tonight, and half your makeup is still on your face."

"Men like you know what to do," she murmured. "You've been through shit. You have the experience of handling shit, you know?"

Was she calling me old?

I gently wiped the smears off, revealing freckles on her nose and a birthmark underneath her brow. The more make up I removed, the more quickly I traveled back to the past, when it hurt a lot less than it did now. Sam's gentle snore brought me back to the present. I stared at her rosy cheeks for what felt like forever. They were plump from smiling and gave her rebellious face an angelic appearance.

The cat jumped off Sam's bed, meowed, and brushed against my leg. It followed me to the kitchen, where it stood by a bowl labeled STAR.

"Are you hungry?" I filled Star's bowl with fresh water and canned food, knocking over some scattered mail in the process. I picked up the letters off the floor and dialed Morgan at Kissed. "Hey, how did the night go?"

"You mean, after you left me stranded?"

"You're alive, so I'm assuming the crowd didn't kill you."

"I'm just closing up. What can I do ya for?"

"Anything in the lost and found tonight? I'm looking for a silver clutch."

"Sorry, not a single item, but there was a creep asking for Kendra."

"What did he look like?"

"Thick Spanish accent, scruffy looking, bushy eyebrows and stunk of cigarettes."

My gut twisted.

Fuck.

"I didn't say anything. He left soon after closing."

"That's good. Thanks, Morgan."

I hung up, set the letters I'd shuffled on the kitchen counter. A note from Sam's employer congratulating her on a promotion stared back at me. I dialed my older brother's number next.

"Can you get a sitter? I need you at 323 Northcliffe Avenue. I have reason to believe Martinez found Kendra. Wear something comfortable. We're breaking in."

"Yeah, sure. Laila's at the sitter's. I thought you'd need help on Kendra's opening night. Give me fifteen." James hung up just before I did.

The best thing about working with brothers who got you was that they got you. They didn't ask pointless questions, and they came to the job prepared.

James was the best father in the world, but given his unyielding job, a surprise baby had introduced him to a life-style he wasn't expecting. And that lifestyle included sleepless nights. He looked like hell.

I checked in on Sam again and left a note on the dining table. I locked her in with the spare key from the kitchen drawer, and took it with me. I hurried to the car and drove to Sam's workplace.

Half an hour later, I watched him pull up to the parking lot and back in beside me. He rolled down the window and pointed to the arched logo.

"We're breaking into McDonald's?"

"No. That way." I repositioned his arm to the building across the street. The modern structure of stacked rectangular boxes had security issues, both IT and physical. I'd broken past their firewall within seconds, and the rooftop patio connected to Sam's office on the third floor had easy access. James studied the blueprint on my phone.

"Sam lost her purse. We may have company, so let's fly low."

"Got it."

We each put on our black hoodies, blending into the night. We crossed the street as silent as cats, without a soul around. At the side of the building by the service entry, before I stepped on the ladder, a rectangular silver-sequined box caught my eye. Except it wasn't a box. I picked up the clutch, immediately recognizing it as Sam's.

"Sam lost her clutch at Kissed tonight."

I opened the flap, but the inside was empty. Nearby, a spill of lip gloss, business cards, a mini-bottle of ibuprofen, and three condoms in their foil packets littered the ground.

"What's it doing here?" my brother asked.

"It brought whoever was looking for Kendra to Sam's workplace. He must have known they're friends."

"Shit. He found her."

"We don't know for sure yet, but if Kendra's dealing, finding her isn't the problem."

"Kendra knows how to keep a low profile."

"Not this new Kendra. And even if that were true, the easiest way to get to Kendra would be through her closest friend, Sam. Her office could be bugged. Let's go."

We climbed the metal staircase that scaled the side of the building up to the rooftop, where James picked the lock on Sam's patio door.

"The lock is clear. No one's come in this way."

We stepped inside and checked her office. A picture of her smiling face and her cat rested on her desk. Her eyes took me back to a moment I rarely experienced and had only shared with Joanne. Her familiar eyes held me back in time until my brother poked me with his finger.

"Aha, now I see why you're so taken by this girl."

"What do you see?" I asked.

"You know exactly what I see. Gabe, what if you're looking for signs that aren't there?"

"I know what I know, and something's off. You can't deny they look alike. Give me a magnifying glass. Sam's…"

"Not Joanne."

Although I was annoyed by his comment, I couldn't deny that what he said was true. I took the round glass from him and brought it to the photograph.

"Fuck…"

My hands shook as I handed the frame to James. He

removed the magnifying glass from my other hand and took his turn examining the photograph.

"Well, what do you know?"

"You see it too, right?"

"The fucking native charm from New Zealand? Yeah, I see it."

"How the hell does *she* have it?"

"How the hell does someone look just like her?"

"They say everyone has a body double, but most people never find theirs."

"A body double with an identical birthmark?"

"So you don't think she's Joanne's double?"

"Give me a couple more minutes to sort this out. I just found out this Sam girl exists. " My brother's dry sarcasm got better with age.

"Do you think she could have like… you know… Joanne's soul?" I tried.

He turned his head to look me dead in my eyes. "Don't let this fuck you up again, my brother. Facts over emotion. Remember? Now come on. Let's do what we came here to do."

I searched through Sam's office for bugs and anything else out of place. I secured a transmitter to a bookshelf and connected the device through the company app.

"Looks clean." James double-checked underneath the desk, behind the corner plant and inside the cabinets. "No sign of intrusion."

"Nothing. That's good. For now."

My brother lowered his hands over his hips and narrowed his brows. "They may wait until the night alarms are off."

"Who are *they*, exactly?"

"Whoever stole Sam's key card."

We left Sam's office and scaled the ladder at the side of the building. A man turned the corner into the alley and stopped mid-step. While we hid behind night's darkness, so did he, and I couldn't see his face. Then he turned around and ran.

"Definitely not a coincidence." James said.

I placed a surveillance team at Sam's apartment while we took turns watching the building from a café across the street. The weekend dragged until on Monday morning, when Samantha Connor walked inside the café. She wore her pencil-tight skirt and strolled across the tiles like she was my past, present, and future. And I knew my life would never be the same without her.

Chapter 4

Sam

The room was hot and very pink. Faint lights glowed from underneath a silky fabric draped over a lamp. The fire hazard didn't hold my attention for long, as Kendra's sexy ass swayed with each step closer to the bed. She removed her pumps, and like a panther, strolled across the plush carpeting towards me. The gold fabric of her top swooshed over her breastbone, and I swallowed hard. My best friend screamed adventure, and at this moment she seemed like a suitable vehicle to scratch such itch. I would have preferred it be Gabe, but my heart was beating so hard that I feared the rushing blood migrating south of my navel couldn't wait to find relief.

Her predatory gaze forced me back to sit up on the four-poster bed. She approached with confidence, and I backed up on top of the mattress until I couldn't get back any further because the headboard blocked me.

"Don't you think it's time you lost your virginity?" Kendra's hands slid up my bare legs, and for the life of me, I couldn't remember when I'd removed my pants. How had we gotten home? I thought I was at the club. Her fingers left a trail of exciting warmth and confusion along my skin. I welcomed her touch, and as she neared my sex, my inhibitions washed away.

"I'm not a virgin." My voice shook, my muscles twitched, and my body trembled. Technically I wasn't, but it had been so long since my one and only miserable time that I totally felt like one. I realized my corset top was somewhere on the floor as my nipples reacted to the colder temperature.

"Casey doesn't count. You said it took less than a minute," Kendra whispered. She was close to my ear by then. Her warm breath flowed along my skin. Truth was, Casey came in under thirty seconds, while I didn't, and Kendra's hushed invitations and promises turned me on more than my ex ever did.

"K, we're friends."

"And what are good friends for?"

She slid her hand down my panties and I closed my eyes. Warmth pooled between my legs right underneath her touch. Her gentle strokes quickened into circles. Her fingers rubbed over my clit. The tender flesh swelled, and she quickened her wrist motion. My body gave into its needs, and I couldn't stop the oncoming release. It had been too long. Way too long.

"Yes!"

I jolted awake at the sound of my voice, heaving in air and coming hard underneath my stroking fingers as a strip of morning light shone between the slit in my sheers. Sunlight beamed at my eyes. I brought my right hand to cover them and groaned at the slickness covering my fingers.

Fucking wet dreams!

I pulled the covers over my head and shifted in my bed to where the cold sheets snuggled against my heated body. Cool and dry. As soon as I located the optimal spot, I realized the sheets were too cool.

I lifted the covers. "Holy shit!"

I was naked – I never slept naked. I checked underneath the covers again.

"What the hell?"

My feet touched the scrunched panties near the foot of the bed. The same panties I'd worn last night. I sat up and tried to remember what had happened and how I'd left Kissed, but I couldn't. My corset top and leather pants lay folded on a chair.

"What the…"

Me sleeping naked in my bed could be understandable. But the folded clothes next to the pile on top of my chair? Those were not. I didn't remember cleaning up.

How did I get home?

My memory fuzzed around the details, but she was the last person I remembered from last night. My head hurt. I grabbed a robe and wrapped it around my body just as my morning alarm chimed.

Confused, I picked up my phone and almost dropped it. It fumbled in my hands before I secured it to check the time. The fairy lights clicked off their timer, dimming the room.

"It's Monday?! How the fuck is it Monday? And what the hell happened to Saturday and Sunday?"

From then on I fell into a madly rushed shower, which brought back a memory of an earlier shower, brushed my teeth, shaved my armpits and legs because my hair liked to grow like grass during the first forty-eight hours, and then dressed for work the fastest I'd ever dressed in my life. When I reached for my house keys, I found a note stuck to the table.

Sam,

I hope you're feeling better when you wake up. I borrowed the key from the kitchen drawer to lock your door and ordered a replacement lock. Yours is easy to pick.

Stay safe.

Gabriel Silver

My face drained of blood as I re-read the letter with his personal phone number underneath his name.

"Gabe was here?" A loud meow caught my attention.

"Star!" I rushed to the kitchen while all the distinct possibilities of what might have happened during the last forty-eight hours flushed my body with an arousing heat. Unsettlement returned to my stomach as I wished I could remember the night I'd apparently spent with Gabriel Silver.

Why can't I remember anything?

I refilled Star's food and water bowls, cleaned the litter, and checked my watch for the time. I opened my laptop to google Silver's full name, but nothing decent came up. Who doesn't have an internet profile? I folded the note into my pocket, grabbed my briefcase, and hurried out the door with just enough time to grab a coffee before work.

A twelve-stop train ride later, I walked into a rush of businessman traffic and hid at the Starbucks on the first floor, across the street from work. Lost in thought, I stood in line waiting for my morning coffee and muffin. My head pounded with the unpleasant reminder of memory loss. I tried my best to figure out what had happened after the nightclub, but nothing helped. Kendra never called—or if she had, I didn't remember picking up. But I checked my phone. And she hadn't called, which wasn't typical for Kendra. She hadn't been herself last night. Or two nights ago. I still couldn't believe I'd lost forty-eight hours. An arousing memory of my friend doing some unforgettable things to my body flashed in my mind. Did that really happen?

I shook it off. A fresh brew trickled into a pot. The coffee shop door swung open, and its bell rang in my ears. The loud echo stirred memories of grinding bodies and bright lights.

"Are you coming tonight?"

I jumped up at the familiar whisper in my ear and turned around to face bright blue eyes.

"Excuse me?" I asked, as recognition dawned. Gabe stood in the line behind me. He sported a fresh shave, and I held no shame for taking a long whiff. I admired his Travolta ensemble

— a crisp white shirt with two open buttons plus a worn-out leather jacket. He pulled off the look much better than Danny. Very suitable for a bartender, especially for one with wide shoulders and ripped arms. Gabe's musky aftershave overpowered the smell of coffee, and my knees softened.

"Gabe. Hi! How are you?"

My nerves often spiked at work presentations, but that was nothing compared what I'd experienced when Gabriel Silver walked through the door. The hot flashes came in waves as the horror and trauma I didn't remember much from Friday night rushed back. I stared at the beautiful man I didn't remember sleeping with, openmouthed and drooling.

He grinned at me in reply. "Great. You?"

"Good. Thanks. Do you have a moment to chat?" I pointed to a booth and checked my watch.

He gestured for me to lead the way.

The barista must have overheard us because she chimed in with a wide smile. "I can bring your orders to your table, Mr. Silver."

"Thank you."

I slid into my seat, and Gabe did the same on the other side.

The barista brought our coffees right as we sat. I stalled with a kind smile back because it gave me a chance to gather my thoughts as I added the sugar I never add. I mean, how could I ask him whether we'd slept together? Wasn't it rude I didn't remember? Wasn't it bad that I couldn't remember? How did I not remember? He could take this the wrong way and never want to see me again.

"Listen..." I started, but as his brow lifted, I lost my words. "Thank you for taking me home." I regrouped, trying to go with the facts. He had definitely taken me home because he left a note.

He leaned back in his seat, amused.

"I... I assume you're the one who took me home?"

"You don't remember?"

I shut my eyes. My face had likely turned burgundy and my freckles wild.

"I'm sorry. I know that's bad. I don't know how, but I don't remember. I woke up this morning and saw your note—"

"—You woke up *this* morning and saw my note?" he repeated, like he didn't understand me.

"Yeah, apparently I slept through the weekend." I rolled my eyes.

His brows drew together in a frown.

"And I can't stop wondering if we... you know..." I leaned forward and lowered my voice. "If we had sex."

His forehead let go of some tension, and the few furrows disappeared. After that, full amusement took over his eyes.

"I hoped the orgasm would stick with you for the night."

"You gave me an orgasm?" I asked, a bit too loud for the morning crowd.

"At Kissed. You ordered the drink?"

Right. That kind of orgasm. I remembered that. And he wasn't mentioning any other kind, so I assumed we hadn't slept together after all. Unless I couldn't get an orgasm? I was sure I'd remember that. My gaze lifted just as he leaned forward and closer to me.

"Nothing happened between us, Sam."

I breathed out in relief.

"And I promise you'd never forget me between your legs."

Tension rushed back to my core, and with it, the yearning for a release. My body couldn't catch a break around Gabe, but who wanted a break with one hundred and eighty-five pounds of beautiful muscle that had put me to bed? And yet I couldn't remember any of it.

"Thank you for taking me home."

He reached inside his briefcase and removed my purse from within. My mouth dropped open.

"You kept my clutch?"

"I found your clutch."

I lifted my chin and angled my attention closer.

"In that side alley by your work." He pointed across the street.

"Thank you. What was it doing there?" I removed the clutch from his hand with the remaining ounce of grace I had left.

"That's what I'm trying to figure out. Check if anything's missing." His brows lifted.

I searched through the few contents. My cheeks heated when my fingertips touched the round edge of a single condom in its foil. I knew I'd had two more attached to the pack, but I couldn't find them.

"So?" he asked.

"My access card. That's it." There was no way I was mentioning the condoms.

He nodded, and for ten blissful seconds said nothing else.

"Kendra doesn't have many friends because the people she hangs out with are bad news. I have a reason to believe one of those friends is trying to get to her through you. What do you remember from Friday night?"

"I think it'd be easier if I told you what I don't remember. Which is pretty much everything."

"Kendra slipped you a pill, correct?"

I nodded.

"Did she tell you what it was?"

If she had, I couldn't remember that either, so I moved my head sideways, cringing.

"The boring me wanted an adventure." It was so much easier to refer to myself in the third person.

"An adventure?" His brows lifted. "Well, you sure picked the right adventure in Kendra. How long have you two known each other?"

Why did this feel like a confession? "About six months," I

replied. It was one hundred and eighty-seven days, to be exact. The half-year mark passed last week.

"She's been a good friend to me, and she's fun. She looks out for me, and I look out for her." I explained in the easiest way possible. "We watch out for each other. But she gets wilder every day."

"Hmm." He snorted with suspicion and relaxed in his seat. "Interesting. And how is it I haven't met you before?"

I tilted my head sideways, mimicking him.

"How haven't *I* met *you* before?" I asked back.

"Rebel." He scuffed with amusement and blurted out, "My answer is simple. I avoid people."

"You're a barman."

He grunted.

"You're not a barman?"

"The bartending position is temporary. Just helping out a friend. Surveillance is my thing during the week."

"Surveillance? Must be a change from making drinks."

He scanned me over, making me heat all over. "It has its better moments. Have you seen Kendra?"

"You'd think as her friend I would know where she is but I haven't been a good friend lately. I've been busy with work, and I was trying to make up for that. I want to be there for her again. Call it a New Year's resolution, but before the New Year. In September."

He laughed.

"What's so funny?"

"You. Your mouth. It's all so...."

I waited for the word *captivating* or *rebellious*, but then he said, "Familiar." Which totally fucked me up.

"Familiar?"

He blinked, looking at me like me like we'd met long ago. "I'm sorry. It's just that your resemblance to—"

His phone rang. Of course, his phone would ring during

one of the most intimate conversations I'd had with a man in years.

"Gabriel Silver." He lifted his finger for me to wait and paused between each of his next four words. "Aha. Yeah. Okay. Thanks."

I mean, who talked like that?

"Work stuff?" I asked when he hung up. "And why do you avoid people?"

He grinned lazily. His blue eyes dazzled and held me captive, yet I didn't understand why. He avoided my question, just like he avoided people.

"Did you hide your house key underneath the mat again?"

"No. I read your note. What exactly happened Friday night? I mean… I lost two days."

He motioned for the barista to bring more coffee. "Call in late to work."

"I've never been late."

His delightful, charming smile held powers I couldn't understand. Calling in late was a big mistake in a newly promoted position. But how could I say no to the person who held answers about the wild weekend I didn't remember?

"Make up a story. Tell them you'll be an hour late. Come on. I thought you were a rebel," he teased.

"You think I'm a rebel?" I laughed.

Today's chaotic morning threw me off. I was one of the most responsible people in my family, yet I'd lost two days. Responsibility was no more, I guessed. On the bright side, since I was an orphan of two orphans with no siblings, it was just me. So that still made me the most responsible in my small family of one, plus cat. Except for last weekend. That didn't count.

Plus Kendra.

"You pee in alleys, take pills from friends, and undress in front of strange men."

Shit!

His words sank in like the first bite of my muffin, which plummeted inside my empty stomach. The thought of him watching me undress revived the tingles on my body. And it made me fucking crazy regretful that I couldn't remember any of it.

"You undressed me?"

"I helped you unfasten the corset top."

I let go of a nervous breath.

"And then you took off your pants." He shifted in discomfort, and I perked up. "Right after you removed the corset yourself." He paused, watching me, then added. "Right in front of me. You showered. I helped you remove your makeup. And then you went to sleep."

Maybe I shouldn't have asked. I was well aware of all the embarrassing possibilities that had led me to sleep naked in bed. Hearing him tell me how he had taken care of me made me understand something I wasn't expecting – he actually cared.

He held my gaze, leaned forward, and whispered.

"It got even better when you got yourself off."

A quick memory of my naughty dream with Kendra flashed through my mind. The wet dream couldn't have been my only one because I remembered more.

Oh, my God! Embarrassment shaded my face. The fact he was still sitting here, worried about me after my careless night, was more than Casey ever gave me in all our nights combined. Part of me wanted to sink underneath that table and die. The other part preferred sinking underneath the covers with Gabe.

What the hell is happening to me?

"I know I've said it already, but thank you. I really mean it." I tried to salvage the little shame remaining inside me.

"You're welcome. Now call."

I picked up my phone and frowned. Casey used to tell me

what to do. But this was different. Gabe had gotten me home safely. That worried look in his eyes couldn't be for nothing. I removed my cell from my pocket, called in, and left a message I'd be late.

He grinned with approval.

"Now what?" I asked.

"Now we wait. Whoever stole your access card will try to get inside. What do you do?"

I turned my head to the entrance across the street. "Insurance underwriter. What if they got inside already?"

"We've been watching the door since Saturday morning. Cards don't work until seven hundred Monday. They screen everyone who enters that building. Has anything odd happened recently?"

"You mean other than me losing two days? Can't think of anything."

"I appreciate the sarcasm. But I still need an answer."

I scanned through the last couple of days in my mind. "No. Nothing out of the ordinary. You sound like a private investigator."

Possibly ex-military.

He glanced across the street. "Just trying to figure out why someone wanted to get inside your building. Was it for someone else? Or was it for you?"

"Shouldn't we call the police if you're that worried?"

His genuine smile was hotter than hell and suited the smug face.

"This is what I do, but today I'm looking out for a friend. Failing women has been my talent recently, so I'd be careful, my friend."

Is that what we were? Friends? Perhaps friends with benefits, if I played my cards right? Then why the morbid warning to stay away from him?

His eyes held something different this morning than when

we'd met at Kissed. They held a sense of bewilderment and care.

"Are you saying orgasms aren't your only talent?"

A lady in the booth behind Gabe turned her head sideways.

He leaned forward and lowered his voice. "From what I witnessed in your bedroom a couple of nights ago, you have no trouble climaxing on your own."

Right. That little number I pulled in front of him could haunt me for a while.

"For what it's worth, you're not the only human who masturbates."

"It was a wet dream," I spat back. "It's not like I had any control over…" I stopped because I realized my voice was carrying too far. A mother in line scowled at me while she covered her child's ears. I sank into my seat.

"It was hot," he mouthed.

And just like that, I heated all over again. I checked my surroundings, and this time it was me who edged closer.

"So, you get off spying on women who relieve themselves? In all meanings of the word?"

"Not before I met you," he grinned.

I shook off his lust.

"What are you going to do if you find the thief?" I tried a fresh approach.

"That depends on who it is."

"Who could it be? The access card could have just slipped out. Maybe they'll return it to the front desk."

I waited, watching his steady gaze on the front door to my work across the street.

"I checked with security this morning. No one's returned a card."

"So now we just sit here?"

"Yes."

I'd never felt uneasy about going to work, but this morning

and the entire weekend had me nervous, and the way Gabe was staring at that door awakened every single last goosebump on my arms.

"Why would someone want to rob an insurance company?" I asked.

"That's an excellent question, Sam."

I frowned. He wasn't easing my worry the way I'd hoped he would.

"Have you heard from Kendra?"

"No. You?"

I shook my head. He clicked something into his phone and received an immediate reply.

"Neither has Julian."

I recalled Kendra mention Julian Silver before. "He's Kendra's ex, isn't he?"

"Not really. It's complicated. Kendra's complicated."

"You know, people keep saying that, but all I see is a girl who wants to live free and have a good time. Since when is that a sin?"

"You don't know Kendra like I do. Trouble is her middle name. It follows her like a newborn pup follows its mamma."

The mental picture I drew of his description forced out a giggle. He noticed and smiled, lifting my spirit.

"As her friends, we should help her."

"That's exactly what I'm trying to do. Where did you two meet again?"

"A strip club," I lied. Explaining to him we'd met while searching for our biological parents fell under the 'too personal' category for now. Not that we hadn't gotten pretty personal in the few hours I'd known him.

"I should have known." He shook his head. "Strip clubs attract rebels and trouble. That's trouble with a capital T."

I laughed. "You talk like you're fifty."

"That's called experience, rebel." He smirked.

"I am not a rebel."

"Said the rebel." He must have noticed my frown. "I'm sorry. I'm teasing, and it's not nice. Obviously, you're a good friend to Kendra. Much better than many of her previous friends have been. I'd love to take you out to dinner tonight. If you're free, that is."

Finally, we were getting somewhere. A date.

"Thanks. I am. So, you and Kendra know each other well."

"Yup. Years."

"Very well?" My brow lifted.

Stupid, stupid, stupid.

Gabe laughed. "We're just friends. Kendra's not my type and she's like family."

"What is your type?"

I shouldn't have gone there. I shouldn't have exposed myself to the possibility of another rejection, but as soon as his lips moved, he opened the door to a possibility which a couple of days ago I wouldn't have entertained.

"You."

The moment Sam got up from the booth and left for work, I wanted her back in that seat. Close to me. Safe. The instinct turned my stomach. The last time I let a woman walk into a building, she never walked out. They carried her out in a box and buried her somewhere in the desert. I finished my espresso and drummed my fingers over the tabletop. Women didn't like men who snooped around, but if I'd snooped around Joanne's—

"Another coffee, Mr. Silver?" the barista asked.

I nodded with a grumpy, "Yes please."

James was sitting in his parked car, and I was losing patience. He was the oldest in the Silver family, and the smartest, but he liked to play it down. Sometimes I wondered what our parents had been thinking when they chose his name as Fox, but the few grey's had set in early on my brother, and Fox Silver lived up to his name to the fullest. James Bond style. He rubbed his marble-toned beard as he focused on his phone.

I turned on the bug app and listened in as Sam realized the small bow of black fabric around the vase of roses I'd sent her were black panties.

"No! Oh, my God, he didn't!" The glee in her voice prompted me to text her.

G. Silver: Thought you could use a fresh pair

Sam: Did you add yourself to my contacts?

G. Silver: Right after I took off your pants. How's work?

A subtle reminder of how close she'd allowed a stranger near her panties ought to make up for my nosiness.

Sam: Nothing unusual. I don't think you have anything to worry about

G. Silver: Says a woman who got drugged by a friend and lost 48 hours

Sam: Thank you for the roses. They're beautiful. But seriously, shouldn't those wait till after the sex? I feel like I owe you at least a BJ

G. Silver: We can fix that next time I see you, Rebel

I thought roses would be a friendly gesture. It had been a long time since I'd wooed a woman. Sam's youthful, vibrant nature intrigued me and made me want to woo her more. A lot. She was the first woman since Joanne who made me want to breathe, hope, and live. So much had changed since I stepped down as a private investigator and turned to surveillance, but for the first time in years, that need to fix things flowed through my veins again.

For now, watching people was my thing. Close surveillance prevented mistakes. For example, like the man in the jean jacket who entered Sam's work across the street sent all kinds of alarm bells ringing in my head. But none of them sounded as loud as the fact that he looked familiar.

Fucking Martinez!

I left a crisp twenty for the barista as she set down my next steaming cup of coffee and sprinted out of the booth like a crazy man, texting James while running across the street. By the time I passed security, the man in the jean jacket was on his way upstairs. I climbed the stairs to the sixth floor, jumping every second one. I pushed the door open and hurried through the hallway, looking for Sam's name.

When I found it, I knocked.

"Come in."

I pushed the door open with caution.

"Gabe? What are you doing here?"

Sam stuffed something in her drawer and sat straight up behind her desk, cross-legged. I glimpsed at her exposed toned thigh from the side. My gaze drifted upward to the valley between her breasts. A black bra strap peeked out from underneath her white shirt. The two popped buttons, rolled-up sleeves, and a slit up her tight skirt completed a tempting secretary ensemble. Like one of those porn office scenes. A pencil poked through the bun in her hair enhanced the naughty image in my mind of her over that desk, hair spilling to the sides. She shifted in her seat, and I noticed the panties were no longer tied around the roses.

Sexy as fuck.

Was she wearing them? The pink tint on her cheeks gave me the answer. Hot wasn't even close to what this woman captured. Black reading glasses rested mid-way on her nose. The complete business attire made her look like a lonely librarian and made me horny like a dog.

I shook my head to clear the porn version of the moment I created in my head. This was bad timing for fantasies.

"A man snuck inside the building," I whispered in my most professional voice. "I notified security. Lock your door and don't leave."

She nodded. I waited to hear the click on her door and hurried down the hallway. I checked every conference room and every stairwell until a brazen secretary stopped my search.

"Sir? Can I help you?" She was carrying a stack of papers out of the copy room.

"I'm looking for someone."

"Do you have an appointment?"

"No. Yes. I mean, no."

"Who are you looking for?"

"A man. Jean jacket. Rough black hair."

From his yellow teeth to his stained cigarette fingers, Joanne's murderer had hunted me every night since her death. Now that he was near, a lust for revenge was making my blood boil. I could feel his presence in my bones.

"Why don't I show you to the waiting room, and we'll make sure you reach the right person." She gestured.

"It's urgent." I looked over her shoulder and down the hall, then back to her again, in hope she'd believe me. "He's dangerous. He snuck inside the building."

She set the papers aside. "Sir, you can come with me, or I can call security."

Just as she finished, I saw Martinez dart from a door down the hallway and to the left. I dropped to my knee and removed the gun from its holster at my ankle.

I pushed the woman out of the way with too much force because she screamed, "Security!"

She followed behind me, running like she had a chance at catching me. I focused on the jean jacket turning the corner. When I reached the spot, the path forked, and I wasn't sure which way he'd run next. I made it too far from Samantha when I realized he'd led me on a wild goose chase. I found the empty corridor that connected back to the main hall with Sam's office and headed her way.

A scream tore through the hall.

"Give me the file!" a deep Spanish voice ordered from within Sam's office.

A gun fired, and blood drained from my face. Three more shots were fired, and I rammed into the office door. Inside Sam's office, a secretary crouched in a corner of the room while Sam stood behind her desk, shaking. Tears streamed down her face, staining her cheeks with black mascara.

Wind blew through the shattered window, and paperwork lifted in a tornado. The door closed, and the click of a gun sounded near my ear. I froze, then turned around in slow motion. Martinez looked me dead in my eyes, and I realized he was as stunned to see me here as I was to see him. A lot passed through my head at the moment. But nothing more important than the odds that he was fucking involved with Kendra's drug problem. Big odds, apparently. And what the fuck did he want with Sam? Rage coiled in my body, reaching its upper limit.

I twisted around and disarmed Martinez. The gun slipped from my grip, crashed to the floor, and went off in a random direction. We both dove for the weapon. I rolled over Martinez before he rolled over me, struggling.

"Her eyes were open when we closed the box." He spat in my face.

I pressed the trigger on impulse, and the gun went off between us. Sam and the other woman screamed, and I hoped that the fact I couldn't feel any pain meant I'd remained intact, because there was blood everywhere.

"You fucker!"

Martinez pushed himself away from me and hopped up on his healthy leg. The other one had a bullet lodged in the thigh. I lay on my back and pointed the gun his way. "Don't move!"

The police banged on the door.

"Police! Open up!"

I'd been waiting for this moment forever, and revenge was only a click away. Martinez smirked. His gaze skidded to the rooftop patio door on his right, like I was bluffing.

"This isn't the last time you'll see me, Silver." His focus returned to Sam. "Because history repeats itself."

I pressed the trigger, but the gun didn't go off. I realized the one bullet Martinez had was in his thigh. The police banged on the door, giving a final warning to get down. Martinez grabbed a file off Sam's desk. I leaped forward, but Sam was quicker. She lunged at him with her full force, retrieved the file from his grip, and landed on the other side of the room. Her necklace broke and fell to the floor. She was so quick, I couldn't stop staring while Martinez fled out the back door.

Fuck!

He ran across the rooftop and down the emergency staircase. I shot up and lunged for the patio as the cops broke through the door. I halted mid-step and lifted my arms in the air. The empty gun dangled in my hand.

"Drop the gun! Drop the gun!"

I slowly crouched to the ground. The police officer pointed her gun my way while Martinez fled. I lowered the empty weapon to the floor. Sam blinked repeatedly, and the image of her fear-stricken face carved into my heart. The secretary was crouching with her in the corner. She grasped at Sam, who was shaking like jelly. I grabbed the necklace Martinez had ripped off Sam's neck and stuffed it in my pocket before anyone noticed.

Fuck. What have I done?

Her mouth was open wide, and as her eyes released the tears into black mascara rivers, all I wanted was to make it all better.

But I couldn't. I'd fucked up before I even had a chance.

"On the floor! Face down, arms behind your back!" The shorter of the two cops pressed her knee between my shoulder blades and cuffed me in one move. I thought I recognized her from somewhere but couldn't place where.

"The intruder's getting away," I yanked my head sideways, noting the name on her uniform.

"Stay still, asshole." The gun's barrel jutted into my back.

"This is his gun," I mumbled to the floor.

"Save it for the judge. I am arresting you for trespassing, possession of a weapon, and assault."

"Assault? I didn't assault anyone."

"Let me finish, asshole. You do not have to say anything, but it may harm your defense if you do not mention when questioned something you later rely on in court. Anything you do or say can be given in evidence."

"You've got the wrong man." I wrestled the cuffs, but the cop wouldn't listen. She was doing her job – even if it was the wrong job.

"Laura, take the statements here, and I'll take him to the car." She turned around, then clicked her two-way radio. "Laura? Where are you?"

"I've got another gem down here. Armed."

James.

"Back up should be here. Take our cruiser."

Cuffed, I left Sam's office. Officer Green took me down into the cruiser. James was nowhere to be seen, which meant he was on his way to the station as well. These cops did not know who they were dealing with.

Fucking Martinez.

The man who'd stolen my life was back. And he was after Samantha? Why her? I was missing a connection between her and Kendra, and I couldn't quite place what it was. Fifteen minutes after they booked me, our family lawyer arrived at the station and bailed us out.

"Thanks, Ace." We shook hands. My cousin's cousin was like family.

"Anytime. My brother's re-opening the club on Friday. The situation has become more complicated."

"You think Martinez is looking for fresh bodies?"

"If it walks like a duck and quacks like laundered money passing through the channels, it means the sex-trafficking operation is picking up steam. I'd increase the security at Kissed."

"This is bullshit."

"Whatever it is, it smells funny. New Zealand would be a safer option."

New Zealand. My home away from home held beautiful but painful memories. It contained the past I desperately fought to fix and forget at the same time.

"Thanks, Ace. We'll stay in touch."

The lawyer mogul waved goodbye and left the station.

"What happened to you?" I asked.

"I ran into a cop." James adjusted his slacks. "Remember the woman I met in Colorado?"

"Yeah? You were into her. What happened?"

"I was into her before I had Laila, and this chick is not into kids. She's fucking ruthless."

"Totally your type, then? No?"

My brother rolled his eyes.

"I guess this one got under my skin. I got to go. Ma's with Laila, and I have a birthday gift to buy. Do you know what to get for a two-year-old?"

"I have no clue, but you should. You have one."

"Laila's eighteen months. This is her first two-year party. I updated your passport and packed your bag. You know, in case you have to go to New Zealand."

"You think I should go?" I had a promise to keep, and Kendra's life depended on my ability to keep her safe. New Zealand could kill two birds with one stone.

"I don't know what you're still doing here."

By the time I checked on Sam, night had fallen. Heavy raindrops splattered on the ground. I ran from the car to the front door with the food steaming from within a paper bag. My foot caught the doormat. I lifted the woven twine and smiled when

I didn't find a key. Sam not only installed the locks I'd ordered, but she'd also installed a doorbell camera.

"Hey!" she said through the two-way speaker. "Hold on. Just in the bathroom, but I'm coming."

She opened the door with a wide smile and threw her arms around my neck. "Thank God you're okay. I went to the station after they took you, but you were already out."

"Our lawyer bailed me out."

"No charges?" She stepped back inside and locked the front door, then slid the deadbolt across, followed by a chain.

I was impressed.

"Our lawyer took care of it." I handed her the white paper bag filled with food.

"Must be nice to have lawyers."

"Family friends."

"Even better."

"I'm sorry we couldn't do a fancier dinner tonight."

"What are you talking about? Come inside. Wine?"

She removed paper plates and plastic cups from the cupboard. It had been a while since I'd lived in what appeared to be half of converted student housing.

"I keep it low maintenance. Busywork means no time for dishes or life."

"So the takeout works?"

She grinned from ear to ear as she took the food from my hand and began unpacking. "It's the perfect dinner to end a day that started at gunpoint. I'm starving."

I'd expected Sam to be more traumatized, but she seemed unfazed. I pulled out the bottle I had tucked inside my jacket. "Great minds think alike. I hope you like red."

I handed her the bottle.

"Red is my favorite color."

The light nerves in her voice sang to me. It had been a long time since I'd heard a woman's need flow from her voice and right to my dick.

"You're soaked."

I removed my shoes only to discover my socks were not in better shape. "Do you mind if I take a quick shower?"

Her cheeks tinted with bright pink.

"Not at all. It's down the hall, second door on your right…" She paused mid-sentence and lowered her hand. "But I guess you already know that. You'll find fresh towels on the top shelf."

"Thanks." I peeled the socks off my feet and went down the hall, noting a flyer for Rebels' opening night. I guessed Club Forever was no more. If there was anyone who could get all the Hartleys out, it was the Wagner lawyers with a chain of strip clubs.

In the bathroom, I removed my jeans and shirt and stepped into the shower.

I pulled back the white curtain. Sam's lilac soap left a note of spring in the fall air.

Once done, I dried myself and wrapped the towel around my waist, but I couldn't find my clothes. I walked along the parquet floor back to the family room. The lights had dimmed. The food was ready on the low table, and Sam was sitting on the couch with a glass of wine. She patted the couch and smiled.

The view of her gave me a flashback as I remembered a moment in my life when this was real. When life at home was normal.

"What happened to my clothes?"

"I threw them in laundry. Don't worry. You look better in the towel than the pants." She winked.

It was a good thing I'd left Sam's necklace with James, who was fitting the charm with a tracker. If Martinez was after Sam, this time I'd stay one step ahead.

"So do you."

"Dig in."

She removed the plate from my hand. "Let me serve you. You had a rough day. Sit and relax."

I caught her drifting stare.

"Did you bug my office?"

Right. That. "I wouldn't be doing a good job at protecting you if I didn't."

"You're protecting me? From what? Who was that man?"

I sighed and lowered my head to where she drew her gaze along my thighs and down to where the towel barely covered my crotch.

"Are you looking at my dick?" I asked.

Her head flew up. "No! I… I was just wondering what you were staring at."

"Not my dick."

Her cheeks flushed with that beautiful pink color that got my dick hard.

I shifted in discomfort. "Tell me about your family."

"My mother's unexpected illness left me with medical bills I'm still paying off. My father died two years earlier in a boating accident." She shook with shivers.

"What is it?"

"I still remember the bloodstained water and the frenzied sharks. It's kept me out of the ocean for years."

"Your father was eaten by sharks?"

She nodded.

"Any siblings?"

"No. My parents couldn't have any kids. That's why they adopted me. Does my family have anything to do with the man at the office?"

I froze. A nerve stilled in my spine as I realized Sam was only twenty-three; sixteen years my junior and eight years younger than Joanne.

"What's the matter?" she asked. "You look like you've just seen a ghost."

"No. It's all good." I dug into the roast of lamb in a balsamic reduction with caramelized pears. A good friend of the family owned a restaurant, and my family's favorite spot never disappointed. Olivier from the Marina had rightfully earned himself three Michelin stars. His food filled me with instant comfort.

"What happened at work after I left?" I asked, meandering back to the conversation.

"They're giving me a week off to help with the trauma. Then we'll have new security briefings."

"Sounds…"

"Boring?"

We laughed at the same time.

"I had no fucking clue what I wanted to do when I went into underwriting and just finished it. And this new promotion is on the line because I underwrote Kissed."

"You what?"

"I underwrote the insurance policy on the club. I think Kendra grew soft on me a little."

While Kendra was never soft on anyone, the fact that she'd chosen Sam instead of one of the well-known insurers surprised me.

"Honestly, she saved my ass. She gave me a chance for a life do-over, and I took it."

Sam grinned, and I decided her mouth was a delightful surprise as well. Yet somehow I expected it.

"What would you do if you had to do it all over again?" I asked.

"I don't know. Maybe ski."

Her surprising answer gave me the shivers. "Why ski?"

"Be like a ski instructor. You know, the simple life in the mountains. I'm new to New York. We lived out in the country in Colorado. My parents kept me pretty sheltered, but they took me skiing all the time."

Joanne had moved to Colorado with me. Her mother never forgave me for stealing her daughter, but Joanne had loved to ski as well.

"All right. Skiing and country. I'll remember that."

"A cottage in the hills with a stream nearby sounds perfect."

"That's great to know. I'll have to take you to Austria."

"Wait, you have a cottage in Austria?"

I nodded. "I don't like to brag, but that place is fucking sick. Runs along a private ski trail."

Her hand stopped halfway to her mouth, and her eyes grew wide and filled with a youthful excitement I once remembered experiencing. "You have to show me. We have to go."

"What happened to the one-night-stand girl I met at Kissed?" I laughed.

"Adventure's bursting through her veins." She wiggled her toes and smiled so wide her stretched grin reminded me of the Cheshire Cat.

"I'm glad to see you feeling okay. That guy in your office, Martinez, is bad news."

"Why was he looking for Kendra?"

"He specifically mentioned her?"

"Right before he stared at me like he'd seen a ghost."

"I have a suspicion, but I'm going to find out for sure. And I'm going to make sure he doesn't come near you again. Here, put your feet up." I sat on an ottoman and lifted her swollen soles to my lap. I pressed near the heel and massaged my way up.

She slouched back against the couch and closed her eyes. A soft moan slipped through her pursed lips.

"Better than an orgasm?" I asked.

"That depends which orgasm I compare it to."

The idea of treating her to a spasming fest which I imagined awaited between her legs appealed to my mouth and my dick.

I pressed my thumb near the ball of her foot, urging her to scream, "Yes!"

She shot up. "What was that?"

"Whatever do you mean?" I grinned.

"That thing you did with my foot." She pointed.

"Was it orgasmic?"

"Yes! Do it again."

She quickly lifted her foot over my thigh. I pressed in a circular motion, and she sank back into the couch, squirming.

"That's so good," she murmured.

She looked glorious with her head resting and blonde hair spilling over her chest.

"I'd love to take you out to a proper dinner, Sam."

"Don't take the fun out of this. The last thing I need right now is proper."

My chest rumbled. "Noted. You prefer adventure." I winked and warned, "But Samantha, I don't do dates. It's my new policy. Why complicate life?"

"Perfect. I don't date either," she said. "No strings attached?"

"None," I told her. I wasn't ready to admit the likelihood we were already attached, was high.

"Wait… you're not married or something, are you?"

"No I'm not. I'm widowed."

"I'm sorry."

"Thank you. Have you heard from Kendra?"

She blinked past the disappointment in her eyes, but I wasn't ready to share. "Her phone goes straight to voicemail, and Kendra doesn't check voicemail. I'm afraid she's in trouble. That man – Martinez. He wanted Kendra's insurance file."

"What? Why didn't you tell me?"

Her foot slipped off my knee and onto the floor.

"When? I was a little busy when he was holding me at

gunpoint. Then I was busy answering a thousand questions and trying to find you."

"I'm sorry. I didn't mean to sound like—"

"—an asshole?"

I couldn't disagree.

"If you underwrote Kissed, it makes sense they want the files. No less dangerous for either of you at the moment. They're likely counting on insurance money, so we'll increase security at the club."

Sam looked absolutely exhausted and didn't press for questions.

I texted my cousin with the recent information and set the phone aside. My eyes grew heavy and the day's toil begged me to sleep.

"Julian, my cousin is looking for Kendra," I said. "He's a partner at Silver Securities."

Her brows drew together, so I explained. "We took over Silver Securities from our fathers, Jack and Fred Silver. Julian and his brother Tristan handle the investigations. My brother James and I take care of the surveillance, and the four of us and the Wagners run Silver Securities."

Her mouth curved. "Not a simple bartender after all. I should have known. So there's you and James—"

"James is the oldest. He's a pro at the job, and he has a toddler in diapers, but he's the best father I've ever seen. He's always there and always makes the time. I don't know how he finds it, but he does. My younger brother Hunter is twenty-two, and the youngest of the Silver brothers. He's bound to join the family business soon. Just needs a bit more practice."

"Wow, that's a lot. I've never had a big family. We kept to ourselves, and after my parents died, it was just me. All I have is what you see."

I eyed her in wonderment because what I saw was so much more than she described.

"So that's how you found where I live?"

"Yes. I'm good at snooping around."

She laughed.

I lifted my head and made sure she looked right at me. "Sam, I want you to stay home this week. I'll get you groceries and anything else you need, but promise me you'll stay home."

Her face sobered.

"All right. I'll stay at home. But you really are Magnum, aren't you?"

The rain pounded against the windows in a lulling rhythm.

"No, still just Gabe."

"But I'm going out on Friday night," she blurted. "And I can't cancel these plans. It's a bachelorette party."

"Let me guess. You're going to Rebels?"

"It's an opening night, and I've been dissing the few friends I have. The evening sounds promising. Not my favorite thing, but definitely a good guess on your part, P.I."

"You saying that I'm a P.I. doesn't make it a fact."

"Yeah, but it's sexy. You're different."

She shifted on the couch and reached for her wine glass. The smell of leather and fruit released from the stirred alcohol.

"Different?"

"That silver streak in your hair gives you an edge and experience."

She bit her lip. Up until I'd met her I was certain I'd remain a single man for the rest of my life, but now I wasn't so sure.

"I'm going to be forty this Christmas, Sam."

She grinned. "You see, for me that translates into amazing experience. I'm looking forward to checking your proficiency because I can't stop thinking about all my promised orgasms. But I'm so exhausted right now."

She yawned, and I noted the dark circles underneath her eyes. My resistance for her waned. We were both lucky she was tired. I lifted her in my arms and carried her to the bedroom.

Her mouth parted, and her eyes rounded. I laid her down in bed and pulled the sheet over her body. She snuggled in the same way she had three nights earlier. I wanted nothing more than to slip underneath the covers, but I couldn't. The urge to lie down beside her warm body grew the longer I stared at her peaceful face, but the questions about her past held me back. I feared the truth I'd find, but I couldn't ignore the coincidences.

I grabbed a hairbrush from Sam's bathroom and placed it in a plastic bag from underneath the kitchen cupboard.

I lay down in the family room. Sometimes during the night, Sam must have covered me with a blanket. I left in the morning before she woke, so I could drop the brush off at the post office. I scribbled her a polite note on the bedside table and locked the door on my way out.

Samantha,

I wish I didn't have to leave you again. Breakfast is ready downstairs.

I hope you're feeling better. I borrowed a spare key from your kitchen drawer. Save your strength for this weekend so you don't fall asleep on me again. I may have to re-assess the quality of my orgasms, as I don't seem to have a lasting effect on you.

Have a good time Friday,

Gabe (not Magnum)

Chapter 6

Sam

opened the window drapes wide.

Ah, shit!

Rain poured and thunder rumbled. Thick streams flowed down the windows, obscuring the view. Black clouds hovered over the city. This Friday wasn't starting out the way I'd planned. I shut the drapes with force and took my remaining frustration out on the vacuum. I cleaned every room, dusted every shelf, and scrubbed every corner.

It had been days since I'd seen Gabe. The man's confidence and level of commitment to his work was attractive. He left a note on Tuesday morning and had called every day since. He asked about Kendra, who'd been flipping the bird to all her friends *I'd* introduced her to since the day Kissed opened. Those same friends were picking me up in less than an hour, and I already had the urge to weasel out of the bachelorette party. The rain must have soured my mood.

I showered and changed into my dress. Half an hour later, the limo honked in front of the building. A night out with the few friends I had was better than moping over a man. Allie enjoyed the takeout so much, we'd scheduled an official date at

Olivier's for tomorrow night. Unfortunately, patience wasn't my forte.

I grabbed my phone and texted him.

Sam: Can't wait to see you tomorrow

It wasn't long before my phone vibrated.

G. Silver: Have a good time tonight

Sam: Thanks

My heart pounded, and Gabe delivered.

G. Silver: text me what you're wearing

I snapped a selfie in the hallway mirror, but I didn't get a reply. He must have not approved of the yellow submarine matching trench coat. The limo honked again. I locked the door and ran through the rain while the girls held the door open.

We greeted each other with the typical squeals, hugs, and kisses. My mood lifted until Reese mentioned the missing person in the party. "What's happening with Kendra? She's ghosting me."

"Me too." Leah handed me a champagne flute.

"Make that three of us," I told them. Truthfully, her absence worried me more than upset me. Gabe hadn't mentioned the guy who broke into my office, and neither had the police. They hadn't mentioned my favorite charm I'd lost during the attack either, and it felt petty to follow up on a piece of jewelry when lives were at stake. What if he'd gotten to Kendra?

"Earth to Sam!" Reese clinked her glass on mine.

"Sorry. Just worried about Kendra." The mood in the limo fell, so I added, "But tonight we're celebrating you, Reese. I promise we'll have a great time. To Reese and Finn! Cheers!"

I lifted my glass, and the six girls followed with a cheer. The cheap bubbles eased my nerves as they fizzed along my tongue.

"All right. Who's the mystery man?" Leah turned my way.

"What?"

"Come on. The guy who got arrested at your work. Leah said he's hot."

"Leah!" I turned to my nosy but good-hearted secretary by day, book nerd by night. It had taken me hours to convince her to come out tonight, but given how our week had taken on one adventure after another, she put her romance novels aside and followed mine in real life.

"He had roses and panties delivered to her office," Leah spilled, and I sighed.

"He's a bartender I met across the street at Kissed about a week ago. But he's also into this surveillance thing, and I thought we'd have a, you know, no strings attached kinda thing, but it's complicated because he knows Kendra."

I missed him. A lot.

"A triangle?" Kimmy's eyes grew wide.

I rolled my eyes. "It's not like that."

Even if it were, it was no one's business.

"Listen, we're not here to talk about me. Tonight, we're here for Reese. To good times!" I clinked my glass against each of theirs once more and finished the champagne. The girls squealed in response, and my minor diversion worked for the moment.

Half an hour later, the limo pulled up to the curb in front of Rebels. I followed the cheering party to a reserved round table set at the side stage and closer to the back of the club. Massive side walls enclosed us in an intimate round booth near a private dance area. We had the perfect view of all three silver dance poles and the amazingly talented dancers. I cranked my head to the side, let out a breath of relief, and sat on the plush red velvet seat.

The table glistened with fresh wood polish. Fabrics flowed down from the ceiling in burlesque waves, and excitement buzzed in the air. While the place needed major updates, Rebels looked promising when with a group of friends.

A half-naked server with sculpted muscles arrived at our table. He closed in on Reese, the obvious life of the party wearing a white veil. His black bow tie and cuffs decorated his well-oiled body. Matching tight shorts outlined everything that made a woman blush.

"My name is Mike, and I'm at your full disposal tonight. What are we drinking, ladies?" he asked.

"Orgasms!" Reese yelled.

I rolled my eyes. Maybe I shouldn't have mentioned the orgasms I'd drunk last weekend, though a tingle warmed in my stomach at the memory of my talented bartender.

The girls cheered. There was a reason we were friends. My small gang of women from work knew how to let go of the stress and tension. My gaze drifted to the bar on the left, but Gabe wasn't there.

Mike took the order while Leah and Reese waved bills at the first act of the night—a police officer with a large billy club at his side. He swung his hips to the left, and the girls screamed. He swung them to the right, and they screamed louder. The lights flashed, and he ripped off his shorts, revealing everything. I glimpsed at his tight ass.

My phone vibrated, and my heart skipped a beat.

G. Silver: Are you enjoying your evening?

Sam: It'd be better if you were here. Can't wait for our later tonight

G. Silver: Me too. Have you heard from Kendra?

Sam: No. Neither have the girls

G. Silver: What are you wearing?

Sam: A short, tight, red dress

"Put that phone down and have some fun." Reese yanked on my hand.

I set the phone on the table and stood up along with the girls as the new act took the stage. The dancer was wearing a pair of angel wings that reached to the floor. A white cloth covered his front, and he held a bow and arrow to complete the Cupid ensemble. The music switched to a romantic beat, and he strolled across the stage. A girl in the front row pretended to faint when she caught one of his foam heart tipped arrows.

My phone's message light blinked just as the server brought a tray full of shots. Leah handed me a shot glass, and I ignored the blinking light. I gulped the shot down. The sweet liquor carried immediate relaxation through my body.

Someone else handed me another shot before I set the empty one down. Between the champagne in the limo and these shots, the alcohol was flowing straight to my head.

The tuxedo-less server set another full tray of shots. "Are you enjoying the orgasms?"

The brightly pulsing light on my phone distracted me, and I ignored the server and checked the two missed messages.

G. Silver: Can't wait to see it in person

G. Silver: Drinking anything special?

Thinking about the dress that complemented my every curve, I wished I'd saved it for tomorrow. I hurried to type back.

Sam: Drinking a screaming orgasm

"Yummy. Is he a special order, Reese?" I heard Leah from the side.

G. Silver: Is it better than my orgasm?

Sam: I don't know yet, do I?

I bit my lip. Excitement grew in my belly as I waited for the light to pulse again. It had been a long time since I'd gotten excited about a text from a man. As the cathartic moment swept through me, the girls quieted and someone poked at my ribcage, "Holy crap, he's hot!"

"Who?" I focused on my phone.

A familiar woodsy scent lifted my attention to a seductive man who stood amidst my friends. Three beats of the song passed before I realize it was Gabe.

The girls stared open-mouthed, star-struck. And drooling. Gabe's torn jeans defined his muscled thighs. The lighter shade of his typical grayish shirt matched the silver spark in his eyes. The perfectly toned physique was every woman's dream. I swallowed hard.

"Perhaps I should erase your doubt once and for all." Gabe stepped in front of the table. He looked me over, starting at my high heels, and dragged his gaze up my legs to my breasts. He paused when our eyes met, and my knees liquefied into jelly.

"Wh…What?" I babbled. What the hell was Gabe doing here?

"You know him?" Leah asked.

I cleared my throat. "This is a friend of mine, Gabriel Silver."

"Are you going to perform for us, Mr. Silver?" Leah licked her lips and snaked her eager hands around Gabe's bicep. Gabe unwrapped her clinging fingers and kissed her hand like a gentleman. She sat down on the plush seat, fanning her face.

"Ladies, my apologies, but I'm going to steal Samantha from you. The next round is on me." He pointed to the table littered with shot glasses.

Reese gently prodded my ribcage. "Steal away!"

I took Gabe's offered arm. My friends' glares burned all over my body as they drooled like fools. But yeah, Gabe was definitely drool-worthy.

"I'm sorry, Reese. I'll be back soon."

"Take your time." Kimmy waved.

A satisfied grin stretched across Gabe's face. I grasped his arm tighter. The lack of air, or perhaps the alcohol, buzzed through me, and I welcomed the support of his arm.

Reese blubbered as we walked away. "Did you see who that was?"

Someone from the table whistled, and my cheeks burned.

"Did you follow me here?" I asked.

"No at first. Yes later."

"I don't understand."

"I got called to upgrade the club's surveillance. The owner is like family. My cousin's cousin."

Shivers scattered over my body.

"He's a good guy. I promise."

"You know, there are rumors about things going on down here. Bad things."

"We're aware. My friend is trying to fix them."

"This way, Mr. Silver." A half-naked maitre d' opened a door, and we entered a darkened room. Another sprinkle of shivers peppered my arms. Low red lighting provided enough visibility to see the outlined furniture. The decor had the same burlesque feel as the rest of the nightclub. Velvety wallpaper walls matched the cushioned seats. The door closed behind us, and I jumped up. Gabe twisted the knob, locking us in the room.

"Are you all right?" he asked. "Am I making you nervous?"

"No, I'm fine," I replied.

He cocked his head to the side. "Samantha? Are you lying?"

"How did you know?"

"You just told me."

I fell for that one. "I didn't expect you here tonight, but I'm happy you're here. I missed you."

"Didn't you say you met Kendra here?"

I did, but that wasn't exactly the first time we met. "Not here, per se. There's a club connected to this one.

Gabe shivered. "There is and I believe that club may have gotten to her."

"Do you know what's happening with her?"

"Julian's dealing with it. He'll make sure she's okay."

Right. Gabe's mysterious cousin.

"I'm… I'm just ready to forget everything and move on, but

I'm worried about Kendra. I'm worried about the man who held me at gunpoint."

"I assure you that people who care most about Kendra are looking for her right now. There's no sign of Martinez either." He gently grabbed my hip and brought me closer to him. "And this is the perfect window for us."

The smell of him and his woodsy musk hit me and my panties pooled.

"For us to do what?" The slight tremble in my voice tickled my throat.

Gabe spun me in his arms and pinned me against the velvety wallpaper. His body pressed over mine. Hard muscles, powerful arms, and the confident hold on my hips helped me forget about everything that I shouldn't be thinking about.

"I had a hard week." His raspy voice hit me deep between my legs. "And thinking about you was the only way I got through."

His grip slid to my wrists. I inhaled deeply as he lifted my arms above my head, hiking my dress to my ass. His mouth lingered delightfully close to mine. The sounds from the outside faded, and his heavy breath warmed my lips as every nerve on my body buzzed with anticipation. My legs trembled, and Gabe pressed his body harder to mine. He slid his hands down my bare arms, over my hips and to the top of my thigh where the hem of my dress ended.

His fingertips touched my skin, and my body melted.

"I want to feel you gag around my cock, Sam, but as I recall, I need to prove the quality of my orgasms first." His lips thrummed against my mouth.

Yes, please.

I tried to swallow through my dry throat. "I... I just had an orgasm."

The room spun some more. The heat between us spread like wildfire.

"Shots don't count." His chest vibrated against mine. "I don't need alcohol to give a fantastic orgasm."

"You keep making these promises—"

His lips took mine, and I lost all my senses. He lifted his hands to my face and held it at that perfect angle, like he knew exactly what I liked. When his hand skimmed back down and underneath my dress, I realized he did know exactly what I liked. With my back pressed against the wall, I had no room to move. And when I did, I ended up grinding against him, which he definitely didn't mind. My breasts pressed against his chest and my thigh over his erection. He eased his eager hand higher along my inner thigh, lifting my dress to my waist. He skimmed his fingers over my panties, and I shivered. I could climax through the black lace right now.

"You're wearing my panties?" he whispered over my mouth. Our nose tips touched, but he denied me another kiss.

I frowned. "Your panties?"

He growled and slid down my body with impatience. My legs parted for him, and he buried his face against the fabric, inhaling. My insides did three point two somersaults and my blood flowed to the only important area between my legs. I fought for air to breathe and concentrated on his deliberate tease below my belt as he moved my panties to the side and licked over my slit.

My legs trembled, and I moaned. "I'm sorry, it's been a while." I breathed.

He pulled his mouth away. "Don't apologize. I love MTP care."

"MTP care?"

I looked down, and he looked up.

"Mouth-to-pussy care."

I shuddered with unexpected pleasure. He yanked on the rim of my panties and tore them off.

"I'll buy you another pair." He pocketed the piece of soaked fabric as if it were a trophy.

His mouth returned to my pussy. I leaned my head back against the wall. My hands grabbed his head, and I held him steady over my mound. I braced my hips forward, pushing myself into his face. His fingers played with me before slipping in. I got lost in his rhythmic pumps, the steady motion of his tongue over my clit and the thick fingers inside me.

A loud cheer echoed outside, and I tensed. "What if someone comes in?"

He looked up. His chin glistened in the red light, and his bright eyes sparked with hunger. "Relax, Sam. It's just you and me now."

Sweat dripped down my forehead and chest. It had been so long since a man had taken care of my needs.

He pushed another finger inside me and resumed kissing over the tender spot. I tightened around him as he stretched me, arching my hips forward to his mouth. My fingers wove into his thick hair. I pressed on his head, guiding it harder against me and swallowed through my moans,

Pressure mounted, and I was running out of air. I shut my eyes until I found the looming release.

"Oh, God!"

"No, just Gabe."

Pleasure spasmed through my body. I shook and trembled at Gabe's deliberate tongue flicks as he finished me, kissing and soothing the heat. He rose, and I fell into his arms. He slid the dress down over my hips. My thighs stuck to one another as the smell of my arousal floated between us.

"Let me take you home," he whispered, like he was reading my mind.

I bit my lip. "I think I really like MTP care."

"MTP is just the beginning. Are you ready to leave, Samantha?"

My body quivered and mind fogged.

"What about my friends?"

"Text them. They'll understand."

"What should I tell them?"

"Tell them that Gabriel Silver is taking you home and you're making it up to them by covering tonight's drinks."

"I am?"

"I already took care of it."

An unfamiliar delight awoke inside me. As much as I didn't want to leave Reese, I was sure my friends would be more upset if I didn't leave with Mr. Silver. My head was still spinning from the orgasm as Gabe took my hand, opened the nightclub side door leading to the alley where we'd met, and guided me to his conveniently parked Bentley. He decided for me. I was going home with Gabriel Silver.

"I've resisted you for too long," he murmured under his breath as he started the ignition.

Our drive remained silent, except for the pounding of my heart, which I was sure even he could hear. My knees bounced up and down as I sat in the passenger's seat. I'd like to say that it was all jitters and butterflies, but truthfully, I was horny. I wanted this man like I'd wanted no other in my life. Mature, experienced and so fuck worthy, I couldn't resist him even if I wanted to, and I didn't want to.

My hand shook as I opened the four locks. Gabe removed the keys from my hand and finished the job for me. We crossed the threshold, secured the door, and I was back in his arms, kissing him like a madwoman. I pulled his shirt apart. The echo of bouncing buttons on the floor carried between our heated breaths. His tanned chest and the sprinkle of black and gray hair heated under my palm. We walked mouth to mouth and body to body until we reached the bathroom. A new piece of clothing disappeared with each moan until I stood bare and an icy water stream showered from above.

"Ouch."

"Sorry not sorry," he said between tender kisses. The water warmed as he washed me with excruciating patience. He started at the hair, which he lathered in slow circles, and then he continued down my body. I savored the delicate sponge scrub filled with suds, Gabe's every touch and tender kiss. He paid attention to every part of my body as I did to his. My palms explored his sculpted abs, arms, and everything else I could reach.

This is not a one-night stand. It can't be.

I sucked in a sharp breath. He set the showerhead he used to rinse me back on its handle, kissed me hard, and guided me to turn around. I braced my hands on the tiled wall, parted my legs, and tilted my ass. When I looked back, I saw him holding himself steady. My urge to touch him grew. But he didn't give me a chance. Instead, he dropped to his knees and started kissing my ass cheeks like he practiced MTA care as well. He held them steady in his palms.

Holy shit!

My ass tensed. I tried to find something to grip, but there was nothing. I expected Gabe to play with me, like he'd done so the first time, but Gabe was all about business. Unfinished business he wanted done within minutes. The thing was, I couldn't hold on. He wound me up to this release like an eighties toy. With his fingers circling around my clit and his mouth devouring my pussy, I let go and screamed out his name.

"Gabe!"

I grabbed the closest thing to my hand and gripped it hard as the orgasm spasmed through my body. Unfortunately, the closest thing to my hand was the shower curtain, which ripped off its hooks near the end of my climax.

"Oh, no!"

Gabe laughed. "Don't worry. I can fix that."

"You're a handyman too?"

"No," he laughed again. "It's just a curtain, though."

Right.

It was a curtain for him but an unmeasurable challenge for someone like my ex, Casey.

Gabe set the curtain aside and turned off the shower. I devoured his soaked body and the muscles, which must have taken years of hard work. I pressed my palms to his chest, sliding them over his abs and to his standing dick.

"You know, I'm pretty good with my hands too."

He removed my hand from his and brought it to his lips for a kiss. "In due time, baby. That was two orgasms, Samantha. Now I get to have you."

His chest rumbled, and the butterflies flapped crazy in my belly.

"How long has it been?"

"What?"

"Since you had sex. You were tight."

"Ahem, it's been a while."

"How long?"

Gabe stepped out of the shower, lifted me into his arms, and carried me to my bed. Soaked, I lay back on the bedding as he took the lead. My heart stopped.

"I lost it when I was eighteen, and it was over quick, and—"

"You haven't had sex in five years?"

"I have toys."

I couldn't believe I just said that. Gabe looked at me like he couldn't believe it either. He lowered himself to my mouth and left a tender kiss.

"I'm going to make sure you don't need your toys from now on. This may hurt, Sam."

"Gabe…" I closed my eyes.

He positioned himself over me, grasped underneath my knee and lifted my leg, slowly guiding himself inside me. The immediate feeling of being filled wall to wall forced my mouth to open. He shut that down with a fresh kiss, stealing my breath. He waited there, then slid out slowly and came forward again. We connected like we'd been together for years.

His left hand braced against the bedding while his right hand lifted to my breast, cupping the flesh. My nipple slid between his thumb and forefinger, coercing a pinch. It zapped through me like a bullet. He knew my body like he'd held it before. I opened my eyes, connected with his, and realized that I never wanted to look at a different set of eyes when I went to bed again.

How did this happen so quickly?

"Oh, my God!" His forehead fell forward to mine. "You're just so… so… perfect."

After another pinch uncoiled my limbs. His hand dropped to my hip and held me steady. Gabe's thrusts grew stronger and quicker. I lifted my arms above my head and braced them hard against the wall. The pumping rhythm moved me up and down the sheets. The fairy lights over the headboard twinkled like stars. I lost myself to the moment, silently wishing this could be my forever. With Gabe. Safe and wanted. I grasped his strong arms and held on as he pumped deeper and harder until he pulled out, grasped himself, and spilled over my belly.

He fell to the side and lay down beside me. We breathed in tandem, watching the fairy lights twinkle above. The moment was magical.

The pitter-patter of raindrops against the window broke through the euphoria. Gabe reached to the side, used a towel he must have grabbed from the washroom, and cleaned me.

"That was amazing," I breathed.

"It was."

His sky-blue eyes darkened.

"What's wrong?" I sat up.

"Nothing's wrong, Sam. I'm just… it's been a while since I lost myself with a woman."

I placed my hand on top of his. "Gabe, you were incredible."

Casey lasted all of thirty seconds and made me feel used, whereas Gabe made me feel fulfilled and wanted.

"I have no doubts about that, baby." He left a comforting smooch on my lips.

"Then what is it?"

Gabe covered me with the duvet and shivers returned as I watched his troubled face. "We've just met—"

"Wait, you're not breaking up with me. You can't because we're not going out."

"We're not?"

"No?"

He leaned forward, kissing me. "You're funny, Sam. There's no way I would ever let you go. You're mine now."

His possessiveness had a totally different effect on me than I thought it would. Unlike Casey, Gabe actually cared. I liked it. I enjoyed being his.

"All right. Then what were you going to say?"

"I need you to stay with me for a while. The guy who broke into your office was spotted today near Rebels."

"So that's why you came to the club tonight?"

"Partially. You're the other reason."

My chest warmed and my heart had flip-flopped like a giddy teenager's.

"I updated the surveillance at Rebels and came to get you because… I wanted you."

Gabe tucked a strand of hair behind my ear. We crawled underneath the covers and I snuggled against his body. I closed my eyes and gave into the fatigue.

"Don't leave in the morning," he asked. "I want to take you out to breakfast."

We made love twice more that night, and by the time I fell asleep in his arms I was convinced I needed Gabriel Silver for more than a one-night stand.

Chapter 7

gabe

I woke to the sound of chirping birds and the smell of coffee and fresh croissants. It smelled like home. It smelled like the past and reminded me of Joanne. I opened my eyes to daylight and reached to the empty bedside.

"Sam?"

I lifted on my elbows. The red light on my phone alerted me to five missed calls and rang as soon as I picked it up in my hand.

"Gabriel Silver."

"The plane is ready for departure as soon as I find Kendra," Julian told me.

Fuck!

We were flying out today, and I still needed to tell Sam I'd planned a trip across the world. I pinched the bridge of my nose and frowned. "You lost Kendra? I thought you had her."

"This is Kendra we're talking about. She always gets lost."

Right. Kendra was the queen of rebels.

"Who's eliminating Martinez?" I asked. "He was by Rebels last night."

"You know this is not a simple matter."

"If I get my hands on him first, I will kill the man, and I'm not a murderer."

"Gabe, we're working on it. I can't tell you how much I appreciate your help with Kendra. Let me know if you hear from her, and be ready to leave."

"Talk soon."

I hung up and rubbed my eyes. "Sam?" I listened for the shower, but she wasn't in the bathroom. "Samantha?"

I pulled the covers aside, got up, and strolled to the kitchen, expecting Sam to be dancing with her earbuds in her ears, but she wasn't there either. Instead, I found a steaming pot of coffee, fresh croissants, and a note.

Good morning,

It's the first sunny day in a week! Went for a run. Make yourself at home.

I'll be back soon.

Sam

"For fuck's sake, Samantha!"

I jumped into my pants like my ass was about to catch fire, grabbed my phone, and checked the map. The tracker showed her in Woodland Park, but the cops could get to her quicker than I could. I dialed the emergency line at work.

"Silver Securities, how may we brighten your day?" answered Greg, the secretary.

"I need a unit in Woodland Park. I'll text the details to the main line."

"Yes, sir."

I was out the door moments later, driving like a madman, ignoring speed limits and my safety. I pulled up to the park's entrance and called out her name. "Sam!"

The tracking app installed on her phone showed her position beyond a bridge, on the other side of the park's pond. I hopped out of the car and left it curbside. My veins were pumping with adrenaline, sweat dripped down my back, and my lungs burned from the frosty fall air as I ran in her direction.

I hurried over the bridge and came to a stop by a willow tree. A familiar silhouette caught my eye near the park's exit on the other side.

"Sam!" I called out, but she didn't answer. I hurried toward her, but as I approached, a man blocked her way just as a cop joined them. The man took a step back, away from Sam. I breathed out in relief, but not for long when I recognized the man was Martinez. He saw me before they did, turned around on his heel, and fled.

By the time I caught up to them, he was gone; I was out of breath, and Sam was shaking like a leaf.

"Gabe?" Sam turned around. "Oh, my God. He was here."

"You know that man?" the cop asked. I immediately recognized her as the same officer who had booked me at Sam's work. What were the odds?

"Yes… well, no…" Sam turned back my way.

"What are you doing here?" I asked.

"Martinez." She could barely get a word out between breaths. "He surprised me. He was looking for Kendra."

"So is everybody else. Are you all right?"

The female cop cleared her throat. "Excuse me, do you know that man?"

My brows furrowed as I turned around, pointing in the direction Martinez had fled. "It's the same guy you let get away last week. At her work. Remember?"

She frowned. "There was no other guy at your work."

"Not when you came into the office, guns pointing. He escaped through the back door while you cuffed me." I shoved my thumb in my chest.

"Listen, I will not apologize for doing my job. I already sent a unit after him. He's obviously stalking this woman."

"No shit, Sherlock," I spat.

He was more than stalking Samantha. He'd connected her to Kendra, who connected Sam to trouble, and I would not let another woman I cared about die.

"You won't find Martinez if he doesn't want to be found." I noted her badge. "It's best you let this one go, Officer Green."

I reached inside my pants, removed a business card, and handed it to the officer. She examined my card and her eyes grew wide. "Yes, Mr. Silver. You call us if you need further support."

She returned to her cruiser, and I took Sam in my arms.

"What was that? What did you show her?"

"Silver Securities has special privileges at the police department."

"Isn't that illegal?"

"Not according to our lawyers. It works nicely when we work together. We do them a favor, and they do us a favor, you know. It's complicated." I stared into the distance. Street cops were like peasants. The county deputies and chiefs were the loyal conspirators who appreciated Silver Securities removing the larger threat off streets.

"Are you all right?" she asked.

"Yeah, are you? I thought I told you to stay close to me all the time."

She frowned. "Gabe, I just went on a run."

Her explanation made little sense. Hadn't I just told her about the threat last night? Kidnappers didn't discriminate between day and night, nor between locations or weather. I clenched my jaw so hard my back molar reminded me I'd missed a dentist visit.

"You're in danger. Deep danger. I need to know where you're at every minute of every hour." I reached for her hand, but she pulled it away.

"You're crazy. This is all crazy. How can he be running around free? Shouldn't that cop do more than take your business card?" Her brows narrowed. "Let me see your business card."

Shit. This was it. This was the moment Sam would realize who I was, and she'd run. I removed another card from within my pocket and handed it to her. I watched her expression shifted as the recognition set in.

"You're *the* Gabriel Silver? I read about a scandal involving your company. A congressional representative's death?"

The story of my life.

"Silver Securities prides itself on personal and professional safety. The business merged after our parents retired. The man who broke into your office runs a drug ring and works for the elite. He's connected to Congress with money and power. Human trafficking is one of their largest operations."

I watched as she swallowed hard and reached for my hand. "You're right. I'm sorry. I should have listened. The last thing I expected was for that guy to find me."

"He won't stop there. Tell me everything he said."

"He asked about Kendra." Her lip trembled. She touched her heated palm to my chest, reminding me I hadn't put on a shirt. "We should get you home. You're half naked and shaking in the middle of a park. You're going to get sick."

The nippy breeze collided with my body. I trembled like it was below zero. It wasn't, but pretty close. I should have at least put on a shirt.

"We can't go home. Not today, at least," I told her, wondering how to break the news to her.

"What are you talking about?"

"I never had the time to tell you, but we're going on a trip."

Her laugh faded when she realized I wasn't joking.

"Martinez is on Kendra's ass, and now he's on yours, too. You're no longer safe on your own, and we have to find her."

She looked me over from the bottom up and back down

again, pausing on my mid-line. She bit her lip and shifted on her feet.

I looked at her the way I would at a teenager who didn't know how to listen.

"Don't get so grumpy. You can't do it all half-naked and sick. You need a sweatshirt."

"I freaked out when you weren't home. I didn't think. I couldn't think—"

"I'm sorry. I didn't realize I had a stalker."

I took Sam's hand. "I'm sorry Kendra drew you into her little sphere of trouble."

"She's my friend, and she's not the trouble." Her eyes filled with concern and kindness. While I didn't agree with the statement, I appreciated Sam's loyalty to her friend.

"That man is the troubled one. She just needs her friends to help her. Good friends."

I pulled on her hand, guiding her across the street to the only open store, but the clerk stopped me.

"No shirt, no service."

She stuck her hand out front and blocked the way.

I gave her one of my charming smiles. "I'm so sorry. A kid spilled coffee all over my shirt, and I had to trash it. It would turn my fortune this morning if you'd be so kind as to allow me to purchase one of your sweatshirts. Please?"

Her pursed lips relaxed, and she pointed to a rack behind her. "Those are on sale. Just don't tell the manager I broke a rule."

Sam leaned in. "Don't worry. Some rules are meant to be broken."

The growl slipped out of my mouth without warning. I grabbed the most expensive sweatshirt in the store with apologies to the clerk.

"What was that?" Sam asked when the clerk turned around.

"Stop breaking rules," I told her, as I tapped my phone for payment.

She grinned with a pasted smile right over her pearly teeth. "If she didn't break a rule, you'd be shirtless."

I couldn't argue with that one. Unfortunately, rule breaking didn't always yield the results we hoped. I'd learned that the hard way.

"Thank you." Sam turned to the lady behind the counter. "We really appreciate it."

I put on the sweatshirt, and we left the store and crossed the park to my Bentley.

"Where to now?" she asked.

"Wherever Kendra's hiding."

"Did you not put a tracker on her phone?" Sam asked. "Because I'm assuming that's how you found me."

Was she upset with me? I must have had a dumbfounded look on my face, because her idea would have solved our problem. But Kendra wasn't mine to track. She was Julian's.

"It doesn't matter." Sam waved. "She's probably locked herself up at Kissed."

"At the club? Why?"

"Because the club is her baby. She's talked about opening it up since the day we met."

"So you think we should go to Kissed?"

She nodded.

"You haven't seen the shit she's gone through to get the club going, have you? She's tried to build a life around blank memories, so to Kendra right now, Kissed is the only thing she can lose. It's the only thing that matters to her. She'll definitely be there."

"It's not the only thing she can lose, and it shouldn't be the only thing that matters." My back molar pinged with pain again, and I loosened my jaw. I'd known Kendra most of her life, and while it might not have been obvious to anyone else, Silver Securities knew exactly what she had to lose.

I opened the car door on Sam's side and waited until she was in the seat to close it. I walked around to the driver's side and was about to ask her about Martinez, but Sam began first.

"The guy said Kendra owes money."

I turned on the ignition as she took a deep breath. Her knees wobbled up and down and her hands shook.

She was breaking.

I covered her hand with mine. She blinked with appreciation, shedding a tear. I reached out to wipe it, and she continued, "And if he doesn't get it, a deadline will pass, and the only remaining payment will be a life. I mean, who the fuck talks like that?"

She pulled in a sniffle, and my heart broke in half. The anger I'd felt when she left this morning faded. I turned the corner and took the highway ramp, which would lead us to the bridge in Manhattan.

"Tell me more." I gave her hand an encouraging squeeze.

"He said he was a friend of Kendra's, which of course I knew he wasn't because I remembered the fucker from my office."

"Martinez thinks he's invincible, but he's not. He works for a man named Hartley. We're collecting proof, but he's well protected. He's their go-to guy. Their cleaner, bookie, pimp and everything else in between. He's the man you never want to see or you'll end up in a tin can full of acid."

A memory flashed through my mind, and I shuddered, adding, "Or buried six feet underground."

"I'm sorry I left this morning." She reached for a tissue and wiped her eyes, then blew her nose. She was adorable, but also so sad and scared. And it pained me.

"Don't cry. I... I should have been clearer."

My phone rang as soon as we crossed the bridge. I pressed the speaker button.

"She's at Kissed." I glanced at Sam from the side and finally saw a smile.

"On my way." Julian hung up, and I turned to Sam, smiling. "You were right."

"Thank God. I'd never forgive myself if something happened to her."

That was the part I didn't understand about Sam. It wasn't like Kendra was a good friend. Well, she could have been, but she'd changed, and I felt responsible for the shit Silver Securities put her family through. Kendra needed help, and it was time to give her exactly that. "She drugged you and stood you up, yet you still stand up for her."

"That's what friends do for each other."

"No. Friends do what you do. Friends don't do what Kendra does."

"Well, you don't know her like I do."

I laughed. She was wrong. So wrong, yet so right. I'd known Kendra since her teens, when she became a client at Silver Securities, and for over a decade we'd been taking care of her wellbeing. But client confidentiality prevented me from giving Sam any of those details. Discretion was our bread and butter. Yet Sam knew where Kendra would hide before I did.

Maybe she knew her friend better than we did after all.

I parked in the club's side alley and nodded to Julian, who parked further down the street. He walked up as soon as he saw us and handed me a small pouch, saying nothing.

"I'll introduce you two later," I told Sam, and opened the club's side door. We walked through the back kitchen, where the crew were prepping for the weekend for the barbecue event on the rooftop terrace.

"Morning, Mr. Silver." The kitchen staff parted in waves like the Red Sea before Moses.

"It's weird when people call you Mr. Silver."

"It's a formality. They know me as Kendra's silent business partner."

"*You're* her silent business partner?" She lifted her hand to her mouth and whispered, "Well, that makes sense."

"I thought I mentioned it before. Kendra!" I called out. "Let's split up. You take the storage room and I'll take the upstairs and her office."

Sam hurried across the empty dance floor while I scaled the metal steps. Kendra wasn't in her office. She wasn't in the sound-room or the dressing room either.

"Found her!" I heard Sam's voice.

I rushed back down the stairs to the storage room, where Kendra was sitting in a corner. She was curled into a ball, with her knees bent high to her chest and arms around them. She was wearing a fluffy pink nightgown that matched her slippers and left little to the imagination. An open bottle of pills waited in her grip.

Sam crouched beside her, and Kendra lifted her face from her knees. Mascara streamed down her cheeks and fresh tears spilled from her eyes. "I just wanted answers, Gabe. That's all. I promise. I just wanted answers."

She moved her hand. Pills spilled to the floor, scattering over the tiles.

"I know you do. Julian's working on it."

"Julian can go to hell!" she screamed, and Sam jumped up.

"K, we want to help you. Now, we can do this the easy way or we can do this the hard way."

"What are we doing?" Sam whispered and shifted closer to my side. The worry in her eyes made me wish she'd remained back home; safe and blissfully unaware of the predators who could snag her and never return. But she wasn't home, and my time to get these women out of the country was running out. Another slip from Kendra could be fatal.

I removed the syringe from its pouch. Sam's eyes grew wide. "What is that?"

"I'm not going anywhere! They have information. They said my parents are alive!" Kendra cried.

"Oh, honey." Sam scooted closer to her friend, but Kendra saw the needle and pushed away. She crawled on all fours, slipping on the freshly washed floor.

"I can't believe you'd stoop to Julian's tricks."

I caught her by her ankle, reached forward, and jabbed the needle in her ass.

"Ouch!" Kendra turned around in slow motion and fell flat on the floor.

"What did you do?" Sam pulled on my sweatshirt as I scooped Kendra up into my arms. She weighed much less than I remembered from the last time I'd carried her.

"I gave her a sedative. We need to get her out of here. Fast."

"Where are we going? What about the club?"

"It's all taken care of, Sam. Follow me."

We left the club out the side door, where Julian waited in the alley with the car door open.

"Sam, Julian. Julian, Sam."

They exchanged a polite nod. My cousin shook Sam's hand and helped settle Kendra inside the car. Sam sat in the back seat beside her while I slid into the leather driver's seat. I turned on the ignition, and the car purred as Julian passed me another envelope.

"Passports, burner phones, and everything else you'll need. The charm bracelet's in a silver box, the way you asked. I moved the bags to the trunk. Thanks for doing this, Gabe. Enjoy New Zealand, and say hello to Marge."

"I will, but this time you owe me," I told him. "Finish what you need and fly your ass over as soon as you can. She needs you."

"I'll see you soon."

I pulled out from the alley and checked Sam's puzzled reflection in the rearview mirror.

"Is he not coming?"

"Julian will join us in New Zealand later."

She laughed.

"What's so funny?"

"That's the second time you said we're going to New Zealand."

"We are."

Chapter 8

Sam

"Gabe, I don't even have a passport."

He parked on the tarmac near a private jet and turned around to face me. "You do now."

"It's expired."

"It doesn't matter."

"Of course it matters."

"Sam, I've got this. It's what I do. Relax."

Kendra stirred in the back seat. Black smears ran down her angelic face. The poor thing likely had no clue we'd abducted her, nor that her life was in danger. I should have been a better friend; maybe she wouldn't be in the trouble she was in today.

"Will she be okay? What did you give her?" I asked, as two guys unloaded the trunk and carried the duffle bags to the jet.

Gabe's brows narrowed, and he combed his fingers through his hair. "A mix of muscle relaxants and a sleeping aid. She'll be fine."

"I hope she doesn't need to pee."

Gabe offered a bemused smile.

"What's so funny?"

"You. Here we are, fleeing the country, and you're thinking about Kendra's bathroom needs."

"Well, if that were me" – I pointed at the drool flowing down her chin, which I immediately wiped with a tissue – "I wouldn't want my bladder to let go because someone knocked me out."

"She'll only sleep for a few hours through the flight. She'll be fine later, trust me."

A top-heavy guy lifted Kendra from the car and carried her limp body up the plane's stairs while Gabe carried the last of the bags. I stopped near the bottom of the staircase before I followed. What the hell was I doing?

"Sam?" Gabe turned around, and I focused on his dazzling eyes.

"What about work? What about my cat?"

"Julian will drop off the cat at Leah's. You're off work on stress leave, so your job is not in jeopardy. It's all taken care of, Sam."

All taken care of wasn't as reassuring as it sounded, but what choice did I have? I stared at the plane in front of me. I'd only met Gabe a week ago, and I was about to cross the world with him. Every time I turned around, he was someone else. A bartender, a surveillance guy, an apparently former private investigator. What kind of private investigator owned a jet? What kind of private investigator gets a passport renewed within hours? An important one, because no one had taken more care of me than Gabe had the past week. Ever. My knees wobbled.

"I... I don't know if I can do this." My hands trembled. I rubbed them to shake off the nerves.

"I won't force you on this plane." His lips firmed and his forehead creased. "But it will be much easier to keep you alive if you come with me."

He hadn't harmed me. In fact, he'd kept me safe. While I'd been yearning for adventure, I hadn't expected to travel across the world in its pursuit. But I couldn't leave my friend on her own, either. She'd been there for me in my darkest hour, and I wouldn't abandon her. She'd experienced enough neglect as it was. I focused on the top of the staircase, where a steward was waiting at the door.

"Ok, I trust you. Let's do this." I took a deep breath and followed him on board. The tasteful interior design and soothing lights resembled a fancy modern hotel. Sleek trim highlighted with beige and black accents reminded me of the Great Gatsby.

I sat in the seat beside Gabe, buckled up, and gripped the seat's rests. The engines rumbled, and my anxiety spiked. Suddenly the couches and the comfort weren't enough to stop my trembling. Gabe removed his shoes and stretched out his legs.

"You're nervous." He took my hand.

"Where's Kendra?" I twisted in my seat.

"She's in the back bedroom. No need to worry. There's a nurse with her."

"Good. That's real good."

Sweat beads trickled between my breasts, and I wished I'd showered before this trip. But the last thing I'd expected when I left for a run this morning was boarding a plane.

"Relax, Sam. It's just a plane."

"It's a plane for you. It's a gazillion pounds of metal miraculously speeding through the air for me."

"Nothing miraculous about that. Just simple physics."

"The same physics that proves gravity always wins?"

He chuckled.

"And we're gonna miss our dinner tonight," I told him.

"We'll have dinner onboard, and I assure you, there's plenty of food in New Zealand."

The cheeky Gabe was much better than the grumpy one. Gabe lifted his feet into the foot rest. "Kendra will join us when she's awake, but prepare yourself. She's not pretty when she's mad." A tone of apprehension drifted over his voice.

"Why would she be upset with me? I'm not the one who drugged and kidnapped her."

I caught his glance from the side, followed by a smirk. "So that's how it's going to be? I do the dirty work and you reap the rewards?"

My mind flew to all the dirty work I'd like him to do.

"It's more than that for Kendra. She's leaving Kissed, and she has a lot of questions she wants answers to."

I wanted to ask him about the questions, but I couldn't because the plane's engines revved up and so did my pulse. My legs trembled. I removed my hand from Gabe's and pressed on my knees to stop the shaking.

"Have you not flown before?"

I kept my eyes shut and paused the Hail Mary in my mind. "Of course I have. In my dreams. Now stop laughing. They say takeoffs and landings are the worst. If you want to kn—"

Gabe silenced my mouth with a kiss. His needy lips took over mine, clouding my mind. I moaned in response, melting into my seat. The unexpected kiss morphed to a delicate touch, which left me shaking. My fingers tangled in his hair, and I forgot about the world around me. He smothered my lips, kissing me like I was his next breath, and when he finished, I was the one out of breath. He coaxed relaxation with his lips like mine were the only ones he ever wanted to kiss. I lost track of time until he pulled away, kissed the tip of my nose, and said, "The takeoff is done. We're at cruising altitude right now, but we can repeat the kissing at landing, if it helps."

It helped. I pulled back and connected my gaze with his to share a moment stolen in time. The smell of his woodsy musk floated between us, and then the smell of my odor reminded me I went out for a run this morning and didn't shower afterward.

"Any way you have some wet wipes?"

His brows furrowed.

"So I can freshen up."

"There's a shower in the back." He gestured down the aisle.

I hesitated.

"What's the matter?"

"Is there a seatbelt in there?"

Gabe's shoulders joined in the laughter. "No. You'll be fine. I'll get fresh clothes ready. Come on."

He took my hand and guided me to the shower. It was larger than I expected, but so was the private jet. I took as much time in the shower as my nerves could muster, hurrying with every delicate yet turbulent and frightening bump. When I turned off the water, a loud argument was vibrating against the wall. I wrapped the towel around me and followed the rising conversation to an office near the front of the plane. I peeked through the thin slit in the door. Kendra was pacing back and forth in her pink nightgown and fluffy slippers.

"I could sue you for this!" she yelled.

"K, I didn't have a choice. Julian agreed."

"Julian? Well, Julian doesn't run my life, does he?"

"He's looking out for you. He cares about you. I promised him to look out for you too, so that's what I'll do."

"If he cared for me, he would have been here himself."

"You know it doesn't work like that."

She let out an exasperated, "Argh!" and threw her arms up in the air. "You're such a hypocrite. Did anyone bother you after Jo died?"

"Don't go there." Gabe lowered his voice, and I grew curious about Jo.

"Did you let anyone help you, then?" Kendra asked.

While eavesdropping on the conversation didn't feel right, its secretive tone kept me frozen in my spot.

"K, I'm warning you. Leave Jo out of this."

But Kendra wasn't one to let an argument slip. "As I recall, last time you tried saving someone, you cost Jo her life. Or do you want someone else buried alive?"

My lungs ceased functioning as Gabe grabbed Kendra's wrist.

"If you weren't high, I'd flip you over my knee and—"

"And what, Gabe? Spank me?" Kendra laughed. "Don't make promises you can't keep."

"You're unbelievable!" It was Gabe's turn to throw his hands up in the air.

"You've changed, Gabe. You used to be fun, and now you're all FBI trying to protect everyone around you. Stop trying. You're not good at it!"

The deafening silence hummed louder than the plane's engines, and I used the quiet moment to walk inside.

"Are you part of this?" Kendra pointed at me, bringing attention to the towel wrapped around me. I wished I'd gotten dressed first.

"Kendra, our lives are in jeopardy. You're high, and you owe money to a mobster who came to my workplace with a gun. Martinez is looking for you – and for me."

"You've been spying on me?"

"No, that's not wh—"

"You didn't leave us much choice, K," Gabe explained.

"Look, there's no point arguing in the middle of the night." I shut my eyes for a moment. The plane hit some turbulence, and I lost my footing and stumbled back and forth. The past twelve hours of pumping adrenaline had taken their toll.

"Where exactly are we going, Gabe?" Kendra asked.

"Kawau Island."

Kendra's eyes widened, her lips curved up, and she let out a joyful squeal. "Yes!"

It wasn't the response I'd been expecting, especially when she jumped into Gabe's arms, wrapped her legs around his waist, and smacked her mouth to his. Gabe's hands took hold of her behind in an attempt not to fall over. They did. Kendra got up with the little grace I recalled her having. And I couldn't do anything else but stand there, stunned.

"Thank you, thank you, thank you!" She blew kisses Gabe's way and ran to the back of the plane.

"What the fuck was that?" I asked.

"That was a combination of benzodiazepines and hallucinogens at its finest. We got her labs back. The pill she gave you last weekend knocked you out and almost killed you."

Almost killed me?

"When did you take my blood sample?"

"We didn't use a blood sample. Hair and urine. It was after I brought you home from Kissed, you peed, showered, and I put you to bed."

Gross.

"When were you going to tell me this? I... I woke up naked."

"That's all you, Sam. I left you in what I thought were comfortable pajamas in your bed Saturday morning."

I sat down in the first seat I could find. A cool breeze swept over my shoulders and reminded me of the towel wrapped around my body.

"Are you all right?"

The two days I'd lost after my night out at Kissed were a lot to take in. A week ago, I was ready for a one-night stand, but I'd fallen into an à la carte adventure of a lifetime. Today, that adventure was playing out in high-definition.

"Yeah, I'm fine. I should get dressed. Who's Jo?"

He froze. I didn't want to sound like a jealous girlfriend because number one, I was not his girlfriend, and number two, I was not the jealous type. Yet a piece of me died every time I thought about Gabe with another woman.

"I heard Kendra mention the name before," I explained.

He sat down on the sofa seat across from me. "Joanne was my wife."

His shoulders drooped, and gloom fell over his face. I rubbed the shivers off my arms as the sense of dread floated from Gabe to me. Goosebumps sprinkled over my skin.

"She was a private investigator and was working with me on a case. It was the first one we'd been assigned together. She didn't make it. That guy from the park is responsible for her death."

"Oh Gabe, I'm so sorry."

I shifted across the aisle to sit beside him and took his hand. He turned my way, opened his mouth, and hesitated for a few good breaths before he found the courage to continue. "You remind me of her. A lot."

"Oh. That's good, right?"

"Definitely good." His low tone lacked the conviction I wished it carried. "Come on. You're cold, and you must be starving."

My stomach growled at the invitation. I grasped my towel and went to get dressed. Kendra must have passed out on a sofa. Gabe moved her to a bedroom, and after a bowl full of oatmeal with blueberries, I passed the time reading all the magazines on board. A vibration underneath my seat triggered my nerves again. My eyes grew wide as I grasped the armrests.

"It's time to put on your seatbelt."

"We're landing?"

"Refueling only."

Before I replied, Gabe's lips took my mouth, slowly manipulating the nerves away. My arms flopped to the sides as he held my face between his hands, and I melted into the seat. His tongue twined with mine, teasing and exploring. Every few strokes, he paused in wonder as if he couldn't believe he was actually kissing me, then resumed even harder, making me feel like his.

I quickly forgot about Kendra's addiction and the fact that my name was near the top of a cartel's hit list. I forgot we were coming down from ten thousand feet, and before I knew it, we were back in the air. Gabe's constant touch brought comfort, whether through a kiss on my head or my shoulder, or a gentle stroke over my thigh when I closed my eyes. His affection warmed my heart and was unlike anything I'd ever received from Casey.

By the time we landed in New Zealand, the sun had set behind a mountain range. I fixed the baseball cap Gabe had given me and asked me to wear, and I stepped down the plane's staircase. As we crossed the tarmac to the awaiting Land Rover, a familiar figure drew my attention. I paused and adjusted my cap. The woman stared our way through her bumblebee sunglasses. An enormous sun hat covered most of her face. With her chin up high so, I could only see its tip from underneath the hat's shadow. Yet there was something so familiar about her that I couldn't take my eyes away.

"Are you all right?" Gabe asked.

Her blonde hair flowed in the breeze, and my heart stopped. When she saw that I'd spotted her, she rushed to her convertible and left. Who had permission to park at an airport like that?

"Do you know anyone here?" I asked. "Because that woman was staring like she knew one of us."

He let out a frustrated breath, and the pulse in his jugular swelled. "That was Mrs. Summers. This private airport belongs to her family. Silver Securities used to have an office in New Zealand. I was at the head of its operations."

He opened the black SUV door. Cool air brought immediate comfort and relief. It was the first heat wave of the summer, and by looking at the fine man sitting across from me, adventure was in the forecast.

By the time we arrived at our destination, the orange sunset glow had disappeared. The car slowed as it entered the security gate. Beyond, a swirling path paved the way. The driveway was lined with trees on both sides, leading into what appeared to be a black forest. The curved path stretched for longer than any I'd ever seen before.

We circled around a fountain and pulled up in front of the house. When Gabe said we'd be staying at a country home, I'd expected a small getaway bungalow. Instead, I stared at a mansion made of glass. Tall metal columns supported the porch roof, and glass walls all around exposed the interior to the outside.

"This is our private residence." Gabe opened the trunk and unloaded the few bags we'd brought.

"Private?"

He must have meant secluded because there was nothing private about floor to ceiling windows in place of solid walls.

Charlie, our chauffeur, stepped out of the SUV to help with the bags. "I got it, sir."

"Thank you, Charlie."

"This is your place?" I gaped at the property.

Gabe secured his arm around my shoulder. "Kendra, you can have Julian's quarters. Sam is staying with me."

He led me to the front door, where the hallway stretched all the way to the back of the house. Beyond, a lush yard ended in darkness. I caught the sound of lulling waves. Gabe touched a keypad, and blue pool light illuminated the back.

"There's a pool?" I gawked.

"See you in the morning!" Kendra waved to Gabe and trotted up the wooden steps, which appeared to be floating in the air, each one on a cloud of soft light. The soothing sound of waves filled the room.

"Is that the ocean?" I asked.

"The steps past the pool lead to a cove with a private beach."

I couldn't wait to check that out. This trip was getting

better and better by the minute, and the reason we were here in the first place drifted away on the gentle sea breeze. While I'd keep my distance from the ocean, I didn't mind catching a few rays on the beach.

Gabe guided me down the hallway and to the kitchen, where a giant conch shell drew my attention to a granite island counter. Dimmed lights from above the white cabinets reflected in the luster. Delicate blue accents tied the coastal atmosphere together. I couldn't wait to see the rest of the house.

"When you said we'd be staying at your home, I didn't realize it'd be a mansion."

My ex still lived in his mother's basement.

"I'm glad you like it. I'll show you the full premises in the morning. Tonight, I have a meeting."

"Do you have to leave? We just arrived." My heart dropped to the floor, and the excitement faded.

"I won't be long. You'll be safe here. Stay out of trouble and stay here." He kissed me on the forehead, making me feel even smaller than I already did.

"I'm not tired," I pouted.

"We crossed more time zones than I cared to count. Your clock will switch in a few days. In the meantime, there's food in the fridge. Make yourself at home and don't leave the premises. It's a smart home, so if you have questions, ask Rona."

Rona?

"She's the AI in this house."

I searched for the meaning in my head as Gabe explained. "Artificial intelligence. Like Siri or Alexa."

"Got it."

He kissed my forehead again, like I was his grandmother, and wrapped his arms around me. He held me tight, like he didn't want to leave; yet he did, and I didn't know what to make of it.

I watched through the glass wall as he opened the door to a Porsche parked in the driveway. He turned the ignition and silently rolled away into the night.

"I know where he's going."

I looked up to Kendra, who was standing on the second floor. She leaned over the glass barrier near the top of the staircase. She'd changed into a matching camouflage outfit that screamed adventure. I should have known that meant trouble.

"You're supposed to be asleep," I told her.

"I thought he'd never leave, and I slept on the plane. Now we're ready to let loose."

"Gabe was specific to stay home."

She trotted down the steps like nothing could stop her. "Rona, open the back yard."

The glass door slid sideways, and warm, salty air hit my face. I inhaled the ocean's breath and followed Kendra to the backyard.

"Where are you going?" I asked.

"To show you the property, silly. Come on. It's unlike anything you've ever seen, and it looks even more beautiful at night."

If she was trying to sell me on some rebellious idea, it was working. Given I was in a mansion in New Zealand, my curiosity didn't need a boost. But when Kendra asked Rona to light the outdoors and the millions of lights lit up the landscape in twinkling patterns, any sense of restraint I had evaporated.

"It's beautiful!" I exhaled. The pool glowed blue in the night. Trimmed hedges supported nests of lights and surrounded the perimeter. As my gaze drifted higher to the decorated treetops, the lights blended with the stars. It was breathtaking.

"If you think this is nice, wait until you see it from the beach."

Kendra turned on her heel and disappeared down a twinkling path. A jolt of joy sparked inside me, as if I were that little girl again, awaiting an adventure. I followed her to the beach and removed my flip flops. The warm sand sunk underneath my bare soles.The sound of an engine drew my attention to the docked boat and Kendra, who sat in the skipper's chair.

"Come on, Sam! Let's go!"

Every ounce of joy inside me drifted away on the cloud of Kendra's stupidity.

I hurried down the dock, where I waved at her like crazy.

"Turn the engine off!" What was she thinking? Number one, it was dark outside. Number two, it was the ocean – where my father had died.

Kendra waved at me to come aboard instead.

"You're crazy! You can't go anywhere! Come on, Kendra. Turn off the boat!" I screamed over the roaring engine, but I was sure she couldn't hear me.

"You're either comin' or stayin," she laughed back.

"Are you high?"

But she didn't reply. Taking a boat out in the middle of the night wasn't a good idea, that was clear, but if she went on her own, I might never see her again. A jab of pity pinged in my chest, and I jumped inside. I got to her fast, and my hand was almost on the key when she pushed the throttle forward and I fell back into the seat. The engine roared, and Kendra sped out onto a dark ocean.

The road ahead of me was as familiar as the road behind me. I gripped the steering wheel and shook off the nostalgia. My knuckles whitened, and I eased the hold, rolling into the cemetery parking lot. I had planned to wait until the morning to come here, but the moment we pulled up to the house, the grief and anger I'd tucked away returned.

I dialed my friend's number in Charleston. "Dave? You got my package?"

"I did, but I don't have good news. There was an accident at the lab. Part of the building burned down. Your sample was damaged, and it'll take a couple more days than usual to retrieve the data."

I let out an exasperated breath.

"I can send it to April if it's an emergency."

"It's an emergency," I told him.

"No problem. Give me four days. Five tops."

"Make it two."

"You're asking for a miracle."

"If the results come back the way I think they will, it will be a miracle indeed."

"Got it. Talk soon."

I put down the phone and turned off the ignition. A somber scent of death and candle wax brought back the darkest and hardest day of my life – when I'd buried my wife. I closed my eyes, and Sam's face appeared behind my eyelids. She pouted in that familiar way Joanne used to, and the struggle inside my chest tightened. Leaving Sam on our first night here hadn't easy, but it was necessary.

"Do you have to leave? We just arrived." Her disappointment rang in my ears. Of course I didn't *have* to leave, but I felt I needed to.

How could you tell someone you met a short week ago that you knew them better than anyone else in the world? How could I tell Sam she reminded me of someone else? Her face, pointy nose, and rosy cheeks were familiar to my eyes. Her body reminded me of everything I'd lost: my past, present and future. Was I falling for Sam, or was I re-living the past I should have lived?

A breeze swayed the trees beyond the gates, where the candles shimmered in the night.

I wanted to tell Sam that I was going to my wife's grave, but I couldn't get the words out. I couldn't have Sam involved in this world I'd been desperate to fix and escape unless the truth pushed me there. I couldn't do it until I confirmed my suspicions with the forensics team.

And every urge to fulfill that fantasy of a happy end would remain paused until I tied up my affairs. I would die before I led Sam down the same deadly path on which Joanne had fallen.

"You don't think Martinez will come to the island, do you?" she'd asked.

"He's done it before."

I gave into the need and took her in my arms, holding her as if I'd been holding her for the past 10 years. After Joanne's death, I assumed I'd be single for the rest of my life. No one could ever replace her, and no one ever would. But when I held Sam, it was like holding the same woman. It felt wrong and right at the same time.

A stronger gust of wind brought me back from my stolen moment in the kitchen before I left. I wasn't sure how long I sat in the parked car, but I sure as hell knew it was long enough to remember the day they took her from me. The bastards had buried Joanne alive. In a box. Alone. Afraid. Waiting for help that wouldn't make it in time. I'd replayed the moment a million times in my head. Was she disappointed in me in her last moments? She should have been. It felt like it was only yesterday when I failed my partner and my wife.

The muscles in my neck tensed, and I let out a scream. A flock of birds resting in the trees awakened and flew away into the darkness. I reached behind the back seat and removed a candle from its package. When I gathered enough courage to leave the car, I walked the moonlit path to her grave like a shadow. It wasn't far. The private cemetery on the Summers' lands revived my grief. My steps underneath the lit pathway echoed through the night. The granite tombstone reflected the night light from far away. Marge must have cleaned it before my arrival. I lit the candle, said the obligatory prayer I no longer believed in, and talked to her as if she were here. Alive and in the flesh.

"Kendra's not an easy client, but I owe Julian."

If it weren't for my cousin, we wouldn't have found Joanne's body.

"I'm trying to right my wrongs, but what if I fail again? I can't let another woman die." My head fell forward and immediately flew up when the echo of a branch breaking deeper in the forest resonated. I listened for further sounds but couldn't hear any, and so I stay seated on the bench in front of the grave. The awareness of someone watching me continued until midnight rolled around and I decided it was time to leave.

"I'll be back in a few days," I told her.

Marge's house rested on a hilltop around the corner. It was lit up with twinkling lights scattered over the hedges. She greeted me in the door with opened arms before I rang the bell.

"It's so good to see you, Gabriel." She wrapped her arms around me in the same way Joanne used to, with the intensity of a woman who believed in someone she shouldn't. Her embrace opened up everything in my heart I was desperate to forget.

Parsley ran up to me, wagging his tail. I crouched to the ground and scratched the Aussie underneath his chin. A new gray streak ran up the middle of his nose to his forehead.

"Good to see you, boy. I missed you."

Parsley jumped up to my face and licked it. His presence soothed the growing anxiety in my chest.

"We all miss you, Gabe."

"I missed you too, Marge."

"Did you get lost at the cemetery?

"Your senses are as keen as ever."

"Come inside. I put on a pot of tea."

I crossed the threshold, and memories flooded in like a tsunami. The smell, the lightly damp air, and wooden furniture, all brought me back to the past.

"You all right?" she asked.

"Yeah."

"It never gets easier, no matter how much time passes."

"I think it may get a lot harder now. Was that you at the airport?" I pulled out a chair for Marge.

We sat down in the kitchen, and Marge poured a steaming cup of chai tea.

"Of course that was me. You can't drop a bomb on me like the one you had and expect me to stay put."

She picked up on my suspicion when I called her from the

airplane. But once I suggested her kidnapped daughter might be alive, there was no going back.

"Her hair is longer, but the resemblance is beyond belief. The birthmark underneath her brow... I really think I found Charlize."

Marge's tears spilled like they'd been waiting to do so for the past twenty-some years. I'd come to New Zealand on a family vacation as a teenager, met Joanne, and went back as often as possible until I finally moved for the girl of my dreams. The back of my throat tingled as I struggled to hold back everything that wanted to spill from inside of me.

"Are you sure?" Marge quickly covered her mouth, closing the echo of her whimper.

"I'll have DNA confirmation in a couple of days."

"How did you find her?" Marge had searched the world for her abducted daughter. So did her husband, Joanne's father, when he was alive. He passed away before Joanne's death. But Marge never found Charlize.

"Coincidence. Pure coincidence. The resemblance is uncanny. I saw a similar charm from a local store in New Zealand in her New York office. She has no clue who I am."

"The charm with her initials?"

I nodded, removed the phone from my pocket, and showed her the photograph of Sam's charm. A tear rolled down Marge's cheek.

"Where is she now?" Her voice broke.

"She's at the beach house. With me. But she's in trouble."

"Well, I'm glad you came to the island this time."

I swallowed past the accusation. Marge insisted Joanne would still have been alive if she'd remained on the island. She was wrong, though. Martinez didn't have barriers, and keeping this trip a secret was essential to the distance between us.

Parsley's head flew up. He looked out into the darkness beyond the garden door.

"Are you expecting someone?" My shoulders tensed.

"No."

"I should mention that Kendra's with me too."

Parsley got up to his feet and paced by the backyard door.

Marge frowned. "Wonderful. The trouble-maker. What if she gets Charlize in trouble?"

"Her name's Samantha Connor, and she's already in trouble. Kendra's her friend. Sam won't abandon her. But you should keep your distance until I get DNA confirmation. I'm keeping a low profile."

"And then what?" she asked. "How do I walk up to my kidnapped daughter and tell her she's mine?"

"I don't know. I can break the news to her on my own, let it sink in, and we can meet up for dinner? I really don't know, but we'll figure it out."

Marge got up and began pacing with Parsley.

"What if she doesn't want to meet me?"

"I don't see a reason she shouldn't."

"What if she thinks I abandoned her?"

I had at least a hundred similar what-ifs running through my mind every hour. I threw my arms up in the air in frustration. "What do you want me to say? How do I tell her I'm in love with her because she reminds me of the dead sister she doesn't know she had?"

Marge's breath hitched. "You're in love with her?"

I sighed and lowered my head. "How can I not be? She's everything Joanne was. It's all so familiar and not painful when I'm with her. But are the feelings really for Sam, or is it the memory I hold of Joanne?"

"I'm so sorry, Gabe." She reached out for my hand, and the house shook as a blast reached us. Vibrations from a sound wave pushed a garden pot off its shelf. It crashed to the ground, and we turned our head in the same direction: to the back garden and the beach below, where a fireball plummeted into the night sky.

"Oh my God!" Marge hurried to the back door, but I was already halfway out, running towards the explosion.

"Gabe! Be careful," she called after me.

Three-quarters on my way to the beach, I heard two familiar voices arguing with each other. I reached into my pocket for the sedative before I got there because there was only one person capable of this mayhem.

Kendra.

Parsley ran ahead, and the voices quieted. I stepped onto the beach and faced two stunned women. Behind them, what looked like my boat was burning like hellfire. Sam's hair resembled another explosion – partially burned on the right and crispy on the left. Black ash smears ran over her face and arms.

"What the hell are you doing here? What happened to you? What happened to my boat?"

Sam's head flew from the fire, back to me, then to Kendra. "I… I… It all happened so fast. I tried to stop her. I really did."

"Kendra?"

My blood boiled. Not that she cared. She danced underneath the moonlit sky as if my burning boat was a bonfire. I placed the syringe back in my pocket and assessed Sam's injuries.

"I didn't want her cruising off into the ocean on her own, so I jumped in the boat," Sam explained.

"Don't worry about the boat. It's not your fault. I should have never left you alone with her."

"I tried to stop her, Gabe."

"I know."

"Hey Gabe! Sorry about the boat," Kendra called out from the shore.

"How the hell did she blow it up?" I asked.

"We ran out of fuel. Kendra said she could syphon fuel from another boat so we could get back home. Then she wanted a smoke. I don't know where she got the cigarettes."

As if the boat wasn't enough to draw attention, Kendra bellowed Michael Buble's *I'll Be Home for Christmas* at the top of her lungs. Her off-key voice echoed through the cove. This might be a private beach, but privacy was earned.

"We have to leave. Now."

I let go of Samantha and reached inside my pocket again. It was time to end Kendra's rebellion. It wouldn't be long before the explosion's news reached the wrong people. Kendra must have sensed my determined walk because she stopped her dance mid-turn and ran away into the water.

"Oh, no, you don't!" she screamed. "Not this time."

I removed the cap from the syringe, took off my shoes, and followed her into the ocean. My feet left deep prints on the wet sand.

"Gabe! Be careful!" Sam screamed from the shoreline. "Sharks everywhere!"

I focused on my target, who flopped on the shore like a beached whale. Kendra's face plunged into the ankle deep water as she tried to swim away. I set my jaw and jabbed the needle into her thigh. She let out a whimper, and soon after, her body flopped. I lifted her before she drowned and carried her back to the beach and up the path around the cemetery that led to my parked car. Sam followed close behind.

As we passed the house, Marge stood in the window behind a curtain.

"Who's that?" Sam asked.

"Marge Summers. The same woman you saw at the airport."

"Someone I should know better?"

The level of her concern in the pitch of her voice was cute.

"Because, you know, we never set limits on our relationship, and I'm not sure whether I should worry about other women."

While her jealousy was sweet, it bothered me she wasn't aware of the extent to which my feelings had magnified for her. It bothered me that I was carrying Kendra in my arms instead of tending to Sam.

"You definitely have nothing to worry about. Ever. Open the door for me?" I motioned to the car. The seating in the back was small, but so was Kendra. I set her in her spot, turned to the passenger's seat, and took Sam's face into my hands. My lips landed on hers in an instant. I savored her mouth and ensured that she remembered the kiss next time she had doubts.

"I'm happy you're safe. Come on. Let's get you home."

I drove back to the house with as much patience as I could muster. We put Kendra to bed, and I clasped a band around her ankle.

"Is that what I think it is?" Sam asked.

"It's a tracking anklet. I should have put it on her as soon as we got here."

"She won't like it."

"Well, it's that, or risking her blowing up something else. Or herself. I've warned her, but did she listen? Of course not!"

Sam jumped up. I finished securing the tracker and turned around. She was shivering.

"I'm sorry. I'm not trying to take this out on you, Samantha. It's been a long day—"

"You don't have to explain."

"It's just better for the two of you to stay in this house for now, at least until I figure things out." I pulled my fingers through my hair. My scalp ached with stress.

"I'm sorry I couldn't stop her."

"She's not your responsibility. She's mine. The device will

keep her on the property, and her nurse will be here in the morning to help with the withdrawal."

I lowered my head.

"What is it?"

"Will you be here in the morning?"

"Of course." I didn't understand where the concern came from, but before I asked, Sam crossed her arms over her chest and whispered, "I'm gonna go wash up."

A sad haze hovered over her, and it wasn't the soot from the explosion. My heart split in half as she turned around and left upstairs.

Shit!

Chapter 10

Sam

I flapped my frozen feet toward the freestanding bathtub by the window. I turned on the faucet and added a bubble mix and then paced around the king-sized bathroom. The exterior walls stretched to the outside. Beyond the glass, mature trees provided natural privacy, except where the balcony faced the ocean.

I opened the door to take full advantage of the ocean's air. The warm, dark night soothed my tired eyes. A stone walkway below led to the private white sand beach where Gabe's boat used to be docked at the shore. In the distance, a peaceful breeze ruffled the perfect mirror of water.

The ocean's air held a promise of a sunny day tomorrow. If Kendra's new medication worked, this trip could be nothing more than a vacation. I hoped. Though with Kendra, vacationing seemed near impossible.

The faint smell of chlorine drew my attention to the infinity pool below. Its surface bent to the wind's dance, creating soft ripples and gentler waves.

Steam lifted in the air. I sat on the edge of the tub and dipped my ice-cold toes in the water. Heat flowed up my body.

The boat explosion flashed in my mind. I shivered and sank into the giant tub.

I closed my eyes and drifted away in my thoughts. Warmth penetrated down to the bones. The suds lifted, and the lavender aroma stirred, masking the burned smell from my hair. For the first time in days, a wave of relaxation floated over my body. Taking a boat out for a spin in the dark ocean was as close to a nightmare as I'd ever had. If it weren't for the onboard GPS, we'd have been lost at sea forever, but Kendra was sane enough to know her way around the ocean. And then there was the hike to a cemetery, where we'd eavesdropped on a private conversation I was too ashamed to mention to Gabe. I missed the chance to come out of hiding when Kendra raced back to the beach for the next adventure that blew up in her face.

A subtle scent of burning fuel from the clothes I'd shed across the room reminded me of the boat accident. The bathroom door opened, and I startled at the gentle breeze. He strolled into the room with a towel around his hips. I swallowed hard, like he was the first meal I wouldn't be able to finish. The memory of him inside of me back home, pushing me up against the bed frame, pulsed through my nether regions.

"Rona – soothing dim."

"Yes, Mr. Silver," the overhead smart speaker replied.

His eyes kept me frozen in my spot. The expectation he'd know exactly what I needed grew in my belly. But would he even touch me? I had been on that boat with Kendra before it blew up.

The glass walls around the house tinted and the lights lowered to a candle glow, emanating from behind the mirrors and around the cabinets. The flames reflected on the surrounding glass.

"Nice touch." My voice trembled.

"I'm sorry for earlier."

"What?"

"I'm sorry. I shouldn't have been so angry."

"You had every right to be."

"Not with you. You were being a good friend when you jumped in that boat."

"I didn't know what else to do."

He stood at the tub side, looking like a sexy, half-naked model. "Kendra's sedative won't wear off for a few hours. May I join you?"

"Define 'a few.' Because we thought she was asleep before." I bit my lip.

"Ten, twelve hours." His mouth curved into a coy smile. "And her nurse will be here in the morning to help with the withdrawal."

The thought of getting a break from that same adventure I'd sought eased my nerves.

"What are we going to do?" I asked.

"You know exactly what I want to do to you, Sam."

"I'm glad you joined me then." I wiggled my brows.

He grasped the end of his towel and let it loose. The fabric hit the floor, revealing him. He stood too many feet away. I ogled the lean muscles over his defined arms and sturdy legs. A perfectly stacked pack of abs laddered right down to the tempting V-line.

I licked my lips.

He strolled to the tub. Proud and confident, he stepped inside. Water lifted from the curve of my breasts to the tip of my chin, and I let go of my nerves. I sat up higher, so the water wouldn't overflow. The beauty of this comfortably deep tub was its mini-pool size.

"You're shy," he said. "Do you even have an idea how much you turn me on?"

"The feeling is mutual." Water rippled through the tub along with my chuckle.

He shook his head in disbelief. "You're this fierce, independent rebel on the outside, but inside, you're a woman who needs proper care."

I settled back in the tub. "A fierce rebel?"

"You risked your life. And from what I gather, you're not a fan of the ocean."

"True. And how do you know I need proper care?"

Gabe lifted my foot above the suds and placed it over his chest. He pressed his fingers to my sole, and I let go of the remaining tension in my body, sinking deeper into the tub. Yeah, that was definitely proper care. Each pressure point he touched beamed a relaxing current through my body. He concentrated on a spot, massaging until a tingling sensation radiated to between my legs. It lingered at my apex before he pressed again. My buttocks clenched, and a delightful need brewed in my nether regions.

"Rona, list number four."

I could barely hear his whisper over all the naughty thoughts I had on my mind. Soft music played overhead, and I quickly decided that I liked his list number four.

His fingers shifted higher to my calf. Each squeeze and rub triggered a relaxing jolt through my greedy centre aching for his experienced touch.

Who would have thought I'd be sitting in a tub across from a man I'd met in an alley? In New Zealand. In a room made of glass. Serenaded by an AI named Rona, who probably knew more about Gabe than I did.

Gabe lowered my left foot and started on the right one. A memory of the ocean's wind against my face flashed behind my eyelids. The more I'd begged Kendra to return to the beach, the harder she'd pushed the throttle. The moment she docked at the new beach, I jumped out and kissed the ground, but Kendra didn't stop. She went right up that hill to the cemetery.

Something tickled my free leg, and my eyes flew open.

"Sam?" he whispered. "Sorry to wake you. You dozed off. Nightmare?"

"Sort of."

"Come here." His raspy voice sent a delectable shiver down my spine.

I slid toward him, and he shifted forward. He drew a sponge full of fresh lavender suds from my shoulder, down my arm, then back up again. The soft cotton scrubbed along my skin in a circular pattern until a layer of lather covered my upper body. I tilted my head to the side, and Gabe pulled the scrub over my neck and then drew it down to my cleavage.

"I'm going to wash you. All of you."

Gabe's silver eyes flamed, and his heated stare intensified. He let go of the sponge and released the elastic from my crisp braid. My curls spilled stiffly to my shoulders.

"I'm not sure I can salvage the hair," I said.

"It doesn't look that bad."

"Liar." I laughed. "I think it needs a cut."

"What it first needs is a wash. Turn around," Gabe whispered.

I pulled my knees toward my chest and swooshed around in the tub.

Gabe's hands wrapped around my waist. He pulled me closer until his front was pressed against my back.

"Tilt your head up a little."

I leaned back against his chest and did as he asked. A thin screen, resembling sheer fabric, rolled down over the window across the room. It flickered with a loop of a crackling fireplace. Water poured down my hair, and I closed my eyes. Every nerve in my body tensed and let go, over and over. He spread shampoo over my hair and massaged the foam into my scalp, working up a lather. When done with my hair, his hands slid down to my shoulders and to my breasts. His pounding heart beat against my back, and I could barely breathe. My nipples pebbled underneath his touch.

Gabe washed each breast with care, then lowered his hand under the water to my tummy and then to the small patch of curls. I pressed into his hand, urging his fingers for more. Instead, his hands slid over my thighs and to underneath my ass, lifting me higher to his lap. He kneaded my behind before drawing his insistent fingers down the crack, washing the one hole no one had ever touched. A jolt of delectable pleasure flew to my pussy, and I felt Gabe smile against the side of my face.

"I'm glad you like that," he whispered.

I never would have thought I'd allow a man to wash me so thoroughly.

"All done," he said. "How are you feeling?"

"Wanton," I replied.

"Well, we can't have any of that, can we?"

He turned me in the tub to face him. I straddled him, feeling his erection slide against my inner thigh. He held me steady as I sank on top of him and tightened. The instant fill was exquisite. His hands supported my ass. I rolled my hips forward, then back, rubbing myself against him. Water waves rolled through the tub, crashing with our rhythm. We slowed until the flow agreed with the movement, but it didn't last long. Impatience guided Gabe's thrusts. I held on to his arms, digging my fingers into his biceps. He grasped my nipple with his mouth and licked around it. I moaned when he squeezed it between his lips. He gave my other breast the same attention, licking and teasing. I didn't want him to stop.

I melted into the bite, and my muscles let go. Like a marionette, I let him take over. He guided me back and forth, thrusting deeper and harder. Water spilled over the tub's edge. Lost in the moment, I rolled my hips forward and back until he stopped, finding relief. His face contorted, but the tension eased after a few seconds. He rested his head against my chest, panting. I slowly slid off him.

"I had no condom," he said.

The thought of having kids had crossed my mind before, but never to the degree it did now. I certainly wasn't ready for kids, but Gabe was older, and his clock was ticking faster than mine. However, fleeing for my life from what I assumed was the mafia didn't provide the optimal family environment I envisioned.

"I'm on a shot."

"Oh, okay. We're okay, then—"

"What if we weren't?"

He stilled. "Are you asking me what would happen if you were pregnant?" His shoulders lowered. "The life I lead now isn't the life I'd want my kids to have."

"But you're not opposed to having a family?"

"Technically, no. I had one before. It worked until my work got in the way. But things are… different now. Chaotic, I guess, is the right word. Unstable. The grief comes back when I least expect it, and it fucks with my mind, you know. I'm not sure I could stand one more person I love dying."

"I'm sorry you hurt so much, but everything you feel is because you care."

I wished I could remove the sorrow, pain, and guilt from his body. I touched my hand to his face. The stubble over his chin scratched a little, but it was as good a time as any to change the subject.

"Looks like you need a shave." I kissed along his jawline until I reached his mouth. He took my face between his hands, and manipulated my lips. His stubble scratched my chin.

He reached under the water and cupped my sex. My eyes flew wide open. "Shave later. Right now I want to make you come and then take you to my bed."

I would be stupid to ignore the warm tingles sweeping through my body.

Gabe lifted me to my feet in one swift move, positioning me over his mouth. Water dripped down my stomach, over my pussy and onto his face, and I'd seen nothing hotter than a man with his open mouth below me. He held my legs apart, looked up at my stunned face, and covered my pussy with his mouth. His stubble on his chin scratched against my inner thighs. My knees softened, and I sank lower. His hands slid up to my ass, where he firmed his hold. I gripped his hair with my fists. Every few strokes, his tongue attacked that tender spot while his fingers explored around my front and back, prodding and teasing. I didn't know what to concentrate on, but his mouth won over. The deliberate licks intensified. I pressed on his head, holding him steady, centering his mouth and tongue on the tender spot that was ready to burst, and he delivered. He sucked on me like I was the best dessert of the century.

I shook in his hold as he left soothing licks around my clit. The orgasm eased, and I looked down. The concern on his face sent shivers up my spine, waking me from my daze.

"What's the matter?" I asked.

Gabe rose and helped me step out of the bathtub. He wrapped a robe around me and leaned in for a kiss.

"Nothing's the matter. I just can't believe I get to have you like that."

I heated. The thought of everything else he could do to me in the tub sent a fresh wave of pleasure between my legs.

He grabbed a towel and wrapped it around his waist.

"What do you mean, you can't believe you get to have me like that? You can have me any way you want, Mr. Silver."

He frowned. "I meant nothing by it."

"It's just the way you said it."

"It was nothing."

He took three long steps to catch up to me and placed his

hands over my hips. My mind fogged, and I forgot what I wanted to ask him.

"What's happening between us?"

My heart pounded in my chest like it wanted to burst out. Whatever was happening, I hadn't expected this one-night stand to turn into anything more, but it had. And I didn't know when it happened or why my body wouldn't stop shaking.

"I'm so comfortable with you that sometimes it scares me," I told him.

His chest lifted with the next deep breath. When he exhaled, the weight of the world he was carrying on his shoulders eased. "If I'm honest, it scares me too."

I gasped. It was dramatic for my usual self, but the atmosphere of the moment and the honesty in his voice called for it.

"I hear your concern, Sam, and thank you for coming on this trip with me. You're a good friend."

Is that what we were? Friends? Because it sure didn't feel like it. Although Gabe was single, it still felt like I had to fight for him, and I couldn't figure out why.

"And I can't get enough of you."

Oh. Maybe I was wrong.

He grasped my robe's front and untied the knot he'd fastened moments ago. The fabric parted to the sides. I removed it from my shoulders, and the robe swooshed to the floor. Gabe's hands found my hips. I peppered with goose-bumps all over.

He leaned in and whispered, "Rebel."

My whimper came out of nowhere.

He kissed my neck, dragging his lips to my collarbone. His hand slid between my thighs, like it was the only spot he found comfortable. My legs parted, and my head tilted backward as he played with my sex. My need returned like a second wave. I cupped his face in my palms and kissed him softly. "You need a shave."

"A shave? Now?"

"All future MTP care deserves a shave. Your beard is scratchy."

He growled.

I pulled a chair from the corner and set it in front of the mirror.

"What are you up to?"

"No questions. Come. Sit." I motioned to the chair and set a towel by the sink. "Get comfortable."

Gabe obliged and stretched his legs out to the front, crossing his arms. He waited patiently.

I opened the drawer under the sink. "Aha! I knew a man like you would use a straight razor."

"Wait – I know how to shave." His voice trembled.

"So do I. I watched a professional barber shave hundreds of men when I helped grandpa at the shop after school."

"But you didn't shave those men, did you?" His eyes fixed on the sharp blade in my hand.

"Do you trust me?"

"I do, but—"

"No buts." I turned on the hot water faucet. Steam rose, and I dipped a face cloth underneath the stream, squeezed it out, and placed the heated fabric just below Gabe's eyes. The chair had been perfectly set so he could lean back, but he sat up.

"It will soften the bristles," I explained.

"I was just going to ask if you're planning on doing this naked?" His warm breath trailed over my breasts.

I lowered my gaze to his hard dick and back to his face. "Absolutely."

He sighed and closed his eyes.

I swirled the shaving cream in the small bowl, mixing the lather. Gabe was reflected stretched out front in the mirror, nearly naked and vulnerable. His ready cock rested on his lower abs. Need flowed to my groin. The urge to touch him and stroke him grew. My mouth watered as I imagined tasting him.

"Enjoying the view?" Gabe opened one eye.

"Always." I removed the cloth from his face, aware of my hardened nipples. "Now, relax."

I brushed the lather on his face, first downward, and then in circles, to swirl the bristles the way my grandfather had done. I moved in closer, careful not to make a mistake. When Gabe's breath warmed my breast, I teased him with my nipple, pulling the nub along his lip.

"First time I've gotten service like this." He took the nipple into his mouth, lengthening it.

Pleasure ran down my belly and to my heated core. "There's a first time for everything." I reluctantly pulled away from Gabe's tender yet oh-so-distracting kisses.

"I'm going to shave you now. No more distractions." I took the straight blade into my fingers.

"Wait." Gabe grasped my wrist just before I touched his skin. "You have done this before, right?"

"I practiced on my Ken dolls." I winked.

He let out a nervous breath and closed his eyes.

"Tilt back and don't move," I said.

Stretching the skin up, I drew the blade from under his sideburn, down the side of his face, with the grain at the same angle I'd seen my grandfather use. Slow and steady. The sound of metal scraping gently against Gabe's skin awakened the smallest hairs on my arms and nape. My hand held steady. The motion of my wrist felt natural.

"So, how does someone like you stay single?"

His forehead creased, and I pulled the blade away from his skin.

"Life. Work. Bad guys."

I got the life part. "Bad guys?"

He opened his eyes and looked into mine. I waited as he took a breath in, then released it.

"My work is not for the faint of heart. Both my brothers and cousins remain single because when you worry about those you love while on the job, you make mistakes. It's that simple."

He shut his eyes. When he opened them again, the pain he was holding in his heart swam in his orbs.

"It's not your fault," I whispered. "Whatever happened in the past. It's not your fault."

I swallowed past the lump in my throat. Gabe closed his eyes, and I resumed the shave. He didn't stir; just breathed steadily through my strokes. The tension in his face eased each time I cleaned the blade over the towel resting on his shoulder. The smell of his skin and the lemon-pine shaving cream wafted through the air.

When I finally rinsed the blade in the sink, he opened one eye. "You're incredible." His relaxed voice held a hint of lust.

"Did you know I can cut hair too?"

"Unbelievable." He leaned forward for a smooch.

"Just glad I can do something for you for a change." I cleaned the remaining cream off his face with the towel.

"You surprise me every hour, Samantha."

"Almost done." I squeezed the tube of moisturizer and cooling lotion onto my palm and sat in Gabe's lap, spreading my legs over chair sides and straddling him.

As I applied the balm to his face, he hardened underneath me. When I finished, my hands slid to his shoulders, and Gabe opened his eyes. The silver shade sparked with bright fire.

"I love that you're so wet and ready," he said.

I circled my hips, feeling him deep inside me.

I pushed myself higher and reached between his legs. I

wrapped my fingers around him and stroked him once, twice, three times, feeling him grow in my palm.

Gabe's mouth found my breasts and pebbled nipples. He rolled the other one between his fingers while biting, sucking, and pulling on the first nub. Heat flowed from there to between my legs, and I centered over him.

"You taste perfect."

My pussy tingled.

"Turn around." Gabe helped me up and off him. He sat straight in the chair, and with one hand on my hip and the other holding himself steady, he guided me down. I opened my mouth in awe and lowered, taking him in. I rolled my hips in an agonizing rhythm, and looked back over my shoulder, watching his face contort from need to pleasure and then more need again. I braced my arms on the counter. He shifted forward as well, lifting his hands to my breasts, cupping them. Our rhythm increased and our skin slapped until he halted from nowhere.

His breaths steamed hot and heavy.

"Samantha, stand."

I stopped moving.

"I want to see your pretty ass."

I stood up and leaned forward, over and against the counter, sticking my ass out for him, and glanced back. "Is that better?"

He stood up, swore under his breath, and entered me in one slick move. His momentum brought an onslaught of bliss. My breasts shook under me. My thighs pressed against the edge, and I secured my hand against the mirror.

Gabe's hands remained on my hips. He steadied me with each thrust as his balls smacked against me. The rough hold would leave me bruised, yet I wanted his ruthless assaults to leave a mark as a reminder. After three thrusts, Gabe stilled and quickly pulled out.

A spurt of warmth trickled down my back. I looked up to the mirror and watched him close his eyes as he spilled. The smallest muscles on his face twitched with pleasure.

The tension in his shoulders eased. He exhaled, smiled, and opened his eyes.

If satisfaction had a face, it would be his. He grabbed the after-shave towel off the counter and wiped my back. He washed the area with a fresh cloth. The circular strokes revived my aching body. I recoiled when his hand slid to between my legs. He paused.

"Are you hurt?"

"No." I shook my head.

"You flinched when I touched you. Perhaps we ought to take some breaks? I don't want you hurt." The distance between his eyes narrowed.

I touched myself between my legs, where the tender flesh was a little swollen from the onslaught. "It burns a little, but I'll be fine." I stepped back.

"Hey, what's the matter?" Gabe lifted my chin to meet his gaze.

"I'm fine, Gabe."

"Samantha, your mouth lies, but your eyes tell the truth. Tell me what's wrong."

"I'm just afraid for this to end," I blurted.

Truth was, I was falling for him, yet I didn't know why or how. The sentiment came from within. I needed him in my life, and I had no clue why. Like I'd met him in a past life. It scared me how quickly I'd attached myself to a man I'd met less than two weeks ago.

"Why would it end?" Gabe's eyes clouded with worry.

"I... I don't know. You're... older and... single and... well... They call it 'no strings attached' for a reason. Strings make things complicated."

"I think it's a little too late to cut the strings, Samantha.

Things change. Life moves forward, and I definitely don't want to move forward without you. Once things settle down."

He slid a drawer open and removed a silver box with a silver bow.

"In the meantime, I would love for you to have this."

"What is that?"

"A gift."

My heart pounded as I pulled on the bow and opened the box he held in front of me. Inside, a silver charm bracelet rested on a pad of cotton fluff.

I gasped – there lay the charm with my initials, hanging between a playful turtle and a sunhat, that I'd lost back home. It was the only piece of me I had from my birth parents.

"How… How did you get this?"

"I found it on your office floor. I put it in my pocket before the cop cuffed me. The new chain is stronger. I hope you like it."

"Gabe, it's beautiful. This is the only piece of me I have from before I was adopted. I thought I'd lost it, but I love this. Thank you." I stretched out my hand so Gabe could fasten the bracelet on my wrist. I shimmied my wrist underneath the light. Each trinket incorporated a sparkling diamond into its design, and the charm with my initials S.C. was plated in platinum. "Does that mean you're not mad about the boat?"

"Of course I'm not mad about the boat. I think the better question is, how quickly can you lie down on that bed so I can massage all those worries away?"

"What?"

"You heard me. Lie down." He pointed to the bed. I obeyed because it would be stupid to turn down a massage, wouldn't it?

My body sank into the sheets, and my face pressed into the pillow. I sighed as he massaged his oiled hands to the top of my shoulders and rubbed in circular patterns.

"I don't want you worrying about silly ideas like our relationship ending," Gabe whispered after a while. "Because I assure you it's not, Samantha. In fact, I think what's happening between us is serious. Very serious."

He continued the massage until I fell asleep. He must have, because his hands flowing over my skin felt like the ocean's waves and were the last thing I remembered.

I'd be out on a boat every day if time, life, and nature allowed me. I gripped the throttle and pushed it forward, guiding my two-seater towards the family yacht. Julian had brought the boat out from Silver's Cove on the other side of the island. Tonight, Sam was in for a treat because I was determined to help her get over her fears.

At times, it felt like I was stuck in the past – a happy past. And then I'd blink and it would be Sam, not Jo, standing by the coffee machine, preparing our morning brew. Every time I saw her, I saw Joanne. And when I didn't see Jo, I definitely felt her in Sam's gestures and mannerisms. We'd spent the last four days between the pool and the bedroom, and every minute I'd spent with Samantha was my favorite as I slowly fell back into the routines from my past.

The cemetery had brought me back to reality the moment I saw Jo's grave. As I waited for the delayed DNA results, the constant worry I held for Samantha never eased.

I pulled the boat up to the yacht side near the stern, and Julian greeted me from above deck. White sunscreen streaked down his nose and underneath his eyes. He looked like a clown trying to pose as a sunbathing football player.

"Good to see you!" He waved.

"Good to see you too. Thanks for bringing the yacht in." I secured the rope and stepped aboard.

"Anytime."

I'd planned a romantic dinner for Samantha tonight. It would be just the two of us, in the middle of the ocean underneath the stars, with a surprise swim afterwards. I made my way up to the upper deck, where Julian was waiting with a couple of guys from his crew.

"Nice makeup."

"We'll compare notes in a couple of hours after your nose fries."

I grabbed the sunscreen tub out of his hand. "Give me some of that."

"I don't know why you need the cages, but I won't ask."

"It's a long story." I set the tube aside and glanced down below, where the divers had assembled a cage underneath.

After a long moment of thought, I sighed and closed my eyes.

"Sam has to face her fears. She doesn't seem to have many, but given we're on an island, I thought it'd be a good idea to make her more comfortable in water."

"Does she know how to swim?"

"I've watched her in the pool. She's good, but she's... she's her and she's not her. Ya know?"

"I don't, and it shouldn't matter. It's about time you dated someone. Sulking in your sorrows doesn't do you any good. This sounds like the perfect opportunity to let the grief go."

Could I? Was it actually possible to move on with a woman who reminded you of your past and twined with your present?

My mouth curved at the corner. "She Facetimed her cat today. I think that's the only thing about her that's different."

"What thing?"

"Jo was into dogs, but Sam has a cat."

He laughed. "You know you can be into both, right?"

"Cats and dogs?"

"You can add parrots and raccoons to that."

"Raccoons?"

"I watched it on the Discovery channel."

"Since when do you watch the Discovery channel?"

"Since the day I met Kendra."

"What?"

"It's calming."

I shook my head. Julian and Kendra's love for the wild and dangerous kept them in the same universe. Still, his 'calming' was my boring. But it worked for them, and that was all that mattered. The sooner Julian cleaned up her case, the better for Silver. It had taken Julian years to cross the age gap between them. I didn't have as much time left to make sense of the shit I called my life. After Jo died, I'd thought my life was over. Yet Sam made me feel like it was possible to have it all again.

"She could be my daughter."

"But she's not."

"I don't feel my age around her."

"You're not old, and women are more mature than men, anyway. That's what Mom says."

"Your parents have always had it figured out."

He laughed. "Bullshit. No one ever has it figured out. Not you, not me, and not my parents or yours. Isn't it Teresa and Jacob's anniversary this year?"

It had been thirty years since my parents married on Christmas day.

"They think we forgot about it, and they said they're going on a cruise." I chuckled.

"How are you going to throw them a party when they're gone?"

"Their travel agent is an old buddy of mine. He didn't book the cruise. They'll be escorted to a private jet at the airport, which will take them to their destination where the family will be waiting."

It was the perfect plan, which we'd had for years, and it was the only plan we weren't allowed to talk about in the house.

"You don't think they'll be pissed about missing their cruise?"

"Not when they see the luxury yacht I rented."

"Nice. Wait – am I going?"

"We're all going."

"Tropical?"

"Yup."

"Good. Doesn't get better than Christmas in the tropics."

A splash on the water's surface brought our attention back to the divers.

"That gate doesn't look straight." I pointed to the cage corner.

"Feel like taking a dive?"

I grinned. Scuba diving was one of my favorite pastimes I didn't get to do much back home. Joanne had been a great diver. Her father used to say she was like a fish pulled out of the water and the ocean was always calling her back. Now the ocean's waves sang to her every night.

"Yeah. Let's do it. How's your brother?" I asked, and we made our way to the stern of the boat where we stored the gear.

"Drowning in self-pity."

"You know he won't stop until he clears the family name."

"You mean until he can keep the family name clean?"

I exhaled sharply. I might have had trouble with Sam and Kendra the past few weeks while my cousins took on a political enemy. Unfortunately, that same enemy had twined its tentacles around Kendra like an octopus and was holding Silver

Securities by the throat. The girl earned her 'Trouble' nickname the day we met.

"Your parents arrive tomorrow night," Julian said.

"What? When did that happen?"

"After their third round of bourbon last Saturday night with Fred and Wilma. Hunter's at the main house already."

My aunt and uncle hosted a monthly game night for their siblings. The tradition had been started by the family patriarchs, brothers John and Jacob, and had lasted for three decades.

"Wait – is everyone coming?"

"What do you think? Your mother hates the cold. It's the start of the best season here."

He was right. My mother would move to the equator if she could.

The blistering sun sizzled against my forehead. Beyond the boat, the blue sky blended with the turquoise ocean. The sun scorched through my thin layer of lotion, and Julian's strategic sunscreen streaks no longer looked funny. I suited up and checked the oxygen gauges, while Julian did the same.

"I'm taking Kendra off your hands for a few days," said Julian,

"Seriously?"

"Yeah, I thought you could use a break. And thanks for taking care of my girl."

"Is she your girl?"

"Fuck off. Everyone knows Kendra's mine."

"Everyone except Kendra?"

"It's complicated."

Wasn't life always complicated? I was back in New Zealand on my deceased wife's home island, struggling to keep two rebels out of trouble and drowning in my past. Quiet time alone with Sam couldn't come sooner.

"I need Kendra well, and I have debts to settle. Martinez is on the lookout for a second employer. Hartley's not paying enough."

Sometimes it felt like we all had debts to settle with the same scum.

"That's bad for him and good for us, I guess."

"It will be good for us once he's out of our lives."

A stronger gust of wind blew by, throwing me off balance. The ocean stirred, and a stray wave swept by.

"Haven't you learned anything in your life?" I eased some oxygen out of the mouthpiece and closed it off again. "Those bastards will never be out of our lives."

Julian's shoulders tensed.

"I wish it was all over. I wish we could turn back the clock—"

"The Silvers did what was right. If it were you, you'd do the same. They had no choice, and no one knew Kendra would fall down a powdered rabbit hole. Her crazy shit is getting out of control, and us dealing with Martinez is just one of them. For Christ's sake, she blew up Marge's boat!" I threw my hands up in the air. "You know she propositioned a threesome to Sam and me the other night?"

"You know that's not her."

"You're absolutely right. It's not her – which means you need to chain her up before she falls into deeper trouble. Take her home, lock her up, and force her through a rehab that will make her never wanna return to this life."

"Ok. I get it. She's not herself. Trust me, I know. Tristan's working with the Congress to close the case. It should be soon."

"They said that last time."

"This year. The company received an invitation from the DEA to work with a narcotics team." Julian checked an incoming message on his phone.

"Silver Securities has certainly grown in the years since we took Kendra on as a client. If it weren't for her cooperation, the company would have destroyed its reputation. We fucking all benefited from her, and at what price?" I removed my wet suit from its compartment.

"You're not wrong."

"So are we going to do something about it?"

"We're doing it. Just too slowly. Are you willing to stick your neck out for the girl a little longer?"

"What kind of fucking question is that? You know I will." Julian threw his hands in the air.

"But not tell her you've been in love with her since the day you saw her on that train?"

He stared at me with his mouth wide open, like he was sorting through a library catalogue in the nineteen eighties.

"That was a rhetorical question."

"She was sixteen, and I was thirty-six. If I'd made any moves, I would have been the same as the pedophile we were trying to capture. Besides, I thought of her as a sister for a long time before, you know, all the feelings got in the way."

I checked the goggles and adjusted the band width. "She's not sixteen anymore."

"Twenty-one doesn't make her much older or wiser. She needs to get well first. When I tell her I love her, it will be when she's sober."

"So, you sleep with her first, break her little teenage heart, and then you wonder what's gone wrong?"

I deserved a punch, but Julian deserved the truth. The solution to his problems was right underneath his nose, but he stubbornly focused on their twenty-year age gap. My Nana always told me everyone had problems. Enormous problems. The trouble with Kendra was that she hadn't been sober in years and piled her problems on like crap.

"Thanks for sending Clara over. She's been like a hawk. Tell her to take a few days off when you get Kendra." The nurse had been tending to Kendra's every need and request without complaint.

"Will do. I'm sure everyone will appreciate the break. I'd make most of the couple of days you've got. The family wants to do a bonfire at the main beach soon."

The old me would have flipped him off. Family time wasn't in my bones. At least not since Joanne's death. But the new me, the one who had fallen absolutely crazy mad in love with Samantha Connor, sort of wanted that happy ending.

"You're right. I will. And thanks," I said.

"I should be the one thanking you. You've helped Kendra more than anyone could have asked for." He reached behind him and pulled out an envelope from his back pocket. "I think you've been waiting for this. It came to our house. April thought you were staying on the other coast."

"You couldn't have mentioned it sooner?" I removed the envelope from his hand and realized that mine was shaking.

"I figured whatever answer you got wouldn't change the fact you're bound to that woman."

He was right, but the results could certainly bring answers to decade-old questions. I tore through the envelope. My hand trembled and my breath stilled as I read Sam's DNA results. Their lab work matched Charlize's.

"Shit..." I breathed out.

I knew it. I knew the truth the moment I saw Sam in the alley.

"It's her," I told him. "Sam is Charlize."

"Great timing, then. I'll take Kendra off your hands, and it will give you two time to... talk."

"Yeah, thanks. Why do I feel like there's a *but* coming up?"

"But I have a surveillance issue on the yacht. If you could have a look at it before you leave—"

"Of course I will." I glanced beyond the deck at the inviting cool water. "I think I need this dive."

While nothing could take my mind off the inevitable conversation I'd face tonight with Sam, then with Marge, a dive would buy me some time and clear my head.

"Make sure Sam locks up when you leave with Kendra. I won't be long." I set the oxygen tank aside.

Julian left on his speedboat, but the anxiety about Sam's true identity remained deep inside me. What would she think of me when she found out the truth? She must have known I suspected... something. Or did she? Truth was, I should have mentioned it sooner, but how do you tell a girl you just met she looks like your dead wife? You don't. I chose to fall in love with her instead. I cranked my neck from one side to the other and back. The sun shone hot, and so I grabbed a beer from the fridge and checked the surveillance. The trouble didn't take long to fix – a broken circuit. I wondered whether the boys had experienced a recent blackout. A breaker was missing, and I'd have to get a spare from the garage back home. I geared up, placed the mouthpiece between my lips, and flipped backwards into the clear water.

Underneath, the crew of two were still struggling to fix the last corner. I swam down and held a pipe while they aligned the middle and upper rods. We fixed the last cage corner and secured the lights to the bottom. A large sea turtle swam by on the other side of the cage. I watched until it disappeared into the ocean's depth. We swam up to the surface and tested the bright lights.

"Are you throwing an underwater party?" one diver asked. "Want me to chum the waters?"

"That's a no to the chum, and the party will be only for two."

"So, the new arrivals in town today weren't your guests?"

"What arrivals?"

The sound of a boat engine drew our attention overboard. That bad feeling you immediately experienced when unexpected news was about to smack you right in the face hit me all over. And when one of our security guards screamed overboard, I knew our peaceful vacation had ended.

"We spotted Martinez in town! And Ms. Connor."

Chapter 12

Sam

The smell of bacon and eggs penetrated my dreams, waking me. Gabe was holding me from behind, the same way he had every morning since our first night together. And he snuck out every night after I fell asleep. I wasn't sure where he went, but I had my suspicions. My heart broke that he didn't think he could share his pain. Still, I was grateful that he always returned before the sun rose to hold me like this in the morning.

Sun streaked between the window curtains. I didn't want to move. For the first time in ages, things were going well. The past few beautifully peaceful days and Kendra's better mood were exactly what we all needed. As much as I missed my cat and my friends, New Zealand delivered on its promise of adventure, safety, and rest.

Gabe stirred behind me and pressed against my back. My limbs tingled with warmth. New aches pulsed through my body, and I wiggled my toes. The delectable sting between my legs reminded me of Gabe inside me. His mouth-to-pussy care brought one orgasm after another. Gabe's experience proved to be exactly what I'd been craving.

"You're awake?"

"Yes." I stretched my arms above my head.

"Good, because I'm starving."

"I think Carla's cooking." I turned around to face Gabe.

"That's not what I'm hungry for." His trademark dimple sank in his cheek.

"No?" I opened my mouth, confused for a moment, but the lust on his face didn't keep me in suspense too long as he closed in for a kiss.

"That mouth of yours is about to get you in trouble." He tapped my chin, slowly moving above my body, and hovered above me. He reached between my legs. "You're still wet."

"That's what happens when a charmer with experience steps into a woman's life." I winked.

"Are you calling me old?"

"No, I'm calling you charming and well… hot, if I'm honest. You turn me on, Mr. Silver."

The rolling growl from his chest was sexier than the single one.

"Well, let me see what I can do about that." Gabe threw the covers aside in a swift move, and flipped me over on the bed.

He slid his hand along my ass, smoothing each curve, teasing a little lower until my pelvis instinctively tilted at his touch. "Push your ass higher for me. Get on your knees," he said.

I did as he asked. An instant breeze assaulted my body, but the warmth of his breath tickling my behind kept my focus on the lower area.

"Your ass is perfect." He kissed one side, then the other. He repeated the pecks, each time moving closer to the center of my ass.

"Has anyone cared for this hole?" His lips tantalized my skin as he kissed his way closer and closer to my virgin hole.

I shut my eyes tight as my face heated. "No."

"Let's see if we can practice some MTA care as well."

MTA... Oh!

His hands took hold of my ass cheeks, parting them. He pulled his tongue from the top of my crack down to the rim of my hole, where he circled with his tongue.

Oh God, that felt good!

I never thought I'd let anyone kiss or lick me there, yet here we were. And I wanted more. Gabe tended to my body like he owned every piece of me. The delicate touch of his tongue in the back sent pleasure all the way to the front. While I wanted his mouth up higher, I needed him there as well.

"We're going to work on you slowly," he said to my ass, gently pressing his finger in its center.

Slowly?

I didn't want slow; I wanted hard and fast because the mounting arousal beneath his mouth zapped to my front.

"But I'm too hungry."

A primal growl echoed from his throat. Gabe slid to my dampened sex. He lay on his back and kissed between my folds, his breath warm against my pussy.

I lowered onto his mouth. He parted the crevice, licking the length of my slit back and forth before resting on the swelling tip. I pressed myself harder to his lapping tongue. He closed his mouth around the tender spot without warning and flicked my clit in an unforgiving rhythm. My body convulsed, and I screamed as his tongue pulled the orgasm out of my pussy. The spasms left me drained as Gabe finished his MTP care.

"That was so good," I said between gasps. My chest heaved, and I struggled to feed my lungs enough air.

Gabe rolled over to his side. He took me in his arms and kissed my shoulder. "I promise you more later, but I'm meeting my cousin after breakfast."

I turned over on my elbow and gazed into his sparkling blue eyes, where the sexual fire had dimmed to a beautiful glow.

"Stay with me. Otherwise I'll have to Facetime my cat again." I pouted and pulled on his arm.

"Clara will be here today. And I'm expecting Julian to stop by later. He wants to chat with Kendra."

"Kendra's been good. I hope he can see that."

I waited, but Gabe gave me no reply. He stood up and proceeded to the bathroom, where he turned on the shower. I quickly jumped out of bed, drew the sheets around my body, and followed him.

"Clara's helped a lot too," I started. "And we've been fine when you leave in the middle of the night. Every night."

I wasn't sure why that came out, but it was enough to halt him mid-way into the shower.

"I'm sorry. I didn't know you knew."

"I'd prefer you told me what keeps you away from a warm bed and a warm body."

He lowered his head. When he looked up again, his eyes had lost the spark they held when I was in his arms. "I know you have questions, and I promise to have answers soon. Very soon."

"I trust you." I truly meant what I said. Gabe had morphed from this mysterious bartender into an even more mysterious surveillance-investigator who never stopped surprising me. We had cleared another week off at work, but I knew I'd have trouble leaving this paradise I'd grown to love.

By the time I brushed my teeth and put on my bathing suit, shorts, and tank, Gabe was showered and dressed.

"Ready for breakfast?" he asked.

My stomach rumbled. With all of our nocturnal activities, it was a miracle I found enough time to eat. And it was a miracle Gabe could remain awake.

"Yeah, let's go," I replied, and hopped first down the stairs and into the kitchen.

"Good morning," Kendra chirped.

"Morning. How are you feeling?"

"Clara's been filtering me with fluids and green concoctions that taste like barf. But I'm getting there." Kendra scanned me from the bottom up. "You are beaming like a glow-bug."

"I don't know what you're talking about." I grabbed a muffin from a delicious carb-filled platter and bit into the fruity, vanilla top. It melted in my mouth as Kendra laughed at my dismissal. Her eyes were still shadowed, and the rims were now pink instead of red, but she looked better.

"What's that?" She pointed to my new bracelet.

I hopped onto the kitchen stool and stretched out my hand. "I got it from Gabe."

Kendra examined the charms. "Looks… familiar."

"Latte?" Gabe asked.

"Yes, please." I swiveled in the chair and connected my gaze with Gabe's. His hair was ruffled in a perfect mess.

"Looks like you two have been busy." Kendra's tone lowered to an explicit insinuation.

"None of your business, K." Gabe smiled. "It's nice to see you feeling better. Clara's been helping you?"

"She has." Kendra rolled her eyes. "And it *is* my business when you're fucking my friend."

"Kendra!" we screamed, turning her way at the same time.

"What?" She shrugged. "It's not like it's not true. I heard you in the middle of the night. 'Oh, Gabe! Yes! Please! Right there!'"

"Kendra!" we screamed again.

"Jesus." I rolled my eyes, grabbed an apple, and hopped off the stool. "Sometimes you're worse than a kid. I'm going to eat elsewhere."

I stormed out the back door toward the poolside and lay on the lounge chair. As I bit into my apple, Gabe came outside with my coffee. He placed it on the side table and sat near my legs. "She can be a handful."

"Yup. She definitely can. Thanks for the coffee."

"You're welcome. I'm sorry I have to leave you two, but I shouldn't be long."

I lowered my legs off the lounge and sat up. "You're going to your cousin's already?"

"He's expecting me." He checked his watch. "And I don't want to be late. Be good and stay out of trouble."

"I'm not twelve." I rolled my eyes.

He was talking to the wrong person. Trouble was Kendra's nickname, not mine.

"You're not, but Kendra acts like it." Gabe leaned in and smacked a kiss on my lips. "I have an errand to run. I'll be back soon."

Gabe grabbed a bag from the garage and left down the path to the beach. He was gone before I realized he was taking the boat. The engine roared from the shore.

"He's meeting Julian," Kendra explained, walking out the patio door.

"Oh. How do you know?"

"Julian texted me."

Right. I'd been so preoccupied with Gabe and sex and more Gabe and sex that I hadn't been paying as much attention to my friend as I should have. I bit into my apple as Kendra came and joined me in the backyard. She set her green smoothie on the table and sat on the lounge chair beside me.

"Hey, listen. I may need a small favor."

Her words sent shivers down my spine, and I definitely regretted not paying as much attention to Kendra as I should have.

"I'm afraid to ask."

"Don't be. It's actually good news."

"Kendra, before you start, I should tell you that Gabe and I—"

"Love each other. I know."

"Well, I wouldn't say love."

"I would, because it's true."

Could it be love? That quick? I checked the horizon. The more I worried about him out there, the harder my heart ached and my head throbbed. I pressed my fingers to my temples. I couldn't concentrate on what ifs right now. "Did you say you need a favor?" I asked.

"Right. I did." She bit her lip. "I squared the deal with Martinez."

I spat out the apple and lifted my hands in the air. "I don't want to know! I. Don't. Want. To. Know."

"But you do, because you're the only one who can save us." She waved her arms around like propellers. Of course, I was 'the only one who could save us,' because in Kendra's language, that meant I could help her do the job she couldn't.

"I'm gonna call bullshit on that, K."

"Well, obviously I'd do it if I could, but I can't get out of the house with the bracelet, right?" She pointed to the metal accessory on her ankle. She was baiting me. I knew she was because that's what Kendra did, and before I knew it, I was hitching a ride halfway back from our failed trip to Vegas.

"But *you* can." She smiled.

I sighed. "I can what?"

"I made a few calls. I have the money to pay up. All you have to do is take a small envelope with instructions and a delivery fee to a boy at a popular café in town. You should see the early afternoon line-up. It's crazy. They have the most delicious local food. That place can never do a siesta. Anyhow, a boy, about twelve, will come get the envelope. I'll text you his picture before he arrives, so you'll know it's him. That's it."

"A boy?"

"Yeah. Easy, right? And it will all be over. No more Martinez, and we can all get on with our lives."

I crossed my arms over my chest and insisted, "No."

"Come on, Sam. You're my only hope."

"Quoting the Skywalkers won't help."

"Maybe this will." She ran my way, opened her arms, and threw herself over me on top of the lounge chair until it nearly flipped. She fluttered her lashes that were supposed to convince me to hand over an envelope to a crooked child. No big deal. Then she whispered like she knew delicious desserts were the way to my soul, "I made cream-stuffed waffle rolls."

My mouth watered.

"They go great with coffee." She grinned.

"Cream-stuffed waffle rolls go fucking well with anything."

She laughed. "I'll bring some over. We'll go for a swim. If the boys are meeting, we have all day."

Kendra hurried to the kitchen and brought out a tray filled with cream-stuffed waffle rolls. We stuffed ourselves full and instead of swimming, lounged on pool floats for the next hour. Kendra flipped over, lifted her sunglasses to the top of her head, and splashed a bit of water my way.

"Hey! Stop that!"

"So, you think you can do it? I doubt Gabe will be back until night."

Seriously?

"I don't know, Kendra. It sounds too easy. Can't we just leave it be?"

"It sounds easy because it is easy, and no. We can't just leave it be. If we leave it be, they will come get us. Believe me, I know. That's how they got Joanne. They'll come with guns and shit. Big guns. Giving the boy a letter would avoid all that."

"That's not quite convincing me to help you."

She froze. "Wait, you actually mean there is a way? You'll do it?"

"I don't know."

"Please? You're only meeting a twelve-year-old boy. In a very public place. No one will ever know."

"I trusted you when you slipped me that pill at the club. I'm not making that mistake again. Where's Clara?" I asked.

"Off. I don't know why, but she left a note, and just… left." She shrugged. When Kendra shrugged, there was trouble; but then the sound of a boat engine turned our attention towards the cove.

I let out a breath of relief. "I guess Gabe is back."

"Shit!" Kendra splashed the water with her hand. I felt sorry for her. "It could have been all over! I had everything ready!" She pointed to the table underneath the awning, where a white envelope had been pinned underneath a flower vase.

The engine shut off, and moments later, the echo of stones scrunching down the path grew louder. Except it wasn't Gabe who surprised us.

"Julian?" Kendra lowered the sunglasses and jumped off her float into the pool. "What the—"

"Before you start, let me explain. I'm taking you for a few days to get things… sorted."

Kendra waded through the water towards the steps, saying, "Okay."

"Okay?" we replied at the same time.

She sat down at the pool's edge. "Yeah, okay. I'll come with you, but you have to get this off." She wiggled her foot.

Julian nodded, removed something from his pocket, kneeled in front of her, and turned the lock on the clasp, freeing Kendra.

"Next time you put a ring around me, I hope it's the right kind." She winked.

Julian made nothing of her comment and turned my way. "I'm Julian Silver. Gabe's fixing a couple of things for me." He pointed towards the ocean, where I assumed I could find Gabe.

"It's nice to meet you. Samantha Connor."

"Yeah, you're definitely her." His odd reply made me pause.

While Kendra got out of the pool and wrapped a robe around herself, Julian kept looking at me like we'd met before.

"I gave Clara a few days off," he said.

That explained the note Kendra had found.

"We can hang around here until Gabe gets here, or—"

"You guys go." I waved. "I'll be fine. Gabe should be back soon. Besides, I'll turn on the alarm, and the property is secure. Right?"

"Of course it is. Have a great day."

Kendra waved before she turned the corner to the driveway. "Don't forget to get out of the sun. There's wonderful shade underneath the gazebo." She pointed to where the letter was waiting on the table. "See you in a few days, Sam!"

Smooth.

As if summoned by her warning, my shoulders pinched, and I realized I was half-naked and burning in the scorching sun. I swam two laps to cool off and sat in a lounge chair, staring at the letter Kendra had left on the table. I could sulk here all on my own and wait until Gabe returned who-knew-when, or I could use my time wisely and get rid of Kendra's predicament once and for all. I'd be back by the time Gabe returned. I grabbed Kendra's stupid letter, got dressed, and went to the garage with the three parked cars. Armed with a set of keys in my hand, I clicked the button on the key. The convertible Miata lights blinked.

"Congratulations! You're the winner today." I said to the car.

I climbed inside and sat in the leather seat, glad it was an automatic and the tank was full. As soon as the engine purred, I rolled it out of the garage, then eased it along the driveway. The sensor opened the front gate, and for the first time in a long time, I felt completely alone and nervous. I stopped the car and turned in my seat to see whether doubt was actually following me. The curved path and trees lining the way blocked the view.

"It's now or never." I gripped the steering wheel, set the car in drive, and turned onto the road. I followed the GPS guide. Within ten minutes, the lush green trees faded, and the horizon turned into rolling hills. Beyond, low-lying buildings with red rooftops spread out in even lines. A sign at the side of the road posted the name of a town. The sun shone directly above me, scorching the top of my head, and I wished I'd worn a hat.

Five minutes later, the town appeared from behind the rolling hills. I weaved through the streets and parked by a fountain in the town square. I checked the address on the envelope from Kendra. The café was across the street. I yawned, and the smell of coffee floated toward me as if summoning me. I rummaged through the glove compartment, searching for spare change. Instead, I found five one-hundred-dollar bills in New Zealand's currency. I grabbed a bill and stepped out of the car.

I headed straight for the line to the café, hoping Kendra would text me the boy's image soon. She was right; the line was long, and I couldn't wait to move forward to underneath the shaded area. A moment later, my phone pinged with an image of a young boy in a striped shirt, cargo pants, and a beige cap.

I looked up, and the replica of that image was standing beside me, staring.

"You've got an envelope for me?" he asked.

"I do."

"Come on. Come on. Make it quick." He pulled out his hand and motioned forward.

I double-checked the perfectly matching picture and handed him the envelope. He stuffed it in his deep cargo pants pocket and turned to leave.

"You know where I can get a cap like that?" I asked. "It looks like it's going to be a hot day."

"It's always a hot day in New Zealand. There's a store over there." He pointed, and I turned to look.

"Your accent... that's not from New Zealand." When I turned back, I saw him disappearing into the crowd. I looked around me at the normalcy of the day and breathed out in relief.

"That's it?" I said to myself, and slowly allowed the smile to return to my face. "That's it."

Kendra was right. It *was* easy.

"Figures." I reached for the money in my pocket, promising to pay Gabe back, and headed for the store on the other side of the street to buy a hat.

The pavement radiated with heat. I lowered my sunglasses and passed through the crowd to the store side of the street. The smell of fresh pastries, fruits, and vegetables wafted from nearby jammed shops. A few clothing racks decorated the sidewalk in front of a boutique, and a stacked pyramid of sun hats topped the rack.

"Perfect." I stepped closer and grabbed the hat on top, then turned to the wall with a mirror. The hat snuggled over my head. To the left of the mirror, a rack with sunglasses, key chains, and bracelets caught my eye. A fan at the entrance blew my sticky hair, and I twisted it into a bun as my gaze came to rest on a section of charms.

I dangled my hand in front for comparison.

"This is impossible," I whispered. They were the same, except Gabe had set mine in silver.

"Possible."

I looked up to the mirror and recognized Martinez behind me. The thick accent sent chills down my spine, and my instincts kicked in. I turned around and pushed my knee up with all the force I had, straight into his groin. He bent in half. I left the hundred for the cashier, grabbed a cap instead of the sunhat on my way out, and ran. I ran as fast as I'd ever run, dashing through the crowd and weaving between people like my life depended on it; which it possibly did. At some point, I crashed into a fruit stand, but recovered just as quickly.

Where's my car?

My head spun. I turned around in circles until I saw Martinez closing in from behind. I pushed my feet harder in the opposite direction. As I bumped into people, excusing myself, the distance between us shortened. Could I outrun him? What if I didn't?

The streets narrowed, and some became dead-end alleys. One wrong turn and I would be stuck. I veered to the right. Someone grabbed me. A large hand covered my mouth and nose. A cigarette stench burned my nostrils. I tried to wiggle out of the grip but my movements forced a tighter hold.

"You try to run, and I'll slice your throat."

His threat held promise. My pulse raced. I gasped for air between his smelly fingers.

"Where is your friend hiding?" he growled. "I'm going to let go of your mouth, but one sound and we'll send you back home in a package."

He slowly released the grip over my mouth.

"Let me go." I inhaled.

The smell of his sweat made me gag, and I wished I'd kept my mouth shut. He gripped me in a chokehold with one hand while his ten-inch blade glistened in the sun in the other.

"Where. Is. Kendra?" He rasped through his gritted teeth.

Whether or not I told him, he'd kill me. Martinez had no other choice. I was useless. But I wasn't a rat. I shut my eyes, hoping to remember something from my college days and the defense class hosted by campus security. In one move, I elbowed Martinez in the gut and forced my foot up behind me, kicking him in his groin for the second time.

He dropped his knife to the ground. The clash echoed in the alley. Martinez yelped in pain. I didn't look back and hoped I'd bought myself enough time to flee. I weaved onto the busy street, losing myself in the crowd. When I looked back, Martinez was out of the alley, scanning the street. I rushed forward to where I parked Gabe's Miata. When I finally saw the car, I froze.

Two men were waiting by its side. They stood out in the tropical crowd with their jeans and long-sleeved sweatshirts. One of them was holding a cell phone close to his ear, and he didn't appear friendly.

Behind me, although he hadn't seen me yet, Martinez crept closer.

I turned right into an alley, but it was a dead end. Before I could turn back, someone pulled me to the side and covered my mouth and nose. "Shh, don't move," a female voice whispered in my ear. As she let go, relief washed over me. I turned around in slow motion, recognizing the bumblebee glasses and a sunhat large enough to give shade to us both.

She placed her finger to her lips and quickly typed something into her phone. She turned around and grabbed my hand with urgency, then let go as if she'd been burned.

"Follow me."

I hurried behind her as she led me through a door held open by a pop can. She kicked it away, and I followed her inside another building. The door shut behind me. The smell of fresh bread filled a bakery.

"Mary, you haven't seen us here," the woman said to an older woman in an apron, who looked like a baker.

"Of course not, Mrs. Summers."

The name triggered a memory of the woman from the airport. I followed her large sunhat through the back. We had just passed the washrooms when the front door opened. The woman dashed behind a curtain and yanked me into a pantry full of sugar and flour sacks. Pure adrenaline pumped through my veins.

"Shh." She placed her pointer finger against her lips.

"When I find her, I'll slice her open, inch by inch," Martinez swore in Spanish.

"Bury her alive. Like the other one," someone else said. It sounded like they were standing within an arm's length of the curtain. The woman beside me began shaking, so I took her hand into mine and held it.

"Hurry with your leak," Martinez warned.

They both stepped inside the bathroom, and I exhaled.

"Come." The woman pulled the curtain away and led us further to the back of the bakery.

We rushed up two flights of stairs, and she pushed open a metal door. I covered my eyes from the bright sun.

"We're on the rooftop?" I asked.

"Let's go." She rushed forward, and I followed her like a pup follows its mama, right across the melting tar. My sandals sank into the heated layer of black goo. Every few steps, the rooftop stuck longer to the soles. The wind blew, and her sunhat floated away on a strong gust. Her golden hair spilled to the sides. She briefly turned back to glance at my bewildered face as I pointed to the gap between the buildings ahead.

"I… I can't."

The roof on the other side of a narrow gap was lower than the one we were standing on. The woman dashed to the edge and jumped over, waving me down. "Hurry!"

I leapt forward with all my strength and launched myself over the alley. To my relief, I landed safely on the other side, and followed the woman over to another row of houses. She crouched near the end and reached out her arm. "I'll lower you to the first floor. Gabe will catch you from there."

Catch me?

She didn't wait for my reply. Instead, she grabbed my arm and lay down on the hot surface.

"What about you?" I asked, inching my way over to the ledge.

"I'm not the one they want. And I have protection." She motioned to the holster around her thigh. "I'll use it if I have to, but I'm not the one they're after. It will be easier for me to sneak away alone. Now go. Hold on to my arm. Gabe will be below."

"Thank you," I said to her, and lowered myself on her arm. As I hung suspended from the rooftop, waiting for Gabe to magically appear in the alley below, I looked up once more. A stronger gust of wind blew the woman's bumblebee sunglasses off her face. Her hair swirled about her face, and familiar blue eyes stared back at me in bewilderment.

I gasped and let go of her hand. Her beautiful, familiar eyes were the last thing I remembered.

I watched Sam let go of Marge's hand and fall in slow motion. I launched myself across the street, stretched out my arms, and caught her before she hit the pavement.

"Wait there! I'm coming!" Marge screamed.

"We need to split up, Marge. It's safer that way!"

I knew she wouldn't have it. It didn't take her long to make it down the emergency staircase around the corner. She got to me before I settled Sam in the car. Once the threat had subsided, Marge would take the Miata to her house.

"She's mine, Gabe. Isn't she?" she accused. I saw it in her eyes and in her face. "Jesus, do you know how hard it was not to take Charlize in my arms?"

"Her name is Samantha, and I haven't told her yet."

"I didn't need a DNA test to know the truth. I mean, look at her!"

"I know, Marge. I know. But you have to wait until I can tell her. Tonight… There are things I need to explain—"

"Under one condition." She lifted her finger. "This time, you bring my daughter back alive."

I glanced back at Samantha.

"I will. I promise. You better go before she wakes up. Be careful, and check in with me when you get home."

Marge hurried to her car, and I hopped in mine. I left the crooks behind me, took the first street out of town, and followed a private path to a beach. Trees opened to a cove, where I parked the car and Sam woke up.

"Gabe? Where are we?"

"Close to home. We're waiting for our ride."

"What happened? What about the Miata?" she asked.

"I'll have it brought back later."

Her eyes grew wide in an instant. Her hair loosened out of her bun, sticking to her cheek. I watched as she bit her lip. My chest swelled with pain. Every time I looked at her, I saw Joanne.

"Oh, my God. Martinez."

"It's okay, Sam. You're safe."

"I fell."

"You did. And I caught you."

"She dropped me."

"Who?" I asked.

"I… I don't remember." She squinted. "A woman. The one from the airport."

I wasn't ready to explain. I didn't know where to start, and truthfully, I was angry she'd listened to Kendra. Julian had been right to test the girls. As solid as their friendship was, Kendra's tactics would eventually expose our location… and Sam.

"Don't worry about it for now. It will come back to you."

"Are you mad at me?"

"A little."

Horizontal lines stretched along her forehead. "Sorry. Wait, did you say we're waiting here for a ride?"

I nodded.

"I hate boats." She crossed her arms over her chest.

"And I hate rebels who don't know how to listen and stay home."

"Oh." Her hand flew up to her mouth. "You're that mad."

I was beyond mad. Frustrated. Confused. Anxious. I wanted to protect her, but this rebel made the job difficult. Fortunately, I spotted Tristan on the horizon and waved him to the beach. Not that I needed to do so, but it gave me something to do other than explain myself to Sam.

She sank back in her seat while I removed my shoes and walked over to the shore.

Tristan Silver, Julian's younger brother, removed his shades. "All okay?"

"Yes. We lost him in town," I said. "Thanks for coming so quick."

Tristan jumped off the boat into the knee-deep water and waded toward me. Sam got out of the car and shuffled her feet over the beach.

"How is Kendra doing?" Tristan asked.

"Better. Getting everyone around her in trouble, as usual." I glanced back at Sam. "You need to be careful. Martinez is one sneaky son of a bitch. I'm not sure how he tracked us."

But Tristan's gaze remained fixed on Sam. "Your brothers arrived with your parents this morning."

"James is working on the security update and the leak."

"Good."

"We'll visit the cove as soon as we can."

He scanned Sam from the bottom up, then leaned in with a whisper. "She looks just like Jo."

"Take care of Martinez, or I will."

"Stay clear of him, Gabe. As much as you want him dead, lives depend on him being alive."

"Fine – just make sure he leaves and stays away, or I'll take him out the first chance I get."

"You'll hear no argument on that from me. Go take care of

your lady. She looks… promising. Maybe Teresa and Jacob's wish will come true after all."

My parents had prayed for someone new in my life since the day Jo passed.

I handed him the car keys. "Speaking of beautiful women, did you get my memo on Officer Green?"

"You sure she's seen Martinez?"

Tristan reached out a hand to Sam, who came up behind me, and she took it. The scar on his upper lip lifted in a lopsided smile that spelled out *I can make your dreams come true.* It was one of his many cheesy yet natural gifts.

"It's nice to meet you, Samantha. Take care of this guy."

"Nice to meet you too, and I will."

I lifted her into my arms before Tristan kidnapped her and carried her to the boat.

"Take one of the back seats," I told her.

"Do we have to?" She grimaced.

"You could have been at home by the pool."

She moved to the back, where she sat and slouched. Yes, I was still upset. In fact, I was mad, but none of that mattered if I didn't tell her the truth about her identity.

Tristan took the Bentley and left the cove. I turned on the boat's ignition and pressed the throttle forward. The ocean stretched ahead, and a hot wind blew past. The boat vibrated with speed underneath my grip as we cut through waves. Five minutes into our ride and far out in the ocean, I slowed and looked back at Sam, who was shaking in her seat.

I stopped the boat.

"Hey, are you okay?"

She trembled, and I hurried to the back.

"Babe, look at me. Samantha?" I crouched in front of her and made sure her eyes finally connected with mine. "Look at me, Sam. The ocean is calm, and we only have a ten-minute ride left. Do you understand that?"

She nodded.

"Good."

"What's going to happen?"

"We're going home. That's what's going to happen. And all you have to do is stay put in that seat. Okay?"

"I meant about Martinez. He found me."

I cleared the straying tear off her cheek with my thumb.

"True, but Tristan will make sure Martinez disappears. You, however, cannot leave the house without me again. Do you understand?" My brows lifted and waited there until she acknowledged me with a nod.

"Good."

I wrapped my arms around her. "Are you going to be okay if I continue? They can't track us on this boat."

"They can't?" she asked.

"You have nothing to worry about. I promise."

"Not even sharks? I saw *Sharknado*."

I forced the chuckle back inside. The last thing I wanted was to joke about her fears.

"Come. Let me show you the joy of boating." I took her hand and helped her move to the bow. She gripped the wheel.

"Put these on."

I clipped a two-way set of earphones over her head and put a similar pair over mine.

"There. Now you can hear me. Just let me walk you through this, okay?"

"Okay."

I covered her hands with mine, and her shaking eased. I guided her to the ignition. The engine rattled behind us. I stood behind her and moved our hands to the throttle. We pushed it forward, and the engine revved. On our way home, I explained the boat's dashboard and taught Sam the basic safety tips. When we docked in our cove and I removed the earphones, a sniffle dripped down her nose. I passed her a tissue.

"What's the matter?"

"I'm sorry I let you down. You asked me to stay home, and I didn't, and he found us."

"Hey, don't cry. You… you could never let me down. You're everything that's been missing in my life, Samantha." I swept my thumb over her cheek once more, wiping away her tears.

"You're so caring and loving, and you don't get angry." She pulled in a longer sniffle. I reached for the tissue box.

"Oh, I get angry all right. I deal with anger every day – just differently. You have nothing to worry about, Sam. I won't let anyone get close to you."

The same words I'd said to Joanne before I failed her hit me deep in my chest, but Sam's fate was different. It had to be.

She stared at me with her doe eyes, open-mouthed, until I pushed her chin up. "You know what your mouth does to me?" My chest vibrated.

"I do."

She opened it again and then smiled faintly. And then she grasped my face between her palms the same way Joanne used to and pressed her lips to mine in a whisper. "Forgive me?"

I pulled her into my body until her feet lifted above the sand. "The boy you met up with was actually a girl."

"A what? How?"

"My cousin. Emma Silver. She's fifteen, and my cousins used her as bait. For Kendra. Kendra fell for it, but she passed on the dirty task to you."

"Shit."

"You were too innocent to see through Kendra's scheme." I kissed her with more longing, taking the time to taste her full lips. I couldn't wait for tonight, except standing on this beach and seeing her so happy, I wasn't sure taking her on the yacht was a good idea.

"Innocent?" She pulled away.

"Is that what you caught from my explanation?" I laughed.

"No, but I truly am sorry. I should have stayed home." She lifted on her toes and kissed me.

"Have dinner with me. Here. Tonight on this beach. There's something I want to tell you."

She swallowed hard. "Really?"

"Yes, it's important. Please?"

"Of course, Gabe. You don't have to ask me twice." She laughed. The familiar sound carried through the cove like it belonged there. It was late afternoon, and I had food to prepare.

"Meet me here half an hour before sunset."

She bit that lower lip.

My psychologist would have warned me I was compensating. She'd have been right. I needed Sam to know how much I loved her before I told her the truth about her family. She had to know she could count on me and depend on me.

We parted our ways to the house. Within an hour, I'd grilled the fish and vegetables and then set up the beachside table underneath an old tree that grew in the middle of the cove.

When I walked out of the shower, Sam was standing in her jean shorts and see-through bra. My dick got hard.

"What's this?" She twirled the boat wheel charm I'd never given Joanne.

"It was my wife's," I told her. "I'm sorry."

"Don't be sorry. It's a shame it's in a drawer. It's beautiful."

"Are you ready?" I dried my hair, swaying Sam's attention away from the charm. Her heated stare focused on my erection until I caught her in the act.

"Like what you see?"

"Aha," she replied, then sized me from the bottom up. Her eyes widened when she stopped at my cock. I grabbed the boxer-briefs and pulled them up, securing myself inside the underwear. She swallowed hard, and I realized I couldn't fit into the underwear.

"Is that what you're wearing to dinner?" I asked as I reached for my shirt.

I slipped my arms through and started buttoning up when my rebel smirked.

"Is this too innocent for you?"

She snapped open the button fly on her shorts and shimmied out of them. She stood in front of me in her white set of barely there panties and a see-through bra that showed her pink nipples.

My dick pulsed at the inviting scene.

"I actually found something comfortable for the beach in Kendra's closet."

As I stood there, dumbfounded, she reached to the door and removed a turquoise silk dress. She dragged the gown up her body, hiding the sun-kissed skin from my view. As soon as she finished, she removed the silky bra from underneath and then the panties, which she scrunched in her hand and set on the bathroom counter near my sink. Her only remaining wardrobe was the bracelet and thin silk.

Fuck me.

"Jesus, Sam. You look amazing. Innocent and… perfect."

I was sure I salivated. She stepped closer and curved her palm around my dick. Painfully slowly, she slid her hand down my shaft, cupped my balls, weighed their size, then slid back up. Her tiny fingers remained around my shaft. "Perhaps innocent is not the right word," I moaned, and finally gave up on the shirt button I fumbled with. I lowered my hand to her wrist, removed it from my dick, and brought it to my lips for a kiss. "Hold that thought for later tonight, darling. Please?"

She sashayed her ass out of the bathroom. Self-control would be impossible tonight. "Would you walk down with me for dinner?" I called out.

She stopped and turned around with a smile. "I would love to."

Moments later, I guided her down the path to the beach where earlier I'd lit the thousands of white lights. They twinkled along the swaying branches. The sun glowed upward, turning the sky pink and orange. The beach curved on each side, forming a perfect exotic bay where the turquoise water, lightly ruffled by the breeze, broke against the shore.

"Gabe, this is beautiful." She pointed to the tree in the middle of the cove where each branch was covered with light. Underneath, a table set for two. Lazy waves lapped along the shore, adding to the atmosphere.

"I love the playlist. Wow!" Sam squeezed my hand tighter. Yes, the scene was picturesque. She had no clue how much she belonged here. She had no clue how much she belonged in my world. The question was, would she want to stay with me after I told her the truth?

When we reached the shore, we removed our shoes and stepped barefoot onto the beach. Grains of sand, still warm from the afternoon sun, heated our feet.

"This is nice." She rubbed the goosebumps over her arms when I came behind her.

"You see that flashing light out in the ocean?" I pointed forward.

"Yeah?"

"That's where we were going tonight."

"Out there?"

"Yes, but after what happened on the boat today, I didn't want to traumatize you again."

The flashing light disappeared and then reappeared in a sequence. I clicked a button on my phone and the yacht lit up with lights all over its sides, shining like a single star out in a dark sea.

Sam's jaw dropped open. "That's incredible."

I tapped her chin up. The wind blew through her hair and I tucked it behind her ear.

"And I appreciate us staying ashore."

"Of course. I should have realized sooner. I hope you're hungry for fish, vegetables, and chocolate brownies. It was the best I could do."

"You baked brownies?"

"They're not the kind a rebel like yourself would prefer, but they're definitely good."

She snickered, and my nerves eased.

"The sand is still warm under my feet." She wiggled her toes.

Unfortunately, my nerves didn't ease enough. My heart pounded in my chest and sweat trickled down my back. "Samantha, I know I've been leaving a lot, and you have many questions. And I need to be honest about some things… in my life… and you—"

"Don't blame yourself for my reckless actions. I have no questions. You owe me no explanations."

"But I do." My heart was pounding in my chest. "I want to give you all the answers, but I don't know where to start."

She patted her stomach and pointed to the table. "Well, if you don't mind, we can start with dinner, because I'm starving."

She curled into my embrace. Her body molded to mine through the thin silk. I dug my fingers into her sides. A warm wind blew, messing Sam's hair. The thousands of lights on the tree above us glistened, and there was no other place in the world I wanted to be. I lowered my mouth to hers and kissed it.

Her insistent hands slid to my dick.

"Is that a gun in your pocket, or are you just happy to see me?" She laughed against my mouth.

"I'm just happy to see you." I slid my hands over her hips. "You should have left your panties on, Samantha. I don't know how I'm going to finish dinner without finishing you first."

"Then I guess we should get started." She pulled out a chair, and I took over, helping her to her seat. I filled our wineglasses, lit the candle, and we dug in. Once Sam took hold of the fork, she couldn't get the food fast enough in her mouth.

"What's the hurry?" I asked.

"I thought that after we eat, we could... I don't know... enjoy the beach?"

"Define enjoy." My mouth lifted in one corner.

"You know what I mean." She rolled her eyes. "I guess I should have said, enjoy each other."

"Now you're onto something."

She sipped on her wine. The tree lights glowed, illuminating the familiar face in front of me.

"What's wrong?" Sam asked.

"Nothing."

"Liar. Did I say something?"

"No, it's not you, Sam. It's the memories that haunt me from my old life."

"Tell me about them."

Could I? Was this my chance?

"You lived here before, right? You had a life here."

"This house and the cove gave me and Joanne two beautiful years together. I've renovated since. Then expanded."

"You must have loved her very much."

"Of course. She was..." I looked up at Sam. "Smart, beautiful, and feisty. Everything I love about you."

Sam's breath hitched.

"I'm not sure if I'm doing it right, but Sam, I'm falling in love with you. Actually, I *am* in love with you. I love you, Samantha Connor."

She reached across the table for my hand. Her warm palm smoothed the top of mine as she whispered back in a teasing tone, "What about the no strings attached, Gabe? I mean, this is our first actual date. I thought you wanted a fling?"

"I know you know this was never a fling."

I lowered my mouth to hers. Her plump lips responded against mine. I loved everything about her.

"If you'll have me, I want all the strings, ropes, chains, and handcuffs if that's what will keep you at my side."

Her brows rose playfully. "Handcuffs?"

"Just keeping it real."

She bit her lip. "I've fallen for you too, Gabriel Silver. And I love you." She took a deep breath, then released it. "I love you hard."

"When I thought you were gone, then when I saw Martinez grab you in that alley... I thought it was over. It can't be over. You're my new beginning." I kissed her again.

As if she couldn't have made my night any better, she said against my mouth, "What do you say we check out that yacht of yours?"

Chapter 14

Sam

Trust was earned, and Gabe had all mine.

Watching Gabe from behind as he maneuvered the boat reminded me of a scene from a James Bond movie. His 007 back was lit by the faint light emanating from the dashboard. That man had a way of making me feel as if I were living in a reality where I could forget about Martinez. I wasn't sure what had come over me on the beach to suggest we go to the yacht, but I couldn't deny my curiosity grew the longer he talked about the vessel.

Gabe turned off the engine and secured the boat to the enormous yacht. Someone had hung lights on every corner of the ship and along its sleek edges and curves, like a white Christmas tree. He clicked a button on his phone and soft music played.

"How are you doing?" he asked.

"It's not as wobbly as your speedboat."

"The yacht is larger, so you should feel less sway. Bigger things are always better." He winked, and I heated.

"Bigger sharks aren't better than smaller ones," I said.

"I'm sorry. I keep forgetting about your fear. For what it's worth, I'm grateful you agreed to come here." Gabe came up behind me. He snaked his hands around my waist, and his heat warmed my back. A chill of excitement ran through my body, concentrating between my legs.

"I'm glad I came. It's not as bad as I imagined. I mean, this boat wouldn't flip, would it?" I reached forward, grasped the waist-high wall, and checked for sturdiness. It held.

Gabe chuckled, and I stepped away from the black ocean.

"You don't seem convinced."

"Let's just take it one step at a time. You said you wanted to talk to me about something?"

"Right. I did."

Was he nervous? I turned around. Jesus, I hoped he wasn't about to do something stupid like get down on one knee to propose. We might have fallen for one another hard and fast, but this was too quick.

"I have a history on the island." He bit his lower lip. Gabe never showed an ounce of nerves, and I wondered how deeply this history was rooted in his heart. Was there any space left in there for me?

"I know. You were married. Your wife has family here. I understand."

"Yes, that's true. But that's not all."

"Gabe, come on. Let's relax a little, okay?" The worry in his eyes kept my anxiety at its peak. He wasn't acting like himself, and whatever was troubling him had to stop. "Why don't we play some music? Rona? Hello?"

He laughed, which made my theatrics of spinning in the middle of the deck in search of an invisible AI named Rona, whom we'd left back home, totally worth it.

"One sec." He removed his phone from his pocket, clicked a few buttons, and the sound of soft eighties ballads echoed through the speaker. It was perfect.

"Come here, Samantha." He took my hand and spun me in a

circle. "I'm sorry for being a douche. I didn't mean to ruin the evening."

He held me close to his chest. I looked up into his eyes again and smoothed my free palm over his cheek. "This is the most romantic thing I'd ever done. I think this is the most romantic thing I'll ever do. It's just the two of us, in the middle of the ocean, underneath a sky full of stars. Tonight couldn't be more perfect."

His shoulders finally relaxed, and he dipped me back. His lips came to rest on my extended neck, and my body yielded to him. I had never felt safer than in Gabe's arms. The wind settled into a light breeze. The music and the gentle waves lulled our bodies in a slow tempo, lifting the ambiance. Gabe traced the line along the peaks and valleys of my spine as he lowered his mouth to my ear for a whisper. "You're so much more than what I could have ever imagined, Samantha."

He skimmed his finger up my arm, from my wrist, curving around the elbow and up my shoulder. The touch sent an army of shivers through my body.

"That only speaks to the excellent company I keep," I told him.

"You smell delicious," he teased, and I wasn't one to give up a good tease. "Like the perfect invitation."

"Then consider yourself invited."

He spun me three times in a row, and I couldn't help but laugh. His lips hovered inches away from mine, teasing, then traced the rim of my mouth. My pulse raced.

"Have you ever done it on a boat?" I asked. I wasn't sure where the question came from, but I had a feeling his mouth could do magic out here. Actually, his mouth created magic every time he went down on me.

"Boat, yes. This yacht, no."

"Really? I'd be the first here?"

"I can't speak for my cousin, but that's a yes for me."

"That's… surprising. I mean, I just thought… you know… I'm sorry. That was stupid. I shouldn't have said anything."

His face sobered. He let go of me, turned away, and walked towards the yacht's side. Gabe braced his hand on the wall and looked out over the dark ocean.

I tiptoed towards him and wrapped my arms around his large body from the back. I pressed my face against him, whispering, "What did I say?"

He turned around and switched our position so that he was holding me. "I'm sorry about this. It's not you. It's me."

"That's a cliché."

"In this case, it's true. I wanted this evening to be… different and unique."

He was kidding, wasn't he? Here we were, on one of the most romantic dates ever, and I couldn't keep his attention.

"It has been. Now tell me what's on your mind. Better yet, what can I do to get your mind off whatever the fuck is bothering you?" I unwrapped his hands from around me and stepped back. I continued backward until I reached the center of the bow, where the light shone the brightest, and scrunched my silky dress up my thighs.

"Sam?"

Once I had enough fabric in my hands, I pulled the dress over my head and threw it to the side. Thank goodness the night was hot as I stood naked in the middle of a yacht, wearing nothing but the bracelet he'd gifted me.

"Is it working?" I stepped forward.

I moved my finger in a come-hither motion. Gabe strolled over with a predatory look in his eyes. My nipples responded to the next breeze. Or maybe it was the hunger in his kiss.

"You look sinful, Samantha."

"Then sin away," I encouraged.

Gabe approached and I dropped to my knees, reaching for his belt. I looked up, licking my lips with a lustful promise.

Gabe stared at me from above with his mouth partially opened as I unbuckled him and lowered his zipper. His pants dropped to his ankles and his dick pushed out on the shirt.

I licked my lips again, tugged at Gabe's shirt, and pulled it over his head. A couple of top buttons flew off, bouncing on the deck, their echo quickly silenced by the ocean's infinite hum.

"Ooops…" I giggled.

"Rebel." The low rumble from his chest immediately brought my attention back to his face and his bright eyes. My mouth dropped open. His perfect chest rose and fell, and I moved in to kiss it. I ran my lips along Gabe's pecs. His hands took hold of my hips, thumbs circling around my hip bones.

I tossed his shirt overboard.

"Now, now. What will I wear back home?"

"Me." I lifted to my toes and grazed Gabe's earlobe with my teeth. The short stubble on his cheek scraped the side of my face. Excitement swirled in my belly. I'd wanted him this vulnerable for a long time. Now that he was mine in all ways, I wanted all of him. He kissed my nose and cheeks before settling on my lips. I curved my palm around his cock. My mouth watered at the flex in my palm as his warm flesh extended in my hand.

Gabe worked his mouth over mine, his tongue playing and teasing. I gripped him harder, stretching his skin up and down. His cock warmed and hardened with each stroke. My breathing deepened until I pulled away, locking my gaze with his.

His eyebrows furrowed then released. "What are you up to?"

"Down, actually." I sat back on the cushioned seat at the bow and looked up. "Enjoy, Mr. Silver."

I wrapped my hand around him, and I stroked him tantalizingly slowly. The thick vein running along his dick from the base to the tip pulsed. The ocean moved the boat up and down, and I mimicked the waves' rhythm. I licked my lips and placed my mouth over his cap.

"Fuck," he growled.

I drew my tongue underneath the ridge, and he gritted his teeth. I followed the encouraging tone and lowered my lips to around his crown, then circled my tongue over the sensitive, heated flesh. I worked over his skin, up and down, licking the drop of pre-cum off his tip. He slid deep down into my mouth. I pursed my lips around him, holding him tight. Gabe flexed his buttocks, releasing a soft moan, and I took him deeper down my throat.

"Jesus Christ!" he continued, and I repeated the motion. I soon found a rhythm that kept him completely pre-occupied and me enjoying cock like I never had. The momentum of the rocking boat measured my merciless sucks. I tensed my lips around him, tightening my mouth around the shaft on the way up and loosening on the way down.

"Oh God." Gabe's strained whisper echoed across the ocean.

His hands found the top of my head, scraping my scalp with his fingers, holding onto my hair to keep his stance steady. I cupped his balls with my palm, gently pressing them up and forward. Gabe's thrusts sped, his skin contracted, and saliva leaked down my chin. His knees softened, then locked, and he pulled out of my mouth.

"Get up. Now." He lifted me by the elbow. Before I knew it, I was in his arms. My legs wrapped around his waist as he guided himself inside me. Gabe supported my weight underneath my ass, thrusting deeper and harder. He hit a spot which zapped exquisite pleasure through my pussy. My hardened nipples rubbed against his chest while his fingers dug into my ass. He took a nipple into his mouth, pulled on it, and I lost it. My legs stiffened around him and my body spasmed with orgasmic bursts. Gabe pushed inside of me three more times and climaxed as well.

After a few moments, he slowly lowered us to the cushions at the bow. My heated skin appreciated the cool fabric. Gabe lay beside me. I wasn't sure how long we watched the falling stars, but it must have been quite a while.

We turned our heads to the center, and he smiled at me. "Hi."

"Hi," I replied. "As much as I hate to admit it, the yacht was a great idea." I turned on my side and lifted myself up on my elbow.

Gabe did the same. "You haven't seen the best part yet."

"No?"

"Not that it matters. Before I knew how much you feared the ocean, I set up a diving cage." He pointed to his left.

"You wanted us to dive with the sharks?" I asked.

"No, not sharks. There's a surprise underwater."

"A surprise?"

A smile played at the corner of his lips and I pictured a pirate ship wreck below.

"So there's a cage down there that keeps the sharks out?" I pointed starboard.

"Yes."

I tilted my head back up to the night sky. Never in a million years would I have imagined that I'd be on a yacht in the middle of an ocean, considering the unimaginable. I sat up and cranked my head to the side, saying, "You never know the cards you're dealt, but I'm ready to play mine."

I stood up, walked to the ship's side, and without thinking, I lifted my legs over the railing and jumped into the ocean.

I regretted the move as soon as I swam to the surface and saw darkness around me.

"I knew you were a rebel the moment I met you!" Gabe

yelled from above. "Except you jumped out on the wrong side, Sam!"

"What?" I swooshed my arms and propelled my legs in a circle. "Gabe! Help me out! Now!"

As I looked up, he plummeted from above. He hit the water's surface with a splash. I turned away and back. White ripples stretched from the spot where he dove. His head finally popped out of the water, his eyes reflecting the moonlight.

"I'm kidding. You're on the right side."

"You mean the left?

"Yes."

I splashed water at his face but couldn't do it more than once because he quickly swam my way and took me into his arms. "Don't worry, Sam. The only kinds of sharks you're swimming with tonight are the safe kind."

"What?"

"Don't panic, but the flood lights will turn on in about thirty seconds. They're attached to the seafloor. There's a high chance we'll see sting rays and some fish."

"Sting rays? Fish? How large?" I fumbled. Maybe this hadn't been such a good idea after all?

"They come here to feed at night, but we're definitely not on their menu. We'd be fine without the cage, but you know, this is safe. I promise."

"Thank you."

He pressed his lips to mine. I snaked my hands around his neck as the gentle waves carried us over the moonlit waters. When our lips touched again, bright lights switched on, illuminating us from below. I pulled away from his mouth and gasped. "Oh, my God!"

Underneath the cage, three enormous sting rays floated through the water like they were flying.

"They're beautiful."

"I can get goggles and a snorkel so we can see better."

"No. Stay here. Please." I raked my fingers through Gabe' hair and kissed him. I expected to get lost in another magical moment, but our kiss broke at the sound of an approaching boat.

"Come on. Let's get aboard." Gabe grabbed my hand and took the lead, lightly pulling me through the water towards side of the yacht. He helped me up the ladder and turned off the ocean lights that had served as a beacon. While I grabbed a couple of towels, he found a pair of binoculars and focused on the approaching boat. I wrapped one towel around myself and the other around Gabe's waist.

"Thanks," he said.

"You're welcome."

Gabe remained focused on the black ocean. "It's okay. It's my younger brother." He lowered the binoculars. "Hunter's staying at our family house on the other side of the coast. My parents should be there soon. He's earning a promotion into the business."

"You have parents?"

"Of course I have parents. Everyone does."

"Not everyone."

"I'm sorry. I didn't think."

"It's okay. It's a slip of the tongue."

"Not the slip of tongue I usually like to make, but it truly was. My apologies." He leaned over and gently kissed my lips. I loved this man beyond anything I had ever thought possible, but I couldn't deny the fact that I'd fallen this hard for someone I just met scared me.

"I should go change before he comes up," I said, as his brother pulled up to the boat.

Gabe shook his head and let out a growl. "Keep the towel on. The dress is much more revealing."

We walked to the stern, where Hunter tied his boat to ours.

I leaned over to Gabe and whispered, "Is he twelve?"

"Young looks run in the family. Turning twenty-two this year."

Hunter stepped on the yacht. Yet he didn't secure his boat. He held the rope in his arm and called out, "No time for chitchat. Your alarm was breached. You can take the boat back. It's less visible. I'll take the yacht."

The next few moments felt like living through a hurricane. Gabe grabbed my hand. We switched rides with Hunter and sped towards the shore. As I stood beside Gabe and held on, darkness stretched ahead. The wind whipped my wet hair around, cutting across my face.

"How do you know where you're going?" I screamed over the engine and wind roar.

"GPS and sonar. These are the coordinates I'm aiming for." He pointed to the dashboard. "This is the coast outline and our position. Similar to what you saw in the daytime. Seafloor level and 3D of the seafloor level to avoid coral."

That was a lot, but it also made sense on screen.

"What do you think we'll find at home?"

"Hopefully nothing."

"Wouldn't it be safer to take the yacht with your brother?"

"It's safer when you're with me," he replied as he docked by the dark shore. I would have never recognized the place without lights. Gabe hurried to help me off the boat. The house lights were all turned off. We waited on the beach as Gabe checked something on his phone. He scrolled through a long list of items and images, clicking on some, then going back until his shoulders relaxed.

"We're good. It's all good. No trespassers."

"What was it, then?"

"I still have to check the security footage."

Feeling a little safer, I nodded. We walked up the dark path to the house. Gabe pushed on the glass door and stepped through first.

"Come on." Gabe guided me to the kitchen counter. "I'll make you some tea."

As many times as he assured me, the assurances made me more anxious every time.

"Do you mind sitting in the dark?" he asked. "Maybe some candles?"

"Sounds wonderful." Shivers scattered over my skin.

"It's just a precaution, Sam. I'll dig through the security footage until I find out who's behind this."

He locked the door behind him and pressed a button on his phone. A double beep echoed through the room, and I jumped up.

"What's that?"

"The alarm system runs on backup power." He pulled me toward the kitchen counter and opened a drawer. "We'll use emergency lights to move around while security works on the power."

"The power's been cut?"

His lack of reply gave me the answer. Hand in hand, we made our way to the bedroom. I showered the salty layer of ocean off my skin. Gabe went straight to work. I put on my night shorts and pajama while he clicked on his laptop. After a while, he turned the bright screen down but continued clicking. He sat at the desk for what seemed like hours. The repetitive tapping on his keyboard made me sleepy. I forced my eyes open, hoping the next few clicks would be the last and I would feel Gabe's body snuggled against mine, but I finally fell asleep. I stirred briefly around four in the morning and noticed that the lamp on his desk had turned on and the light from the pool downstairs emanated up toward our floor.

Sometime in the very early hours of the morning, his cool body met mine in bed. He cocooned around me, held me tight, and fell asleep, and the only thing I could do was lie there, thinking how to ease his worries.

"Where is she?" I jolted up in bed. Sunlight was streaming through the window, hitting my eyes. I glanced at the empty pillow beside me and grunted.

"Sam?" I called out louder.

"In the kitchen!" she replied, and I released my anxious breath.

The smell of coffee and fresh pastries hit my nose, and I finally relaxed. The night had passed too quickly as I searched through the cameras. I found nothing, and Marge would be calling soon to ask about Sam. I planned to tell her about the DNA results she didn't know I'd received, but my plan didn't pan out and we ended up in bed. Again. How the fuck was I supposed to tell her when the timing wasn't right?

"I'll be down in a few," I called out to her.

I took a quick shower, pulled on a pair of comfortable sweats, and headed to the kitchen. Today would be the day I broke the news to Sam.

My bare feet met the cool floor, leaving footprints on the marble behind me. As I turned the corner and saw Samantha lying flat on the kitchen island, I froze.

She turned her head my way. "You made dinner last night. I thought I would make breakfast this morning."

Well, I'll be damned.

A sprinkle of flour decorated the floor around the counter. The dinette held a platter of muffins, pancakes, and croissants almost toppling over.

"I figured we can clean up after we make more mess," she explained.

"Rebel." I scanned her naked and prepped body, stepped closer, and admired the strategically placed cream and fruit over her nipples and pussy. My dick hardened.

Fucking delicious.

"I'm going to make a huge mess," I growled, and she trembled. "How long did it take you to make this appetizing breakfast?"

"A while." She giggled. "I highly recommend the peaches and cream."

She pointed to her lower area, and my gaze found the fruit slices in the shape of a flower around a single strawberry covering her pussy. I stepped closer to the counter and lowered my mouth to one breast, sucking the raspberry and whipped cream along with a pink nipple into my mouth.

She whimpered.

"You brought this on, Samantha." I licked my lips. "What else have you got?"

"I wanted to ease your worries." She writhed underneath my skimming fingers, and my dick twitched.

"Well done. It worked. I'm not worried about anything." That was a lie, but there was no fucking way I could concentrate before I properly feasted on the most imaginative breakfast of my life. I paced around the counter to the other side. My dick pulsed as I went for the other breast. I removed the cherry with my mouth and passed it between her lips. She crunched the sweet fruit and I returned to her breast, sweeping all the cream with one long lick. I swallowed, then pulled on her pebbled flesh with my teeth.

She moaned again.

"That's two already. You're too fast," she complained, twisting on the marble surface.

"Two for two. And if you like it slow, I promise to take it slow from now on." I walked to the end of the counter's shorter edge, dragging my finger along her skin from the undercurve of her breast, down her belly, over her thighs and knees toward her feet, where each toe held a blueberry in between the grooves. Dressed in fruit and cream, Sam looked like a goddess. I tapped at her ankles and spread her legs. The blueberry spilled. She gasped.

I turned to the side, took her foot in my hand, and pressed on her sole. She squirmed as I gave her a preview of what I'd do to her body.

"You're not playing fair," she accused, giggling. Her breasts, topped with pink nipples, bopped up and down.

"Who said anything about playing fair, Samantha? Are you being fair, covering up the most delicious parts of your body?"

She giggled again.

"I hope you greased that counter." I gently pulled on her legs to bring her closer. A cherry rolled off her navel.

I set her feet at the edge and focused on the flower between her legs. While the fruit salad there looked delicious, her glistening pussy looked even better. I kissed my way along her inner thigh, inhaling her fresh scent. I shifted my dick in discomfort and focused on the cream dripping down her lips. I licked up the crevice, just beside the fold, and she squirmed. I licked up the other side as well, then licked towards her clit.

The longer I licked, the more she swelled. Sweet cream leaked from above, and when Sam was about to come, I paused and cleared the sweetness above.

"More," she breathed. "I'm almost there."

"I know." I soaked a cloth and cleaned everything below her navel and around her pussy. This time when I tasted her, I wanted only her in my mouth. I climbed up on the counter and slid up her body to kiss her mouth. "I love you, Samantha."

"I love you too, Gabriel."

I slid back down and pushed up on her thighs, lifting her ass off the counter. She glistened with deliciousness.

I lowered her legs. She lay spread open in front of me, waiting. I slid a finger inside her and watched her smile. I closed my mouth over her pussy. Her ass clenched. I added another finger, pumping her. She tightened around me, and I flicked her protruding clit. She swelled in my mouth. Her whimpers fueled my tongue and I flicked faster, sucked with precision, and finger-fucked her, hooking that g-spot on my way out.

"Gabe!" she screamed out. I held my mouth over her spot and licked as she came. Her body thrashed and convulsed until she couldn't come any longer. I rose to my knees and slid my throbbing dick inside her drenched and swollen pussy. Her eyes flew open. "Oh, my God!"

"Nope, still Gabe." I replied, and she laughed. Her second wind kicked in.

"Harder, Gabe. Please."

Her voice sang to my cock, and I braced my arms on the corner. I thrust forward as hard as the slippery kitchen counter allowed me. Thirty seconds later, I spilled inside her warm pussy and held still.

"Fucking best breakfast of my life."

I lowered myself to her body and kissed her.

"Shower?"

She smiled, and we hopped off the counter. I took her hand and led her to the poolside shower. Outside, the sun reflected in the pool's surface. Waves beamed over the shrubs around the area.

"How are you feeling?" Sam asked, as I turned on the

shower. She stepped underneath the first stream. "You were up most of the night."

I turned on my shower beside hers.

"Better. Much better. There are some things I have to clear up today, but I'm confident a herd of wild boars caused the security breach."

"Oh, that's good, then, isn't it?"

"That's excellent. Also, Tristan confirmed that Martinez is on his way out of New Zealand."

"Oh, my God, Gabe. That's fantastic!" She crossed over the foot-high hedge between the showers, threw her arms around my neck, and pressed her naked body to mine. As I held her, I remembered I owed her an explanation. After last night and this morning, I could no longer hold the secrets of her parentage to myself. But as of last night, I also realized I couldn't do this by myself.

I kissed her and helped her wash up. Once we dried off and dressed, I sat beside her by the pool where she dipped her feet. "There's something I need to tell you, but before I do, I need to do something."

"Okay?"

"I don't want to wait until the middle of the night to do what I have to do. I want to go now, so I can come back as soon as possible, and we can... talk. About everything. I wouldn't be long."

Her face drained of blood. "You're not proposing, are you?"

"No, no. I'm not."

"Good." She breathed out.

"But I would like to move forward from a one-night stand to an official relationship status. You know, no more the 'one-night stand' kind."

She smiled, then her brows scrunched. "All right. So you want to go now?"

"I'll secure the house. No boar could pass through without

me knowing. And honestly, I'll only be a five-minute drive away."

Her quiet laugh shook with nerves. "It's okay. Go. I'll be fine."

"I won't be long. Twenty minutes, tops." I kissed her plump lips and headed for the garage. On my way there, I veered through the laundry to close the side door, then upstairs to lock the balcony window. The instinct was stupid, since the property was secure enough for us to sleep with open doors and windows.

I took the Bentley past the gates, locked them, and double-checked the security on my phone before leaving. I drove to Marge's, tapping the steering wheel, wondering whether I should have prepared something for when Marge came to meet Sam. I'd thought about breaking the news about Samantha's family all night and stupidly came up with the idea to just bring Marge to the house so we could do it together.

I pulled up the Summers' driveway. Parsley ran up, greeting me with his face licks. He ran around the car, barking and wagging his tail like he couldn't get enough of me.

"Come on, Parsley. Let's make some tea."

"Marge, we have no time for tea. You need to come with me."

"Something happened to Charlize?"

"No. I mean, yes," I sighed. I wanted this over with. I was sure the moment Sam saw Marge, they'd instantly connect. They said seeing was believing, and breaking the news to Sam with Marge at her side, made sense. "Samantha is fine. You know what – let's have that quick tea."

We went to the garden, where Marge had already set up the tea with a fruit platter.

"You knew I was coming?"

"No." She poured the tea, sat down, and gave me that stern

look mothers-in-law are famous for. "But I like tea. Now, when are you going to let me see my daughter?"

"Today. We're going to tell Sam today, and I don't know how to tell her on my own."

Her eyes popped open like bottle caps as she held the teacup in mid-air.

"Wait, you want to take me to see her? Now? Let's go!" The tea cup shook in her hands as she set it down.

"It's why I came to get you. She'll hate me. She'll think I'm with her because of Joanne. I wanted to tell her sooner, but I wanted to be sure, and the timing was off—"

"Jesus, Gabriel. You're shaking."

I wasn't sure why my nerves were showing. Working under pressure was my thing, after all. But this was different.

Marge smoothed her hand over mine. "She won't hate you. She'll understand. I'm sure of it. "

"I was trying to tell her," I explained, remembering. "But things got in the way."

"Have you killed Martinez yet?" she asked.

"Marge—"

"I'm a woman of faith, and I mean no harm to anyone, but that bastard does not deserve to breathe."

"We'll get him if it's the last thing I do."

"That's bullshit. He's protected by your cousins."

"It's much more complicated. He's the key to an under-ground sex-trafficking ring that must be destroyed."

"At the cost of him ruining lives? Is that what Silver Securi-ties represents now?"

Parsley barked from inside the house, and our heads turned. Marge narrowed her brows. I quickly finished my tea, lightly burning the roof of my mouth, and asked, "Ready to go?"

"I've been waiting for this moment my entire life."

I helped her carry the dishes back inside the house when Parsley barked again from upstairs.

"Parsley?" Marge called out, but the pup didn't reply.

My heart skipped a few beats at the concern on her face.

"I'll go check on him." When something clattered upstairs, though, we both rushed up. As soon as I stepped onto the second floor, Parsley ran to me, wagging his tail and spinning in circles.

"What is it, boy?" I followed him down the hallway, wondering about the item he must have knocked over with his tail.

"Something's off," Marge whispered from behind me.

We followed Parsley as he took us to Charlize's room. I halted mid-step when I saw a familiar back. A broken picture frame lay scattered at Sam's feet in the fairy-lit room. She turned around in slow motion, holding a photograph of Joanne as a child, sitting on the living room couch and holding a baby. Tears streaked down her face as she looked up at me and asked, "Why does this girl look like me?"

Chapter 16

Sam

Maybe Gabe was right to call me a rebel. Something snapped in my head at his mention of leaving me on my own.

Twenty minutes.

My pulse raced, my vision blurred, and sounds faded in and out. Twenty minutes was enough time to kidnap someone.

I'm not a wuss. I'm ready to play my cards. And I'm ready to see his.

I grabbed my shorts from the chair, slipped on a shirt over my bathing suit, and followed Gabe. He grabbed the keys to the Bentley and hurried upstairs. I snuck inside the garage, opened the Bentley, popped open the trunk, climbed in, and gently shut the lid over me. Moments later, Gabe returned to the garage.

The engine's vibrations rattled through my body. Gabe pulled out of the garage, and I breathed out in relief. Wherever he was going, I knew I'd be safer with him nearby. When we returned home, I'd sneak back out, and he'd never know the difference. I braced my arms and feet against the trunk walls to hold steady. Gabe was a fast driver: much faster than when he'd driven with me. Five minutes later, he parked the car, turned off the engine, and left in a hurry. I lay on my back, waiting for him to return, until I heard a dog's bark outside.

Is the dog in trouble?

The pup wouldn't stop. He circled the vehicle, yelping, and so I pushed on the back seat and climbed out of the trunk through the car. Outside the window, a golden retriever stood on its hind legs, his front paws and nose against the glass. His tail wagged back and forth. I opened the door and stepped outside.

"Hi, boy." I crouched and reached out my hand. Instead of sniffing me, the dog lifted on his hinds and secured his paws over my chest. I braced myself against the car and he licked my face.

I laughed. The dog spun in circles and weaved around my legs. After a good five-minute scratch under his chin and over his belly, he finally calmed. I checked his tag and stood up. "So, who do you belong to, Parsley?"

He spun in another circle when I said his name. I admired the beautiful brick house at the end of the driveway. The sound of the ocean drew my attention to the shore, where remains of a burned boat rested on the beach. I realized we were at the same cove where Kendra had blown up Gabe's boat.

My attention went back to the dog, who grabbed at the hem of my shorts and pulled me towards the house.

"What are you doing?" I asked.

Parsley persevered. I followed him to the side door, which had been left open, but hesitated. This was someone's house, and I had no right to come inside. But then I heard Gabe's voice in the backyard.

"I can't wait for you to meet her. She's incredible."

Was he talking about me?

Parsley returned and nipped at my shorts, pulling me inside. He wouldn't let go, leading me towards a staircase. I followed the happy pup up the stairs and to a room. He pushed it open with his nose. The predominantly lavender bedroom was likely a girl's and in pristine condition. Fairy lights hung in the window, and I smiled. I clicked a button on the cable, lighting up the room. More fairy lights hung over the closet, and I turned those on, too. The room twinkled with cozy lights and brought back a memory of my lavender room back in New Jersey. Parsley rubbed against my leg and let out a bark. I jumped up and snuck a peek at the door, realizing I shouldn't be here.

"Shh, you'll give me away. Come on."

I turned to leave when a picture frame on a dresser caught my gaze. I picked it up for a closer look and my breath hitched. I rubbed my eyes and examined the photograph of two girls again. The older one was sitting on a couch and holding a baby in her arms.

"Whose room is this?" I said to myself.

A tear rolled down my cheek. I didn't know where it came from. I stared at the photo and couldn't keep my eyes off the older girl, who looked just like me when I was a child. I quickly removed the photograph from its frame and turned it over.

Joanne and Charlize, 1997

When I flipped the photograph over again, I brought it closer to my eyes and dropped the frame. It hit the corner of a desk, shattering. I picked up the picture. My hands shook, but I could not take my gaze away from the bracelet around the baby's wrist. I lifted my left hand and compared it to my bracelet. The charm set in silver was identical to the baby's.

"Oh, my God," I whispered.

Tears streaked down my face as the connection clicked. Parsley wagged his tail, brushed by my leg, and left my side to head to the door, which prompted me to turn around. Gabe was standing there in the doorway, with a woman who stepped out from behind him. It was the same woman who had helped me flee Martinez in town.

I lifted the photograph in my hand.

"Why does this girl look like me?" I asked.

"Sam—"

"The truth. Please, just tell me the truth."

He took in a deep breath. "The girl sitting on the couch is my wife as a child. The baby she's holding is you. She looks like you because she was your sister."

The weight of his words crushed my chest inward, forcing all air out of my lungs. I shook my head. "Your Joanne?" I asked. "This is impossible."

"They stole you from us." The woman stepped out from behind Gabe.

"You? You… you're… you helped me in town."

She nodded.

"And you?" I said to Gabe. "You knew?"

The room spun. My head throbbed, and my heart pounded even harder. I found it difficult to breathe.

This whole time, he knew.

"We've been searching for you since the day they took you from the stroller."

"I wasn't taken. I was adopted."

"The kidnappers sold you as a black market baby." Gabe reached out.

I jumped up. "Don't touch me."

A lump formed in my throat. "I… I thought I knew who you were. If you were who I thought, you would have told me. I trusted you. I was so wrong."

My vision blurred, my head pounded, and every muscle in my body ached. I pulled my hand across my eyes and glanced back at the photograph.

"And…" Gabe hesitated. When he didn't continue, the woman stepped forward. "We searched for years until we received information that… that they'd sold you for organ donation."

What? My insides twisted, and nausea filled my mouth.

"Are you my mother?" While I asked, I already knew the answer. From her fair hair to her eyes and frame, the woman was an older version of me.

Marge let go of all the tears she'd held back over the years.

"This is me?" I pointed to the baby in the photograph.

A gentle smile tugged at the corner of her mouth. Part of me wanted to run into her arms. Another part of me wanted to get away from them both. I'd been searching for my birth parents for years. That was how I'd met Kendra. And now I was in the same room with my mother.

"How long have you known?" I asked.

"I was suspicious when I met you. I mean, the resemblance is uncanny . . ." He paused. "Then I found the charm in your office, and I knew I had to dig deeper."

"My charm has my initials on it. SC, for Samantha Connor."

"The SC stands for Summers Charlize." The woman reached out her hand where a similar charm hung on a Silver bracelet. "It was a family thing when we first moved to New Zealand."

"It's a coincidence." I whispered, shaking my head. Yet I knew the opposite was true. This wasn't a coincidence, and Gabe had kept the secret of my identity since the day I met him. My stomach swirled.

"I'm going to be sick. I need air."

I ran out of the bedroom, past Gabe and the woman.

"Sam, wait!" Gabe called after me.

I rushed down the stairs and out the side door. They followed me, but somehow my feet were quicker and more determined. Parsley stayed at my side the entire time.

"Charlize, please." I heard the woman's broken voice behind me. I tried to connect it to my mother's, but I couldn't. My mother had died two years ago.

I lowered myself to my knees on the grass. My stomach squeezed upward, and I threw up. Gabe rushed my way.

"Get away from me!" I cried out.

"Sam—"

"Please!" I sobbed and got up from my knees. "Just leave me alone."

The world around me shifted. Objects faded in and out of focus. The blue sky blended with the green. I shut my eyes, braced my hands on the grass, and stood.

"I… I can't do this." I ran across the lawn, with Parsley at my side.

Gabe called after me until we reached the beach, where the endless ocean stretched in wonderment. I wished Kendra was there. She understood the art of living a life without a true identity. I'd searched for mine for years, and when I couldn't find it, I created my own. Except it was all a lie. Samantha Connor was a lie… and so was Gabriel Silver.

I removed my shoes and hurried across the sand to the shore as Gabe appeared from within the tall grasses.

"Samantha!" he called out.

I dashed along the shore towards Gabe's boat carcass. When I reached the dock, I sprinted to the boat Kendra had used to syphon the fuel from our first night in New Zealand. I hopped on without thinking. Parsley remained on the dock, barking.

"Keys, keys, keys…."

I found the keys in a compartment and turned the ignition, trying to remember everything Gabe had taught me about boating. It wasn't a lot. I untied the boat and gently pushed on the throttle, steering towards the open waters.

"Samantha!" Gabe screamed at the top of his lungs, running down the dock. But he was too late. The boat pulled away from the dock. I wanted to be alone, and there was nothing he could do to stop me. He plunged into the water, swimming after the boat he would never catch.

The front cut through the waves like a hot knife through butter. The wind howled past me as the sun reached its highest point in the sky. It was just me and the ocean. Never in my life had I thought I'd take a boat out in the ocean, but here I was, stealing one when I didn't even want to. Fifteen minutes later, I was out in the open water with no land in sight… when the boat rumbled and steering wheel vibrated. I gripped it tighter, but the engine shut off. The fuel gage showed empty.

"Shit!" I punched the steering wheel, screamed out, and slouched in the chair. I should have known the tank would be empty because Kendra was the one who had syphoned off the gasoline. Clearly nobody had refilled it. I switched off the ignition and checked the GPS. The dot on the screen wasn't far from the coast, yet it felt like I was in the middle of nowhere. I sat on the skipper's chair and sobbed. When the tears ran out, I lay down on the boat's floor and closed my eyes. The sun shone with intensity as I bopped over the waves. How had my life gone so wrong? I had trusted Gabe enough to follow him across the world, and he'd lied to me about the one truth I sought.

As I pieced the day's events, nothing made sense. How could I be from New Zealand? That country had never come up in my research. When I had met Kendra, we hadn't been able find an ounce of information about my adoption.

"They stole you from us." My mother's voice resonated in my ears.

My mother.

Fresh tears filled my eyes again. I turned on my side into a fetal position. My body shook and my heart ached until the sound of an engine caught my attention. I stood up and looked over the bow at the approaching yacht ahead.

"Shit!"

I lowered myself from view. The yacht was close enough to recognize that it wasn't Gabe's. Shivers ran down my spine. I rummaged through the boat looking for a snorkel, but I couldn't find one. Then I remembered I couldn't snorkel. I opened the next compartment and grabbed a pair goggles and a bottle-sized oxygen cylinder with a mouthpiece. I turned the knob. Air fizzed through the mouthpiece, and I twisted the knob to the off position.

Sharks or Martinez?

My gaze darted from the water to the approaching yacht, and I quickly chose the former. Although I knew Martinez had supposedly left New Zealand, I didn't want to take the chance. I hurried to the stern, climbed down the steps, secured a pair of flippers, adjusted my goggles, and slid into the water. I held on to the rope at the side of the boat, careful to remain on its hidden side as the yacht closed in, secretly praying for no sharks. If the people were friendly, I would come out and ask for help.

"It's abandoned."

"Check everything. This boat belongs to the Summers. Burn it."

My breath locked in my lungs. Martinez's voice sent a sprinkle of shivers over my skin. I secured the goggles, turned on the oxygen, placed the mouthpiece in my mouth, and dove under the boat, near the front. I wasn't a splendid swimmer, but I liked living. The survival instinct guided me towards the yacht. I swam as deep as possible without surfacing. By the time I reached the yacht's bow and came up for air, they had set my boat on fire.

The yacht's engines roared, startling me. I dove under again as it pulled away from the inferno. Moments later, the sound of an explosion rippled through the ocean. The boats' scattered remains burned on the surface, and then most sank beneath the waves.

I came up for air after they left. As I treaded water in a circle, the enormity of my situation hit me. The stupidity of my actions had left me stranded in the middle of the ocean, floating on a current, which was pulling me further away from the shore.

As if things couldn't get any worse, a shark fin surfaced on the horizon.

"Sam took Marge's boat. I need the speedboat and all resources available to find her. By sea and air!"

I gripped the phone until my knuckles ached.

"We'll be there in twenty minutes," Tristan replied, and hung up.

"She may not have that long." My jaw clenched until the back molar ached.

I checked her location on my phone app. The tracker from Sam's charm pulsed on the screen, moving further away from land. I looked out into the ocean in the direction Sam had left.

"I need a boat."

"Jack's old one is in the garage."

The next five minutes took forever. As my brain buzzed with the possibilities of what could happen, I hooked up the boat to Marge's Rover and guided it to the launch pad. After what seemed like an eternity, I sped on one engine at a snail's pace.

"Fuck!" I screamed out.

It wasn't long before my cousin sailed the family yacht behind me.

"What are you doing with that?"

"Shut up and get closer!" I called out.

I boarded the yacht while Julian's crew took Marge's boat back home.

"What happened?" Kendra asked "Where is Sam?"

"Sam is Charlize Summers. Something you would have fucking known if you'd had the sense to notice how much she looked like Jo."

"What?!"

"Yeah, that's pretty much how Sam felt when she found out."

"Sam's Jo's sister?"

"Yes!"

"And you didn't tell her?"

"I never had the chance. Where did you meet Sam?" I forced restraint through my teeth.

"What?" That dumbfounded expression she was faking to avoid confrontation did not work on me.

"It's a simple question, K. Where did you meet Sam?"

"At an ancestry conference. We were both looking for our parents. She was trying to find her biological family."

"And that didn't click anything?"

Kendra jumped up, and I immediately regretted the harsh comment. Kendra and Sam's strong bond made perfect sense, but Kendra wasn't safe for her friends. It was one of the reasons she didn't have many.

"Your parents have been gone for a while."

The accident that had taken her parents was another reason.

She shook her head. "I don't think so. I think they're still alive. I can feel it."

I lowered my hand over hers. "K, they're gone. The accident... they couldn't have survived. We all saw the explosion."

A deafening boom thundered from the ocean like I'd

summoned it. A visible explosion lifted a plume of fire and smoke into the sky.

"That's Sam's location." Julian pushed harder on the throttle.

The pulsing light on my app disappeared. "No, no, no! I lost her ping!"

Kendra sat in the chair, shaking. She gripped the sides, holding steady. I removed my binoculars from their pouch and scanned the horizon. A yacht was sailing away from the explosion.

Martinez.

My face twisted into persistence as I focused on the burning vessel. Marge would never forgive me if I lost her second daughter. I would never forgive myself.

A debris field of wood, metal, and unidentifiable pieces was scattered over the surface.

"Sam! Samantha!" But my voice fell prey to the ocean's power as soon as it left my lips.

Julian anchored the yacht.

"I'm going down." I grabbed a handheld oxygen flask, goggles, and flippers, and dove underwater. While I searched for her body, I prayed I wouldn't find her – because if I did find her here, it would mean she was dead. Twenty feet lower, the shallow ocean floor was littered with debris, but her body was nowhere to be found. I surfaced and removed my mask. "She's not here. She must have lost the bracelet in the explosion."

"When a body explodes, there's nothing left," Kendra cried out overboard. She was hysterical.

"She's not dead!"

My jaw tightened. She couldn't be, and I wouldn't give up before I found her. I boarded the yacht.

"Send this location to the search and rescue party. Tell them to hurry."

"Already done." Julian checked the currents, turned on the

engine, and headed in the likely direction the water would have swept Sam away.

The sun scorched from above until it set, and we were still empty-handed. Marge organized over twenty private rescue boats and kept in touch over radio.

It was past midnight when I heard the most beautiful words in my life: "Over there!"

I dove overboard and swam towards the spotlight before they confirmed it was her. We found Sam barely conscious, holding onto a piece of floating debris in a near-hypothermic state.

"Gabe?" she mouthed before passing out in my arms. After I brought her on board, I wrapped another blanket around her. We called Marge to give her the news and hurried home, where she met us.

"Thank God!" She ran across the dock towards us.

Sam startled in my arms. "Help!"

"It's okay. I've got you."

She sighed, closed her eyes, and sank back into my hold.

"We'll see you in the morning." My cousin waved and left on the speedboat with Kendra.

"The doctor's in the house," Marge said. "And I'm not leaving until she's awake."

I carried Sam home in a hurry, where I covered her with even more blankets. Marge brought warm tea, but Sam passed out before she drank any.

The doctor took her vitals while she slept. "Let her be like this until the morning. Her blood pressure is getting better. I think she's exhausted and needs sleep, but she'll be fine. The IV will help with re-hydration."

I made the sign of the cross and thanked God for returning Sam safely. I cranked my neck from one side to the other as Marge set two glasses of bourbon on the rocks on the living room table.

"Thank you. How did you know I needed this?"

"It's what we all need. You look awful."

"Thanks." I touched my glass to hers. "I'm just happy we found her."

"Thank you. I mean it." She paused. "When we tracked down the dealer ten years ago, and he told us they'd sold my baby for parts… I thought I'd lost her forever. I thought she'd joined the angels."

"I'm sorry we've put you through so much pain. Losing two daughters—"

"It's not your fault, Gabe."

I took another sip. It certainly felt like it was my fault. I could have done so much more to protect both Joanne and Samantha, but I had failed. Joanne died on my watch, and the same almost happened to Sam. I downed the rest of my drink and poured a second glass.

"Gabe, if you don't stop blaming yourself, I'm going to smack you silly."

"It comes with the territory."

Marge lifted her arm and gave me a gentle smack across my head. "Then get on a new territory."

"Is that a Kiwi thing?"

"It's a motherly thing. Speaking of which, your mother called."

"Let me guess. My aunt called as well?"

"What do you expect? It's been a while since we all hung out on the island."

Island getaways called for family time, and Silver potluck styled picnics were a tradition my mother and aunt would never miss. The sisters-in-law insisted on everyone's presence.

I grunted. "This isn't a good time. I need to find out why Martinez is still in New Zealand."

"We both know why he's here." She set her drink aside and

crossed her arms over her chest. "Your friend is trouble. Mischief follows her wherever she goes."

"Kendra's a good person, and Silver Securities owes her. That includes protection, and that's what she'll get."

Marge sighed. "I'm sorry. I just wish Charlize hadn't gotten caught up in her troubles with the mafia."

"Her name is Sam. I know she's your Charlize, but when she wakes up, I imagine it will take her some time to come to terms with her identity. She thought her parents were dead."

Marge lifted her head. "Well, I'm not. And a name is just a name. I will love her whether she's Sam or Charlize. It doesn't matter. I'm just glad I have my daughter back."

We sat in silence until three in the morning.

Marge removed the empty bourbon glass from my hand. "Are you going to take her back to the US with you?"

"I don't know. I really don't know. Wherever we go, I need her to be safe. The ring will continue operating for as long as Hartley and Martinez are alive. We'll stay off the grid until he's caught."

"She should stay here. This is her home." Before I could argue, she added, "I'll take the guest bedroom. Get some rest, Gabe. Today is a good day. You found my daughter. Tomorrow will be even better because she's here. Good night."

I knew Marge hadn't forgotten how they'd stolen Sam right from underneath her nose, and I didn't have to remind her Martinez knew where she lived.

She kissed me on the cheek and left upstairs to the guest bedroom. I poured myself the last glass of bourbon and went up to my bedroom, where I sat out on the balcony, watching the ocean until I passed out.

"GABE! GABE, WAKE UP!"

Marge's panicked voice vibrated in my eardrums. Her fingers clenched my arm until I opened my eyes.

Morning light blinded me. I lifted myself to a sitting position. Sun sparkled through the broken glass scattered across the tile. I shot off the floor like a spring.

"Sam?" I whipped my body towards the empty bed. Glass shards cut into my foot.

"I checked her room. She's gone!" Marge cried. "I already called Julian. What the hell happened?"

"I… I don't know. Samantha!" I checked every bedroom, nook, and hall on the second floor, then hurried down the stairs, leaving a track of bloody footprints behind. I searched the downstairs and the garage before going to the backyard.

She wasn't there either.

My chest emptied as if someone had knocked all the air out of my lungs. My heart froze as the realization sank in. I'd had her in my arms mere hours ago, and now she was gone again. My stomach tightened as the acids turned. Bitter bile filled my mouth. The back of my head throbbed. I lifted my hand to where warmth oozed from underneath my hair.

"Where is she, Gabe?" Marge followed me outside, where she touched the back of my head. "You're hurt."

The world around me faded in and out of focus. I lifted my hand to where Marge had touched my head again. A bruise had formed over the wet gash under my fingers. I turned to Marge, "I don't know where she is, but I'll find her. I need my phone. Are you all right?"

"Yes – I didn't hear or see anything. But there's blood in the kitchen, and I don't think it's yours."

Shattered glass littered the patio, reflecting the sun like diamonds. I looked up to the broken window by the balcony off my bedroom. How the fuck did the alarm not go off?

I followed Marge back inside, where she hopped over the bloody smears to the kitchen sink and soaked a cloth under cold water. She pointed to a chair. The room spun around me and my vision blurred. I sat down, and the light-headedness eased. While Marge cleaned the cut, I checked my phone with Julian's text from ten minutes earlier. "On my way."

"Ouch," I whined.

"I'm sorry."

"It's okay. How the fuck did they get through security?" I scrolled through the cameras when a flashing time-clock caught the corner of my eye. The oven display showed three in the morning. I checked my watch.

"They took out the power and the generators, and they have a three-hour lead on us. Fuck!"

The security gate opened. I got up to my feet, nearly tumbling over, and headed to the front, but halted two feet from the entrance.

History repeats itself.

The taped note to the door brought up bile in my throat.

Martinez's scribbled message held a familiar tone. He had lured Joanne into a trap before burying her.

"They're going to bury Sam alive, the way they did Joanne," I whispered, and heard Marge thud to the floor behind me. I hurried and helped her to the couch as Julian and Kendra entered.

"You've checked all the trackers?" he asked, as I lifted Marge's legs in the air. He pulled out his phone and swiped through what I assumed was the Silver tracking app.

"Of course. She only had one, and she lost it yesterday in the ocean."

While I propped up Marge's feet to restore blood flow, Kendra brought her a glass of water. Marge came to moments later, and I lowered her feet to the couch. "What's going on?"

"I have no time to explain, but Sam's missing. We're going to use all our resources to find her, Marge. I promise."

I'd never forget the look of terror in Marge's eyes as she

grabbed my wrist in her hand and locked her gaze with mine. "Gabe? Find her."

I nodded. Kendra passed her the water.

"Put on some clothes, Gabe."

That's when I noticed I was still in my boxer briefs. "Julian—"

"Hold on!" My cousin lifted his hand. His brows narrowed, and the room fell silent. The next three seconds felt like three hours as I watched Julian's expression shift from despair to hope.

"What is it?"

"It's Joanne's old tracker."

"That's upstairs."

"Then why is it beeping on my phone, showing it in the middle of a field, an hour away?"

I skipped upstairs every third step and ran to the bathroom, where I confirmed Joanne's charm was missing from the drawer. I dressed in a hurry: a pair of sweats and t-shirt, plus socks I pulled over my bloody feet. When I returned, Kendra's phone rang.

She passed it to me in a hurry. I pressed the speaker button and waited.

"Her debts had to be paid with a life." A raspy Spanish voice sounded on the other end.

"Where is Samantha?" The molar in the back of my jaw pinged with pain.

"Closer to hell than you think." Martinez laughed. "Tell your little druggie it was supposed to be her, but she wasn't home. She's next."

"Listen to me, fucker! Tell us where she is, and we'll settle the payment."

"It's too late for your bitch."

"I swear, I will find you and rip out your throat," I threatened.

"That won't settle the payment either. You know I'm just a messenger doing his job."

"Then take this message. We're coming for you, your boss, and your boss's boss."

A click, followed by deadly silence.

"Shit!" My gaze connected with Julian's.

"I'm so sorry, Gabe. It should have been me." Kendra slumped to the couch beside Marge. "I'm so sorry."

But I had no time to pay attention because time held Sam's life in its orb. I turned to Julian, "We're going to need shovels."

Chapter 18

Sam

bopped with the waves like a perfectly edible seal. Up and down, up and down. The shark fin turned out to be a floating piece of wood. I grasped a corner of larger debris, climbed up as far as my strength allowed, and held on as the current swept me away from the sinking boat carcass. Around me, the endless ocean stretched into infinity. I lifted my wrist to the front of my face, but the sun's reflection I'd hoped to catch in my charm wasn't there. The bracelet must have slipped off.

The sun seared over my forehead and arms. It bounced off the water, blinding me, and so I kept my eyes closed when I could. The waves' repetitive sway was making me nauseous. After a while, my stomach gave in and I emptied until I had nothing left inside. I lifted my legs higher onto the platform and curled into a fetal position.

Deep regret filled my chest. This level of stupidity was new, even for me. What had I been thinking, running away from the people who loved me? I should have never taken the boat. Except I hadn't been thinking. I was mad and fleeing from a liar. Or at least, I thought he was a liar.

And he called *me* the rebel?

Gabriel Silver had been married to my deceased sister. One I never knew I had. He had known who I was the moment he met me, but he didn't tell me. He knew my mother better than I did. How was this even possible? I had so many questions I didn't know where to start, and now I could possibly never get my answers.

The hours I drifted out into the ocean deflated my lungs. By the time the sun dipped, my breaths had shortened. I held my knees close to my chest and curled into a ball as night fell. The sun lowered, and the water temperature dropped. The moisture didn't bother me at first, but as I remained soaked, the gentlest of breezes shook through my body with the force of a thunderstorm.

I might have avoided quick death by the sharks, but hypothermia didn't discriminate between victims. I missed Gabe's arms, which held me warm at night. I missed his confidence and safety. Gabe would know what to do. He always knew what to do, but I never listened. I never gave him a chance to explain.

The fear and lies in his eyes had pierced through my chest like sharp knives, cutting off my trust. The plea in Marge's eyes, though – that ached the hardest. I flipped onto my back and spotted the first dangling star in the sky. I imagined hugging my mother, and I shivered. The possibility I'd never get to do so grew with my shallower breaths.

I'd never had a child I'd lost, but I'd lost a mother. Twice, apparently. No – three times. And I'd left a mother who thought she found her daughter grieving all over again.

Maybe I am the rebel. Coward, more likely.

The moment I found the one person I'd been searching for my entire life, I ran. I whimpered and lowered my head over my arm to rest. I must have dozed off because when I opened my eyes, the sun was just above the horizon. Its orange glow spread across the ocean. I swept my tongue along my dry gums and lifted my head. The hours I'd spent out here dragged on, and there was no landmass in sight. I searched the horizon every few minutes until a fin cut through the water.

I stiffened.

The shark approached without fear, curving around the platform at the last moment he could. I positioned myself in the center and watched as its circles narrowed. The shark's sudden turns toward my floating debris shot a jolt of adrenaline through my body. I stiffened when it bumped the board.

"What do I do? What do I do?"

Don't panic.

I remained still. The fin disappeared underwater and reappeared closer than it had before. I drew my hand across my face. Salty regret stung my eyes. My body tensed as I wondered whether a shark could sense fear. The uncontrollable pounding in my chest pumped like a beacon.

This was it. The stupid shark would eat me alive, and there was nothing I could do.

Another fin surfaced in the distance. I positioned my body to face the sun. As the glow blended with the water, it was becoming more difficult to see.

Life definitely flashed in front of your eyes before you died. When I closed my eyes, I didn't like the scene I saw. I'd searched for a new family after my parents died. I'd inched closer and closer to that happiness I'd read about, but when I finally had it, I ran.

"I'm such a loser!" I screamed.

The shark must have heard my agony because it turned away from its circular pattern and headed straight for me.

"Shit! Shit! Shit!"

I watched it swim towards me, desperate to remember whether I should stick out my hand now, so I could poke its eye, or after it grabbed me? The water splashed off to the side, and the shark veered off its course. But he wasn't quick enough for the dolphin , which rammed its nose into its side. At least I thought it was a dolphin. More fish splashed around me, attacking the shark. The dolphins chased the predators away in the most *National Geographic* way I'd seen in my life. When the predator disappeared, a dolphin lifted its head above water, like he wanted to tell me the threat had left, then floated on its belly beside me.

Or maybe it was one of my last most beautiful hallucinations as the last sliver of the sun's orb disappeared underwater and the night fused with the ocean.

Exhausted, I lowered my head over my arm, saying, "Thank you," and closed my eyes, letting the ocean drag me into the night.

MY LIMP LIMBS hung in the air, flopping. Someone was carrying me across a beach. The powerful arms, secure hold, and familiar scent forced my eyes open.

"Gabe?" I tried to speak through my hoarse throat and dry mouth, but I couldn't get a word out. The world faded in and out of focus. One moment I had been in the ocean, the next on a boat. Moments later, I was in my bed. Gabe was sitting beside me, holding my hand. The repetitive sound of a heartbeat thrummed. My upper arm ached under some pressure, but I couldn't lift my head. An intravenous machine was hooked up to a butterfly in my arm and dripped with fluids.

Someone else was in the room too, but I had no strength to turn.

"Stay still, Sam. You're home now, but you're weak. There's an IV in your arm."

Home. His hot lips pressed to my forehead, and I sank deep into the mattress and the pillow. The moment of relaxation was short-lived, though, because when I opened my eyes again, my head was pounding. It was the middle of the night, and the smell of rotten eggs, soil, and dirty socks filled my lungs. I smacked my cracked lips together. My mouth was dry, and my arm ached where a bandage was wrapped around my elbow.

What happened to my IV? Where am I?

The soft sheets were gone from underneath me, replaced with wooden planks. My pulse picked up. I opened my eyes as wide as I could and waved my hand in front of my face, but I couldn't see it.

"Gabe?" I whispered again, reaching out to my sides. Each of my elbows hit what felt like a wooden plank.

"Ouch." I rubbed the spot and extended my arms, searching the rough surface with my palms. A splinter gouged into my thumb, and I stopped. I lifted my arm above my head and further out behind me, but hit another wall.

My breathing quickened into uneven gasps.

I slid my hands across the wood in search of a hinge or an opening. My palms ached and my fingertips, punctured with wooden slivers, throbbed and bled. I had cut my palm on a protruding nail, and the laceration burned.

"No, this can't be happening." Fear crept up my body as I followed the wall's line until I reached a corner above my head. My palms felt over to the wooden ceiling less than a foot away from my face. I pressed up and against it, but it didn't budge. They had trapped me.

The smell of earth and soil magnified each minute.

"Help!" I screamed in a hoarse voice, though I could barely hear myself. Was it all in my head? "Help me!" I slid lower, but my feet touched the end of the enclosure. I hit my knees on the low ceiling, trying to push myself back up, only to reach another wall above my head.

"Gabe! Help me, please." I released a long wail and let the river of tears flow as my limited time ticked away, somewhere underground.

I shut my eyes, and a memory flashed through my mind. A familiar voice had laughed when I first woke. Tie tags sliced through my wrists as they secured my hands behind me. My ankles ached where rope burned around my bound feet. The knot dug into my skin, and I wished for Kendra's anklet, so Gabe could trace my location.

"History repeats itself, Ms. Summers," Martinez said in an amused voice. "The last one was conscious when we buried her, and you will be as well."

Was that how my sister had died?

The stench of a homemade cigar burned my nose. Martinez dropped me in the back of a truck and cuffed me to a metal rod. We drove for a long time, and I heard no other cars pass us as I fell in and out of consciousness. The asphalt pavement turned into gravel and then dirt. The truck wobbled over frequent bumps, its wheels crunching under the vehicle. I'd passed out before they removed the ropes from around my wrists and ankles, and I didn't wake again until it was too late.

Hours or days could have passed, and I wouldn't have known the difference. It felt like weeks and months, even though I knew that wasn't possible. I pulled my hand over my face. I could no longer cry, and my eyes stung. Blood oozed down my legs from having scraped against the wooden ceiling with my knees. I repeatedly banged them, like I could somehow get out. The survival instinct continued until I ran out of strength.

My breaths slowed. There was barely any air left in the coffin. Deprived of oxygen, my lungs squeezed in from the outside. Beads of sweat dripped down my forehead and face. The pounding in my chest slowed to a quiet, rhythmic thump. The smell of death surrounded me as I mumbled my Hail Mary.

"**S**traight ahead. She's not far. Hurry."

Julian had insisted on driving, which was for the better because the pain in the back of my head ached from the whack. He pressed his foot harder on the gas. Focused on the ping from Joanne's charm, we'd been driving for the past hour, getting closer.

The good news was that location had remained in the same spot. The bad news was that we were out in the middle of wild Maniototo Plains.

"Come on. Come on." I pressed my foot to the floor as if I were the one driving. Harder. Faster. Yet not fast enough.

"You want to get there alive, don't you?"

I had faith in my cousin who sped over the dirt road, but if I lost Sam…

"I can't lose her," I said.

"I know. I get it. If it weren't for you, I would have lost Kendra. I'm sorry we got Sam into this mess."

"Silver Securities has a lot of cleaning up to do."

"Tristan's working on it. A few more months and it will be all over."

"You think Kendra can survive this?" I asked.

"She has to." He gripped the steering wheel harder. "Just like Sam has to survive this."

Please be alive.

Julian followed a set of tire tracks and turned left.

"That way." I pointed off-road toward the mountains as we closed in on the ping.

He swerved right and into the bushes. The Rover lifted in the air as we crossed a ditch and passed the shrubs. The car's bottom scraped against the rocks. Julian propelled forward, and the car bounced up and down, swaying right and left over the uneven terrain. As I kept my focus on the blinking dot on my phone, dust rose around us.

"I can't see." Julian had run out of windshield fluid, and the wipers smeared the dust into a streaking paste.

"A hundred yards further down. Don't stop."

Julian pressed his foot on the brakes instead. The tires locked in, and the Rover stopped. The smell of heated iron filled the car. He scanned the rocky plains ahead.

"I'm not crashing into a wall. We have to go on foot from here."

I opened the door and dashed out. "I can't lose her!"

I ran as fast as I could until my muscles ceased and lungs burned. I reached a small area where a pile of fresh soil was drying in the heat, and I dropped to my knees. The dirt cooled an inch deep, and I feared I was too late.

"Joanne…" I whispered. "No."

I dug my hands into the dirt and pushed scoops aside. It had taken us forty-eight hours to find Joanne buried in the Colorado mountains. We didn't get to her in time, and she'd suffocated. My wife had died for the work we both loved.

"Joanne!" I screamed.

"Sam, Gabe. Sam."

But I barely heard my cousin as he passed me a shovel. "It will be quicker with this."

I pushed the blade into the ground.

He grabbed my hand. "We got to her quickly. She should be alive, but she'll need you to be strong. Do you understand?"

I nodded and resumed the task. Julian bore into the ground with his spade.

"Sam!" I screamed. "Hold on, Sam! Please hold on."

We removed the soil from the grave like two well-oiled bulldozers. There seemed to be no end to the hole. This one was deeper than Joanne's, and the further we reached, the more fear crept up my spine. I dug relentlessly. The sun blazed from above. It felt like hours passed before my shovel hit a hard surface. I connected my gaze with Julian's and we fell to our knees at the same time. We removed the remaining soil from the makeshift coffin. I slid the edge of my shovel underneath a board and pried it open.

Sam's pale face and blue lips appeared from within.

"No, no, no."

I lowered myself to the open slit and placed my mouth to hers. I blew a breath into her lungs while Julian stripped away the remaining boards. I lifted Samantha into my arms and lay her limp body on flat ground, where I checked her airways.

She didn't stir.

I pressed my ear to her chest and listened for a heartbeat, but I couldn't find a pulse. Not on her neck, nor on her wrist. Was I too late? I breathed another breath inside her, then started the rhythmic chest compressions while vultures circled above us.

One, two, three, four, five, six…

One, two, three, four, five, six…

One, two, three, four, five, six…

One, two, three, four, five, six…

One, two, three, four, five, six…

I breathed into her again, and she gave me nothing in return.

"Come on, Sam!" I started the next round.

One, two, three, four, five, six…

One, two, three, four, five, six…

One, two, three, four, five, six…

One, two, three, four, five, six…

One, two, three, four, five, six…

I inflated her lungs once more, and she gasped for air. Sam rolled to her side, heaving. When she had enough air, I helped her sit up. Her body slumped against me. She could barely open her eyes.

"Water," she said through her cracked lips. Julian ran back to the car as I held her in my arms, rocking.

"I'm so sorry. I'm so sorry, Sam," I repeated.

Julian returned with a bottle of water, and I placed the nozzle to her lips. She couldn't drink fast enough.

"Slow down," I whispered, but she wouldn't have it. She emptied the bottle and fell into my arms in exhaustion. I lifted her and carried her back to the Rover. She stayed in my lap while Julian drove to the hospital.

"I'm out," I told him. "I don't know what happens from now on, but I'm out until this shit clears and Kendra's case is over."

He glanced in the rear-view mirror and met my eyes.

"I understand you. Completely."

We had months left before Congress voted on new sex-trafficking and pedophile legislations. If the vote passed, we'd expose the billionaire moguls who thought they could run the world according to their rules. If it failed, the cases Silver had been working on since its merger would be a waste. Worse, lives were at risk.

Predators would prey, and our lives would never go back to normal again.

I sat by Sam's bed, listening to the monotone beeping of a monitor. The smell of antiseptic and red roses filled the room. I'd hung fairy lights over the window and decorated the space with comfortable pillows and blankets. Samantha had been asleep for thirty-six hours and was due to wake up at any moment. The doctors said her exhaustion and dehydration had nearly caused kidney failure, but she would be okay.

I smoothed the back of my hand over her cheek, and she stirred.

"There you are," I whispered.

She grabbed the bedside and jerked up. "Let me go!"

I touched her hand and eased her grip off the rails.

"Shh, shh, it's okay, Sam. You're safe now."

She lay down at the sound of my voice.

"You're in a hospital, Sam, and you're doing great."

Her eyes darted from side to side. "Kendra?"

"She's with Julian."

"Martinez?"

"He'll get what's coming his way. There's a security guard outside your door and downstairs. No one's getting in here, and honestly, I'm not leaving without you."

I hadn't left Sam's side since we'd found her, and I wouldn't leave her again.

"I… I thought this was it. The soil… the coffin… How did you find me?"

I removed Joanne's sail-wheel charm from within my pocket and placed it in her palm. "Joanne's charm had a tracker, and you had it in your jean shorts. It was meant to save her life, but I never had the chance to give it to her. It saved your life instead."

Sam took a deep breath and released it with relief. She rested her head for a moment and closed her eyes before sitting back up again.

"I wanted to have it set for you the way you set mine. I put it in my pocket but never got the chance."

Every time she spoke through her hoarse throat, my body ached. Her bandaged hands looked like small boxing gloves. They'd started pumping fluids through her body the moment we arrived. She was so dehydrated, the nurses had had a tough time locating a viable vein in her arm. I remained at her side as they cleaned her raw knees, cuts, and lacerations.

"I'm glad you did. Otherwise… well, let's not think about it. I'm just happy you're safe now. We're getting out of here as soon as you're cleared, and I'm never letting you out of my sight again."

She shut her eyes tight. "I can't believe I took that boat out."

"I can't believe you dove underwater. At least, that's what I'm assuming you did before the boat blew up."

"I had no choice. It was either the sharks or Martinez."

"You chose wisely."

She chuckled.

I took her bandaged hand in both of mine.

"What's wrong?" she asked.

"Nothing. I promise. I just wanted to apologize, Sam."

"For what?"

"For not telling you who you were when I met you."

"Did you know right away?"

"When I saw you, I thought it was Joanne. I thought I was crazy."

"And it's all really true? I have a mother?"

I nodded.

"Knock, knock!" The hospital door squeaked right on cue.

Sam turned her head to the side, and I rose in my chair as Marge peeked through.

"Can I come in?"

Sam's face brightened.

"Come in. She's awake."

Marge removed her bumblebee sunglasses and the sun hat. She moved forward with caution. I pulled another chair closer to Sam's bed.

"Hello," she said.

"Hi… Mom," Sam replied.

Marge's eyes welled. She wiped her tears and lowered her hand to Sam's. It felt like someone had sucked all the air out of the room. A fresh chorus of tears spilled when she blinked. "I've dreamt about this moment my entire life, and… and I can't believe it's here. I can't believe this is real."

Sam's eyes filled as well. I passed her a tissue, and she wiped them. "I looked for you, but everywhere I turned, I found nothing." Sam said.

"They covered their tracks well. They told me they sold you… for…" Marge shook her head, and I gently touched her shoulder.

"She's here now. That's all that matters."

I never wanted Marge or Sam to see or fear Martinez again.

"How are you feeling?" Marge smoothed her thumb over Sam's cheek, wiping away a tear.

"Alive," she smiled. "Grateful and stupid."

Marge placed her hand over her daughter's bandaged one. "All that matters is that you're here. With us. Today is the best day I've had in a long time."

Sam turned her head my way. "Is it really true? I'm not dreaming this?"

"It's all true. Samantha Connor, meet your biological mom, Marge Summers."

They both laughed and cried as Marge leaned in for a giant embrace. For the first time in years, I felt like life would fall back into its place. And it was all thanks to my rebel.

Chapter 20

Sam

"I know you'll miss your family and work. But this is for the best." Gabe lifted my suitcase out of the trunk.

I stared in awe at the house nestled in a deep valley, thinking about how anyone could miss anything if they lived in a mansion like this. In place of glass walls, stacked wooden beams supported the structure, their horizontal lengths running to each end where they interlaced with the other side at the corners. The cottage-style home smelled of pine and freshly cut wood. Above the steep shingled roof, smoke strayed in silver puffs into the night sky.

Gabriel Silver always delivered with perfection. While he didn't flaunt his wealth, he certainly knew how to use it. There was something so sexy about a man who knew how to lead and take care of… well… everything.

"I think I really like Austria. It's beautiful," I said.

Evergreens surrounded the property against a backdrop of snow-capped mountains. It was the perfect spot to settle while Silver Securities went after Martinez, his boss, and his boss's boss. Those were Julian's words, not mine. Kendra had stayed with him in New Zealand to prepare a trap. While I missed her, my cat, and my friends, staying out of their way was more important. Kendra's health and our safety were all that mattered. Julian promised her case would close soon, and once they caught Martinez, we'd both return to her club in Manhattan and celebrate.

Gabe set the luggage on the front porch and opened the door. Inside, fairy lights sparkled along the staircase. More hung from the beams underneath the ceiling. In the middle of the room, a wood-burning fireplace crackled like the heart of the house. Gabe pulled me quickly through to the backyard, squeezing my hand as he opened the patio door.

My breath stilled. Beyond the rectangular infinity pool, Vienna's lights glistened in the distance.

"Oh my," I whispered.

More lights twinkled over the hedges, making me feel at home and safe, with enough air around me to breathe forever. Chills swept over my arms. Could my forever be truly with Gabe? Was he ready to move forward with the person who reminded him of a painful past?

I trembled in Gabe's hold. He grabbed a blanket off a chair and wrapped it around my shoulders. Gabe's hideaway in Austria would give us some peace over the next few months as the other Silvers tackled a cartel. At least, that's what Kendra had told me; Gabe rarely mentioned the case.

My mother was due to arrive in Vienna in three days. Parsley was coming with her. She was closing her house for the next little while to come live with us. For the first time in my life, I felt like the family I'd always wanted was coming along, in more ways than one. I lowered my palm to my stomach and adjusted the button on my fly. It wouldn't be long before the pants tightened.

"I love it here." My breath left a trail in the air. This was the perfect place to have a family. "And have I told you lately that I love you?"

I turned around to face Gabe, and I froze. He was standing in front of me with a rectangular gift box in his hands. "Come on. Open it." He shifted from one foot to the other.

Intrigued, I stepped forward. The box seemed too big to contain what I thought he'd been hiding for the last week we'd spent at my mother's house in New Zealand. I pulled on the wide silver ribbon and lifted the top of the box. Inside were two shot glasses, a bottle of Amaretto, coffee liquor, and Irish Cream was nestled in the soft paper.

"Orgasm?" Gabe offered.

"Not the kind I had in mind, but all right," I giggled. "I must tell you, Mr. Silver. I like this welcome a lot."

Too bad I wouldn't be able to drink for a while.

His eyes sparkled. "Be careful what you ask for, Samantha. Let's take this into the kitchen, shall we?"

"Yes! We definitely have great kitchen memories," I laughed.

Gabe's eyes brightened as we made our way back inside.

"Meow."

I stilled. "Did you hear that?"

"Wh—"

"Shh!"

"Meow."

"There it is again!"

Gabe laughed.

"Star?"

"Meow."

His head peaked out from behind a wall, followed by his puffy tail. Star ran to me and jumped up in my arms. I held the cat close to my chest.

"You brought Star? Thank you! Oh Gabe, this is so perfect." I set the cat down and let him brush against my legs. "What about your allergies?"

"I'll get in touch with a naturopath and we'll figure it out."

Gabe took my hand and guided me to the kitchen counter

where another box awaited, an identical silver bow wrapped around its edges. It was half the size of the first one, but still not small enough for what I'd thought Gabe hid.

"For me?"

"Open it." He squared his shoulders and focused on the box.

"Well, you're full of surprises today, aren't you?"

I untied the ribbon in a rush and removed the top. My charm bracelet lay within a black velvet backdrop.

"You found it?"

He shrugged as if searching the ocean floor for a charm was no big deal.

"I hope you don't mind. I added your sister's trinket to the bracelet. It saved your life."

The new silver charm in the shape of a sailboat steering wheel glistened with diamonds fitted between each silver spoke.

"Oh, Gabe." I threw my arms around his neck. "I love it. Thank you."

"I love you, Samantha. You're everything to me. May I?"

I held out my eager hand, and Gabe hooked the bracelet around my wrist. The touch of his fingers along my skin reminded me how much I'd missed him. The man who I'd dreamed of one night with and who had agreed to stand by my side for a while. He knew what he wanted, took what he desired, and gave what I needed.

As if reading my mind, Gabe leaned in and whispered, "Let me show you the bedroom."

"You know I'm planning to christen each room of this house." I slid my hand to his crotch.

Gabe's bright eyes flamed with a surprise.

"I hope so." He lifted me into his arms and closed his hands underneath my behind, supporting my weight. I wrapped my legs around his waist. His needy fingers dug into my ass as he carried me to the fluffy white rug at the foot of the glowing fireplace. I pressed my mouth to his.

He lowered me to the floor and unwound my legs from around him. With one swift pull, he removed my leggings.

"Wait – there's something I need to tell you," I said.

"What?"

I swallowed hard. Technically, we'd never talked about kids, so I wasn't sure how he'd respond.

"I won't be taking my next contraceptive shot, and I hope you're okay with that."

He blinked three times, and his brows relaxed. "All right. I'm game."

"Game for kids?" I laughed. "Really? I thought the solitary life was your thing. You know, because of work—"

"Wait – are you saying you're pregnant?"

"Shh. Less talking and more kissing."

He kissed me like he was kissing me for the first time, making me forget what I wanted to say. Oh, these hormones were a wonderful thing. As soon as he let me breathe, I pulled my sweater over my head.

"No bra?" His brows lifted along with the coy smile on his face.

My breasts had been waiting for his touch for hours, but Gabe had seemed too nervous the past few days to touch me at all. With all these new hormones controlling my body, I couldn't wait to be with him, and one less item of clothing to remove meant his hands had quicker access to my breasts.

"I thought I'd surprise you too." I said.

"You have." He lowered his mouth to the left nipple and licked around its rim, teasing.

Relief and a fierce need mixed into a frenzy. I pushed my chest higher, but Gabe didn't need encouragement. He grasped a nipple between his lips and stretched the tender flesh out, then let go. The bounce zapped to my sex. He trailed a row of kisses along the shallow valley between my breasts to the other side while his hand took over my reddened nipple.

He pulled away and kneeled between my legs. The fire cast its orange glow over the right side of his body as he stared at my lace panties.

I propped myself up on my elbows. "You're hesitating. Why?"

"I don't want to hurt you." His fingers skimmed over the freshly healed wounds on my knees.

"I'm fine, Gabe. They're just scrapes. And I really, really need you."

His gaze darted toward the stairs before returning to mine. He grasped the bottom of his gray V-neck and pulled the shirt over his head, exposing his chest.

I sat up higher and ran my finger down the trail from his navel to below his belt line. I dragged my finger to the button of his slacks and popped it open.

"What do you want me to do?" The need in his ragged voice curled through me.

"Stand," I said.

He listened.

I lowered his pants and stood up to meet him. Fire sparked in his eyes. I took Gabe's hand, guiding it between my legs.

"Oh my God, Samantha." He closed his eyes as his fingers spread my need.

I lowered his briefs, and he sprang free. I wrapped my fingers around his cock, stroking up and down. His hips joined the motion. I parted my legs, letting his fingers work their magic inside me.

Gabe grabbed my hand. He knelt in front of me and removed my panties with his teeth, then stood and lifted me up into his arms.

"Where are we going?"

"Upstairs. And we're not coming down for three days."

I laughed.

The master bedroom was even grander than the one in New Zealand. A fireplace set between the en suite and the bedroom flooded both rooms in orange tones. He set me down in front of the bed, where a silver box with a sparkling black bow glistened in the light. My heart picked up its beat. A sudden wave of nerves flew through me.

"Open it." He nudged me forward.

I hesitated before taking the perfectly sized box in my hand. I breathed in as deeply as I could and exhaled while lifting the cover. "It's empty." I turned around to face Gabe, who was kneeling naked on one knee.

"I may have forgotten to put this inside." He held a sparkling ring between his fingers with an amethyst stone set in white gold.

I held my breath.

"Samantha, will you date me for the rest of your life? Will you marry me?"

Tears flooded my eyes and spilled down my cheeks. I threw my arms around his neck. "Yes, Gabe, I will."

He took my hand in his and placed the ring on my finger. As if on cue, Gabe's cell phone rang from downstairs with the Silver Securities tone.

"I have to get this." He grimaced.

"Their timing is always so perfect." I rolled my eyes playfully. "Come back soon. I have something important to tell you."

While he rushed downstairs, I lit the candles set in the bathroom and turned on the faucet to fill the tub. The suds reached the top, and Gabe still hadn't returned. I slipped into a robe and tiptoed downstairs to find him sitting on the couch in front of the fireplace. He was holding a glass of bourbon in his hand and staring at the flames in front of him.

Cold air blew from where he sat. His cheeks sagged, and his face was pale.

I sat beside him and took his hand in mine. "Gabe? What's the matter?"

"Kendra's been kidnapped."

Chapter 1

Tristan

I stood in the middle of 5th Avenue as the city's nightlife and all its thugs awakened. The intersection lights changed, and cars passed me on both sides. Spotlights lit up the sky on my right, where luxury cars were parked along the curb in front of Kendra's thriving nightclub. The crowd in line shuffled forward. If she had been here, my client would have been happy, and Silver Securities would have had no problems. The problem was, she wasn't here.

On my left, the charred ruins of Club Forever lent a burned stench to the air. Obviously, nothing lasted forever. We'd intended for the abandoned property to solve our problems; instead, the purchase magnified them. A flashlight beam cut through the darkness in a broken window, and my focus shifted to the front door of an adjacent hotel, where a girl stepped out onto the sidewalk. A john followed her. The couple slipped into a black SUV, and my insides twisted. If it hadn't been for the failed bust and the fire, we would have shut down the cartel. But we didn't. Hartley had his security change names and locations. On top of that, they had kidnapped our client.

The flashlight shone again on the lower floor. I waited for a clearing on the road and hurried across the street. I pushed open the side door and stepped into the shadows. Inside, a distant echo of noises carried through. I followed the sound down the stairs to the basement, where the fire hadn't damaged the building.

I reached the lowest step. I followed a shared stairwell to the basement, which connected to the hotel. The voices became clearer, except they weren't really talking. The deep moans, heavy sighs, and uncontrolled breathing could only mean one thing around here: an orgy. I moved from beyond the shadows. The handful of naked people in the middle of a candlelit room completed a jigsaw puzzle I had no intention of solving.

What the fuck?

They lay on scattered blankets across the old couches and floor, all somehow connected. I opened my mouth to get the crowd moving, but closed it just as quick when I saw her. Dressed in a cop's uniform, she was standing across the room, staring at the act. Her drawn gun rested at the side of her strong thigh as she watched them in wonder. She licked her parted lips. Her breaths deepened and became heavier as she took a step forward.

What the hell are you doing? I shook my head in disbelief.

She bit that lower lip and leaned her shoulder against a wall. She switched her crossed legs in the process and adjusted her crotch.

My mouth curved. She looked too young to be a cop from a distance. And she was definitely too small. Too vulnerable.

Further back, something was creeping in the shadows. Yet she remained still, unaware of the approaching danger, leaving me with no choice.

"Behind you!" I stepped out into the faint light, pointing her way.

Startled, her head flew up and her eyes grew wide. She whipped her body around on instinct, but the creep in the shadows had disappeared.

"This party is over! Get dressed and get out!" I called out.

The cop spun around once more and paced forward with her gun held forward, pointing the weapon in random directions.

"This is the police. Nobody move!"

The orgy scattered. They all grabbed whatever clothes they could find within reach and ran.

"Don't move!" she yelled out.

As expected, no one listened, and I wasn't about to stop them, either. I needed the place to clear. Scar Wagner was starting renovations next week. The posh club would be the perfect lure for perverted predators.

"Get out of here!" I yelled, heading across the room to the cop.

"Hey, you!" She pointed the gun at me. "What do you think you're doing?"

"I'm saving you from embarrassment."

"They're getting away!"

She hurried after the last one, but I was there, so her attention turned my way. I grabbed her arm, disarmed her, and drew her to my body, then spun around before I pushed her face forward, right against that wall. She yelped out in the process. I pressed my body hard against hers, constricting her.

"Let me go." She writhed in my grip.

I had to hand it to her; she was definitely strong and feisty.

"I'm gonna have you arrested for this!"

Her lips parted, and she looked back over her shoulder, catching my gaze. The patch of moonlight that snuck in between burned boards from above reflected in her cat-like eyes. It was then that I noticed her true beauty – her caring eyes, pointy nose, and freckles. She was the most gorgeous woman I'd seen in a long time. I inhaled her scent. She must have had wrapped her auburn hair in a hurry, before it dried, which resulted in a magnified aroma of lavender and strawberries.

"Your dick is against my ass," she growled. Little did she know, to my dick, her noises translated as an invitation. The challenge in her tone added an extra spice to the mix, and my mind flew straight to the gutter. It had been a while since someone this young had held my attention for longer than a blink. As much as the idea of having her fight her way out of my grip turned me on right now, consent wasn't up for negotiation. I tightened my grip around her and shrugged. "So? You're messing up my game."

Scar Wagner had called earlier and told me we had visitors across the street. While it was unlikely Martinez would show up, I couldn't chance he would.

"Fuck your game! You've just assaulted a police officer! Step away so I can do my fucking job and make an arrest!" Her anger vibrated through my body, and I liked it. "Unless you're in on this?"

I laughed, and since everyone else had left, I let her go. Another outburst of hers and I'd be the one bursting.

"The only person who should be arrested right now is you," I said.

"Wait – let me guess. Because I'm absolutely sinful?" She rolled her eyes.

"I was going to say because you're trespassing."

The certainty on her face faded. She looked me over, swallowed hard, and laughed back in a challenge, pretending she didn't recognize me. I liked her keeping some cards to herself even more. I had to hand it to her; she did a decent job.

"Is my uniform not enough for you to notice who I am? Oh, wait, of course not. It's because I'm a woman, isn't it? Why would you notice anything else about me?"

"That's sarcasm, right? It's cute, but you really are trespassing. Check the records. This is private property, and I presume you don't have a warrant."

She frowned. "If that's so, you're trespassing as well."

I held my stance.

"Am I supposed to let these… these…" Her cheeks flushed red as she pointed to the spot where an orgy had played out moments earlier. "… these scoundrels run?"

"They looked more like swingers to me."

"Argh… that's even grosser."

"For what it's worth, this place will be undergoing renovations soon."

"Wonderful. Another club on the same street. More places to sell drugs and bodies." She paused, scanned me over, and froze. "I can't believe you let them get away. Did you know they used to run a swingers' club down here?"

Unfortunately, that wasn't the only club they ran.

"You would have gotten nothing out of those kids," I told her. "They were acting out fantasies they heard about the brothel, and they're not the people you should be looking for."

Her forehead creased. "Where's your ID? What are you doing here?"

She slid the gun back inside its holster and crossed her arms over her chest. She'd interrupted my scouting; that was what I was doing here. Silvers used to own the building in partnership with the Hartley's. This place had given birth to a lifelong lie, and we'd worked for years to lure all the wrong people into our trap. Scar Wagner planned to clean up the place and the fire on the one night he closed was a warning.

I looked around the dark room. Flipped cushions, torn fabric, broken lights, and cigarette butts littered the ground. Cuffs, whips, chains, and dildos hung on a sectioned wall spared by the fire.

"Sex-trafficking, slavery, blackmail, and auctions. Bodies

sold like chattel," I said under my breath. "That's what went on here. Girls like you used to meet their hell in this basement."

"Girls like me?"

"You know – pretty, young, and delicate. Are you even old enough to be a cop?" I leaned in closer to her face. In hindsight, that was a mistake because her scent made my head spin. "You look too young to be a police officer."

"I have good genes. What do you know about the auctions?" she asked.

She definitely had good genes, but did she seriously not know who I was?

Impossible.

Maybe it was better this way? My name came with too many caveats and broken bridges.

"I know everything about them and not enough." I lowered my shoulders. "My name is Tristan Silver. My buddy takes care of this place. I saw flashlights in the windows. We've had reports of loitering, so I came to check it out."

She stilled, which told me she definitely knew who I was. I didn't partake in name-dropping often, but the stunned yet relieved look on her face was worth it. I had yet to determine the reason for her relief, but the last thing I wanted was to be seen here, standing with a cop.

"Of Silver Securities?" She stepped closer for a better look.

"Yeah, that one."

"I've heard of you." She swallowed hard and shifted from one foot to the other. "It looks like the… scoundrels left."

I chuckled… *scoundrels*. If scoundrels were my only problem, I'd be a free man. If they were the issue, Kendra would be here, and I wouldn't have a missing client.

"Sorry." I cleared my throat. "That wasn't funny."

"If you're Silver, then you know something more about this place."

"A cartel kidnapped my friend last week," I said. "She owns

the place across the street, and they'll sell her at an auction if I don't find her. "

"An auction? Like sex-trafficking? How do you even find out about those?" Her voice quivered.

"Years of intel. Connections."

"I've heard about Silver. I mean, everyone's heard. I'm sorry about your friend. Have you filed a missing person's report?"

I shook my head.

"You should call the police. They have resources."

I laughed. "The police?"

She was right about one thing: the police had a resource all right, and their best resource was me.

"You don't think we can do our job?" Her brows lifted.

I looked her over from the bottom up. Her muscled thighs and wider shoulders showed strength underneath the uniform. Combined with her delicate lips and doe eyes, the officer could definitely do her job.

"That's not what I'm saying."

"But you won't report a missing person?"

I wouldn't waste any more time in this dump. Scar would clean up the mess tomorrow, and I was nowhere near finding Kendra.

"The police can't help." I glanced at her badge. "Stay away from this place, officer… Green."

Green… Green… Green… Why does that name sound familiar?

Her brows narrowed. I turned to leave, but she grasped my wrist.

"Why stay away?"

I spun back around to face her and lowered my voice. "You shouldn't hang around dark basements because evil men come here to do bad things to girls who don't listen."

She appeared unfazed and tilted her head to the side. "Sounds to me like this is exactly where I should be. You know, because I'm a fucking cop and all!"

She was undoubtedly… something.

"Your name wouldn't be Allie, would it?" I swallowed hard and felt my dick react to the realization. She wasn't supposed to be this delicate and perfect.

"Yes. I'm Allie Green. How did you know?"

Well, well… what were the chances?

Allie and Tristan's sizzling adventure continues in *Silver's Pawn,* Book 3 in the *Silver Brothers Securities Family Saga.*

ABOUT THE AUTHOR

USA Today Bestselling Author Lacey Silks crafts riveting romantic suspense filled with heat, spice, and pulse-pounding tension. Many of her endearing characters are inspired by her own life, and her loved ones often find themselves playfully woven into her tales. Her two children and her dog, Kygo, keep her days lively with homework queries and affectionate slobbery kisses (courtesy of Kygo, of course).

Outside of penning intense love stories, Lacey is an avid camper and skier. Naturally an early riser, she often finds herself reaching for coffee over water, crediting her billionaire heroes for her packed schedule.

Lacey's characters, replete with flaws and quirks, evoke laughter, sass, and emotion on every page. She cheekily measures men by their foot size, has a penchant for sultry lingerie, and harbors dreams of exploring the nation in a motorhome.

ACKNOWLEDGMENTS

Silver's Rebel has been marinating in my brain for over a decade after I wrote it. When I returned to the original work, I quickly realized that not only the novel, but the entire series needed a major re-write. And so the journey of the Silver brothers began.

I couldn't have done the work without my reader support or the ever-inspiring indie author community filled with a wealth of knowledge. The continued encouragement and faith in my work, along with the outpouring of love, replenished my muse.

To my amazing editor who always finds the time for me, thank you for making my life easy and my writing understandable. I will chuckle over those 'silver eyes' for a while.

To my beta readers, thank you for your keen eyes! Once I read a story twenty times (or more), the details aren't easy to spot. Your feedback is invaluable and makes the novel what it should be.

To my family, the past few years have tested us in more ways than we would have liked, and I could not do what I love without you. Thank you for your support, faith and encouragement.

Maya, thank you for your artistic eye and cover design. I'm honoured to watch you grow and develop as an artist. Alex, your loving heart and sense of humour are a constant inspiration.

To my parents, this book would not have happened without you. Thank you for believing in my dreams.

www.ingramcontent.com/pod-product-compliance
Lightning Source LLC
Chambersburg PA
CBHW032245310726
48973CB00008B/2302